EYES OF DECEPTION

A NOVEL BY

STAN C. GAILLARD

Eyes of Deception is a work of fiction. Names and characters are from the imagination of the author's mind.

For more information,address:kaisheem7@gmail.com

ACKNOWLEDGMENT

This book is dedicated to all of my family and friends who stood the test of time.

To my Mother and Father who I put through so much, yet stood by my side, believed in me, and motivated me to stay on course.

To my beautiful wife whose courage, sacrifice and commitment guided me along the way. Thank you for riding this rollercoaster called life with me.

And a special thanks to my brother, Kelvin Gaillard. I will never forget the time we shared. I am Always, Always, Always fighting back the tears. R.I.P., my brother, we will meet again.

PROLOGUE

In a world of million-dollar homes, expensive cars, and opulent lifestyles, Ron Harper moved effortlessly. He was accustomed to the good life, and he lived it to the fullest. Once his father passed and left him as the CEO of his multi-million dollar investment firm, Ron's spending habits and Reckless investments took a turn for the worst.

The Board of Directors caught wind of his investments and learned of the millions that were missing from the Company's accounts, they alerted the Fed's and upon further investigation, found out about several offshore accounts and shell corporations.

And if that wasn't enough, his past and his Company's past were about to re-emerge and run head to head into several unsolved murders. Now a thorn that was once removed from his side, would be firmly placed back into its position.

Detective Demitrious Blane never forgot about Ron Harper and the tragic incident that occurred at his home years earlier. He couldn't wrap his mind around some of the inconsistencies, which led to that incident becoming a cold case. Now that Ron Harper was in prison, Detective Blane would once again be thrust back into the lifestyle of the rich and powerful and travel down a winding road filled with plenty of twists and turns.

A new day always brings about new possibilities, whether good or bad. And this day was no different

CHAPTER 1

As the sun rose on the breezy spring morning, a yellowish red reflection was cast on this Harlem neighborhood, exposing the concrete jungle at its quietest. A bark, a chirp or an occasional beep of a horn, was all that could be heard from a city that never sleeps.

For Eric Sanders, the morning started out like all the others. A quick shower, a small energy drink, and a light breakfast were all he needed to maintain his slim physique. He was 5' 11" with light brown eyes, and his coffee-colored skin blended well with his sculpted cheekbones. He wore a sharp line up on his close to a bald head, which added to his youthful looks and confidence.

Eric's world revolved around computers, he was infatuated at an early age. He learned everything he could about programming and coding through trade magazines and hanging out with the so-called computer geeks in high school. After graduating and receiving a degree in Computer technology, he couldn't wait to see what the world had to offer.

Little did he know that the world would have to take a back seat to the unexpected turn that sent him in a different direction.

CHAPTER 2

Running late, Eric checked his watch, then grabbed his duffle bag off of the couch, he gave his mother a kiss and headed out the door. As he exited the Brownstone, he reached in his pocket for his phone.

"E, what's taking you so long?"

"Take it easy, I just walked out of the house, I'll be there in a minute."

"You should've been here an hour ago, you know how busy it gets in the morning."

"Alright, don't panic, I'm on my way"

He cut off his phone, put it in his pocket, and headed for his car. "I don't know why I even got started with this dude. I can't wait for this to be over with." Eric mumbled to himself as he got closer to his car. When he popped open the trunk to put his bag inside, he didn't notice the police car that as slowly approaching. As they pulled beside him, he slammed the trunk closed.

"Good Morning Officers." He said, with a calm but serious look on his face.

Both officers exited the vehicle, but only one spoke.

"Do you have any I.D. on you, Sir?"

"Yes I do Officer, Why?" Eric responded

"Uh, no particular reason," He said, as he stared at Eric's car.

Once Eric handed him the I.D. he continued with the questions, while the other Officer walked over to the side of the car.

"How long have you lived here?"

"Why?" Eric asked with a frown on his face.

"Just calm down Sir-"

"I'm late for an appointment."

"Sir, Please calm down, this will be over with shortly. Now, this is your car, is it not?"

Eric's frown now turned to anger. "For what? you don't have any right to search my car. What's the reason?"

"You know what I've had enough of this, turn around and put your hands on top of the car, now!"

"Sir, this is your last warning put your hands on top of the hood now."

He was about to comply, the thought crossed his mind, but when the officer approached him, he turned and ran up the block faster than an Olympic sprinter. The Officer let off two rounds, and that was the last sound ever heard.

XXXX

Ron Harper was a savvy businessman, in the fifth decade of his life, who started out in the mailroom of his father's Investment

Firm R.H. Holdings. His father took him through various stages of the Company until he became a day trader himself. Due to his uncanny ability to predict the market, he quickly made a name for himself. He started out by taking little known, Companies, investing heavily in them, then banking on a rally of its stock in the coming months. After the price of the sticks rose, he would quickly sell them, thereby bringing in enormous profits.

His father Ron Harper Sr. was hard on him, but he knew that he had to be if he was going to leave him his lucrative Firm. Eighty-two and suffering from a bad heart, he didn't have long to live, so he drafted his will leaving specific instructions on what to do with his Company.

Upon his death, the will would be revealed that Ron Harper Jr. would be made C.E.O. and Chairman of R.H. Holdings he left him 49 percent of the Company and left the remaining 51 percent to the Board of Directors. He wanted to make sure that his son's erratic spending would be monitored. That monitoring would prove to be unsuccessful. With a surplus of Trust Funds, Pension Funds, and Private Equity Accounts, it was like leaving a kid in a candy store.

Ron Harper started making those same risky investments he did as a day trader. It turned out to be the beginning of his demise. To the bewilderment of the Board, a 2.5 Billion dollar cash crop was reduced to half in a matter of months. Millions were disappearing from the Company's financial accounts to personal accounts overseas. Limited Liability Companies were set up in the United States, but had business accounts offshore, directly doing business with R.H. Holdings. The Board was fed up, they knew that there was only one person able to authorize such transactions.

Hawks were circling above, as two black tinted Cadillac Escalades pulled in front of the Federal Courthouse in Manhattan.

An army of television and Camera crews, from all the major networks and Reporters from every News Paper in the City, swarmed the trucks. With Microphones in hand and cameras flashing nonstop, the Press waited for Ron Harper to exit the truck. He watched the circus from inside the truck, and thought, "My father must be turning around in his grave."

XXXX

This picture-perfect morning was disturbed by two gunshots from an Officer's handgun. The bullets hit two bricks on the side of a building, missing Eric Sanders by a fraction of an inch and sent debris scattered in a compass-like direction. He looked back just in time to see the speckled dust from the bricks falling to the ground. As he concentrated on getting away, he didn't see the car that was flying down the intersection, the time he did, it was too late. The driver stepped on his breaks, coming from zero to sixty in a matter of seconds. Eric tried to brace himself from the force of the car, by stretching out his hands, but the force was too strong. He tumbled into the middle of the street before he could shake it off and roll on to his hands and knees, he heard those familiar words.

"Stop, stop, or I'll shoot! And this time I won't miss. Place your hands on top of your fucking head, now!"

This time Eric complied. The Officer eased close, with cuffs in one hand and his gun in another. After he placed his gun in his holster, he forced Eric's arms behind his back and cuffed him. Before he picked him up off the ground he gave Eric a swift kick to the ribs. He knew it was coming that was his punishment for running. They hate you when you run, makes them do extra work.

Once Officer Rodriquez cuffed and read Eric his rights, he

notified his partner that the suspect was apprehended.

"Get up, have you lost your mind. I almost killed you."

"You don't have any right to search my car or shoot at me for that matter. I'm gonna sue you and the whole city, by the time I'm finished, you'll be a crossing guard at a high school."

"If you didn't do anything why did you run?"

"None of your damn business."

"Yeah yeah, I've heard it all before. You guys are all alike, now let's go see what's in that car."

When they got back to where Officer Rodriquez's partner, Officer Pertelli was waiting, they approached the white Lexus, but the trunk was already open.

"What do we have?" Officer Rodriquez asked.

"I don't know let's see what's in the bag." When Officer Pertelli unzipped and opened the bag, he pulled out two perfectly squared bricks of cocaine. He looked at Eric and smiled.

"That's not mine!" Eric said in a defiant tone.

"I see why you were running now," Rodriquez said

"You didn't get that from me!" Eric was becoming more and more hysterical. "That's not mine, somebody put that there. You put that there!" He yelled and looked at Officer Pertelli.

"Shut up put his ass in the car," Pertelli said.

While he was being put in the back of the police car, a voice came from a neighbor's window

"Don't worry Eric I'll go down to the police station and tell them what I saw."

By now, half of the block was outside, watching in disbelief. When Eric looked up, he found his mother watching him from their Brownstone window. As he focused on her short curly grey hair and thin face, his eyes started blinking to hold back the flood of tears. She gave him a look that only a mother and son could understand. His head became too heavy to remain upright on his shoulders. He knew without the extra money, there would be no way to help her.

CHAPTER 3

They exited the Escalades one by one. Ron Harper was surrounded by a group of lawyers from one of the best law firms in the City, Cooper and Cooper. They were followed by his best friend and Senior Executive at the Company, Brian Scott and Ron's assistant, Felicia Hernann. As they exited the trucks, they were rushed by reporters

"Why did you do that to your shareholders Mr. Harper?" One reporter asked.

"Mr. Harper, Mr. Harper.Are the allegations true?", Another yelled.

"Mr. Harper, do you have any comment whatsoever?"

He didn't, he remained silent as they walked towards the building.

"My client has no comment, I will speak for him, and I can tell you that he is innocent of the charges lodged against him. Thank you." Joseph Cooper said.

As they entered the Federal building, they made their way past the metal detectors, down the hall, and around the corner to the elevators. They got off on the second floor and were immediately ushered into the main courtroom. News cameras and Reporters were not allowed inside.

The inside of the Courtroom was a sight to see. The ceilings appeared to be a hundred feet high, pictures of past presiding Judges lined the walls and the American flag was in full view. The Judge's bench was so far from the ground, it seemed as if God was looking down on his children. To Ron, everything in the courtroom screamed guilty until proven innocent.

While everyone began to take their seats, small talk and whispers emanated throughout the Courtroom. The Lawyers sat at the defense table, preparing to represent their client. Brian Scott and Felic Hernann sat directly behind them. At last, Ron Harper got to see his adversary, U.S. Attorney Richard Goldston, who fit the part. A short pudgy man with wired rimmed glasses that sat on his stout nose, who for some reason, made it his crusade to crack down on corporate corruption.

Judge Anderson entered the Courtroom, a woman of many years. She went about her usual routine before sitting down, always looking the defendant in the face, staring at him, waiting for a certain level of eye contact. It gave her a feel of who she was dealing with. Out of all her years on the bench, she knew one thing, that there were a lot of overzealous Prosecutors, and that all things were not what they appeared to be. No case was ever open and shut. She learned that early on in her career when she was presiding over a drug case against three defendants who were charged with conspiracy. One of the defendants chose to testify against the others. His testimony was convincing, he grew up with the other defendants and gave so-called information that only a co-conspirator could have known. Then suddenly his testimony fell apart. He began to break under cross-examination. The times and dates that he said drug deals were taking place, in which he was involved, couldn't have happened because he was locked up in an upstate prison. At that moment, she realized that the scales of Justice would remain balanced in her Courtroom.

After taking a sip of water, she sat down and slammed her gavel. "Are both parties here?"

"Yes, your Honor." Both parties acknowledged.

"Good, let's get started. What do we have here?"

"Your Honor, this case is Docket Number 37201-02, in the matter of the United States Vs Ron Harper. It is the United States' position that Mr. Harper, along with known and unknown persons, set out to defraud the shareholders of his Company, by creating various Shell Companies in the United States, but doing business with those same Companies outside of the United States. In other words your Honor, the shell Companies were just fronts, just incorporated names with account numbers. We have evidence that Mr. Harper was siding money to those accounts directly from R.H. Holdings accounts, while all along making it look like investments.

Once the money was safely deposited in these Shell Company accounts, they simply extracted the money, then folded the Company and filed for chapter 11, thereby bilking investors out of millions of dollars. We have filed a four-count indictment so far. Count one is Conspiracy to commit fraud and count two is the actual carrying out of that crime. Count three is money laundering, and count four is wire fraud. It is the United States' position that all of Mr. Harper's assets be frozen until our investigators can continue to fill in the blanks. This is still an ongoing investigation."

"Your Honor." The lead defense Attorney Joseph Cooper screamed. "I've heard enough. I think that we are getting way ahead of ourselves here. It's the defense's position that this indictment should be dismissed and thrown out altogether, with prejudice."

"Why would I do a thing like that Counsel?"

"Your Honor, all we have here are accusations, nothing concrete. My client is being charged with Conspiracy, how is that possible if he is the only defendant being charged, who did he conspire with?"

"Your Honor, may we please approach the bench", Goldston asked

Joseph Cooper and the U.S. Attorney walked around their tables and towards the Judge's bench.

"Your Honor, this is a bogus attempt to paint my client as a criminal, when he didn't do anything wrong. There aren't any Co-defendants, and especially no witnesses in this case."

"Your Honor." Richard Goldston said. "There is a witness who has agreed to testify against Mr. Harper."

"This is exactly what I'm talking about your Honor I received a copy of the discovery, and there isn't any mention of a cooperating witness."

After she gave the U.S Attorney an angry look, Judge Anderson gave herself a second not to explode. "Is that true?" she asked calmly.

"Your Honor this is a witness we've been talking to for months, whose just been sworn in as a government witness."

"This is not fairyour Honor," Copper said in a demanding voice. "We would like to meet this witness and have a chance to question them since the Government decided to play this little game."

"It's no game, your Honor. This witness has testified to actually being the one who has received money transfers to accounts in their name."

"Uh….. I agree with the defense in this instance, you've had ample enough time to produce whatever witness you may have had. Since they have been sworn in this morning, I would like to know who this witness is as well." She made a gesture with her hands, sending them back to their seats.

The U.S. Attorney paused for a moment, trying to decide what to do next. Everyone in the courtroom looked at each other in suspense, not knowing what the conversation was about.

"We're waiting for Mr. Goldston." The Judge said as she tapped her pen on her bench. "You are wearing my patience thin, as well as being in contempt of court, I want to know who that witness is now, or I am throwing this case out."

"One minute your Honor." Goldston took time out to confer with his Assistant Attorney. "Okay your Honor, the witness is Kathlin Harper, the wife of Ron Harper."

The courtroom erupted in disbelief.

"Order, Order." The Judge yelled and banged her gavel numerous times. "Order in this Courtroom."

As the noise died down, she spoke

"In light of this recent development, I hereby order all accounts and assets frozen, until investigators can get to the bottom of this alleged fraud. I'm also remanding Mr. Harper into custody. This court is adjourned."

When she let go of the gavel, the courtroom went into a frenzy people could not wait to go into the hallways and discuss the recent developments.

Leaving the Federal Courthouse was equally hard to get past reporters, as it was getting in. Brian Scott and Felicia Hernann were visibly shaken as they walked to the Cadillac trucks waiting for them out front. Before Joseph Cooper got into the truck, he stopped to speak to the media.

"I would like to say that today was a sad day for the criminal justice system. Whenever a man can be swooped up and have charges brought against him, with virtually no evidence to support those charges, none of us are safe. I will, no we will be working day and night tirelessly to prove Mr. Harper's innocence."

"Mr. Cooper, what do you say about his wife testifying against him." A reporter asked.

"I haven't had time to assess that information, but I will tell you this. I'm confident that once all the evidence is presented to a jury of his peers, He will be fully exonerated. Thank you, no more questions please."

Once on the passenger's side of the truck, Joseph turned and said. "I can't believe that bitch is testifying against Ron."

XXXX

Ron Harper was being processed at the Metropolitan Correctional Center. It was a long and tedious procedure. The wait alone could drive a person insane, not to mention being put in a cell with around thirty to forty people, with barely enough room to use the toilet. Dry paint was peeling off the metal bars and walls, and it reeked of urine and feces. The perspiration from the men added an even stranger odor to the air. As he looked around, Ron felt as if he was in an insane asylum, not a federal holding cell. The desolate faces took on a consequence of its own, yet left no room to wonder. The inevitable was near.

The Federal prison system was no longer the same, it took a turn for the worst, the days of the drug kingpins, organized crime figures, and people like himself, faded into despair, In its place was every petty offense known to man.

Ron's falling asleep on the cell benches, was short-lived. He would have to sip pina Coladas on the white sand beaches of Costa Rica some other time.

"Ron Harper! Ron Harper!" The officer yelled, waking him up from his fantasy, and bringing him back to the harsh reality he must face.

He was taken to an empty room, where he had his fingers and thumbs dipped in ink and pressed on a small paper. After he was given a wet piece of towel to wipe the ink off his hands, it was time to take his mug shot. He was told to stand next to a chart that measured his height and took his picture at the same time. He faced the front and stood still as the flash went off. After blinking he went over his hair with his hands and thought about all the ways he could get back at the Board of Directors.

After answering a few questions it was time for the most degrading part of the process, a full-body search. He was told to remove all of his clothing, and stand there naked, while every part of his body was explored. When that horrible experience was over, he was given the customary garments, a brown Jumpsuit, slippers, and a bedroll. The bedroll consisted of blankets, sheets and a small bag filled with toothpaste and soap. He was put back in a holding cell until a permanent cell-block was found for him.

Some places in the Correctional Center were so violent, that even the most hardened criminals didn't want to go there.

"Ron Harper, are you ready to go to your new hotel suite?" The C.O. yelled.

He stood up and grabbed his bedroll then was taken to a cell block, where he would be staying until his trial, or until he made bail, whichever came first. When they got to the cellblock and the metal doors opened, he hesitantly walked inside. The living conditions were unbelievable, he thought. Even though he was a little nervous, he learned to mask his fears, due to the constant pressure put on him by his father.

He was greeted by the head orderly, the person who keeps everything in order in each cell-block.

"What's up man, everybody calls me old head, follow me" He looked around for an empty bunk, then saw a guy in a cell designed for four people. "Hey, do you mind being cellmates with this white dude."

"Nah, it's alright let him in" The guy in the cell answered, as he stared at Ron.

Ron walked inside, looked around and put his bedroll on an empty bunk. "So, I guess the top bunk is mine huh?" he said trying to break the silence.

"Yeah, yeah, yeah, that's yours. Listen, I'm not hard to get along with. Don't bother me, and I won't bother you."

Ron shrugged his shoulders and said. "Sure, no problem" He glanced in the mirror, and rubbed his hand over the two or three extra grey hairs, that propped up since the morning. By the time he was processed through the system, it was already late afternoon.

"Chow time!", the old head yelled from the day room.

"It's time to eat, let's go get our treys. I hope you have a strong stomach."

"Why would you say that?", Ron asked.

"You'll see in a minute." His cellmate said, with a smirk on his face. "Oh, by the way, my name is Eric Sanders, but everybody calls me E.

CHAPTER 4

A couple of months had passed since the fall of Ron Harper. He had developed a good relationship with Eric and the Old Head and was looking forward to his day in court. As he stared out of the window in his cell block, he couldn't get his mind off of his assistant Felicia Hernann. He could remember the first time he saw her, at the front desk in the trump towers. She had dark curly hair, vanilla complexion, and hazel eye. Flawless was the only word he could use to describe her. When she walked around the counter, to hand him his keys, it was the simple touch of her hand that took him over the edge. No one had ever brought that kind of reaction out of him before, he found himself for the first time, infatuated.

Once he gave her a job at his Company, he lavished her with expensive gifts, and an apartment on the Upper East Side. Although he was amazed by her, he soon found out that no one could pry him away from his true love, money.

"Snap out of it," Eric said before picking up the receiver.

Ron shook his head to see Eric getting on the phone. "I don't know how you stay so upbeat, young man."

"Upbeat, shit I'm just trying not to lose my mind." He said while he dialed the number to his house. He let it ring a couple of times, knowing that when Lisa wasn't there, it would take his mother a while to answer it.

"Hello" She said.

"How are you doing ma?"

"I'm okay, I'll make it."

"Is Lisa taking good care of you?"

"You know your sister, family first."

He laughed and said. "Yeah I know, Family first. " So, what did the insurance company say?"

"They said that I can't be covered by my policy, because I have a pre-existing condition."

"What, that doesn't make any sense, I don't understand-"

"It means that before I got diagnosed with Cancer, I could have already had it long before I got the policy."

"That's crazy, that doesn't even sound right. How could they not want to cover your treatment, when you've been giving them your money. We got to be able to do something about that." He said while wiping the tears from his eyes.

Ron was still looking out of the window, while Eric was on the phone, and overheard part of the conversation. After listening to Eric he started to ponder his own situation, then in an instant, figured out a way to help both of them.

When Eric got off the phone, he went to the cell and sat on the bed. A couple of minutes later Ron walked in behind him.

"How are you holding up?" He asked.

"How do you think I'm holding up, do I look like everything is alright?" He responded with a look of desperation on his face.

Ron figured this was his chance to present Eric with his idea, so he took it. "Sorry to hear about your mother."

Eric's desperation switched to anger. "How the fuck do you know about my mother?"

"I overheard you talking on the phone."

"You did what?" He jumped up and grabbed Ron by the throat. "You were eavesdropping on my conversation."

"Wait, I'm sorry, I didn't mean to..., I can help." He said barely audible.

Eric loosened his grip. "What do you mean, you can help?"

"I have an idea, I need to get out of here, and you need to get out of here, right?"

Eric nodded in agreement

"I have a way for us both to achieve that."

Completely away from Ron at this point, he weighed and judged the proposal. Eric knew Ron said he was rich, but then again, he said that everything was seized by the Feds. What could he be talking about, escape? He didn't know what to think, but when a picture of his mother flashed across his mind, it didn't matter what Ron was offering, he was in.

The front lawn of this palatial home was sprawling and beautifully manicured. The sprinklers were spinning in an earthly pace, while bushes were being trimmed to perfection. The pathway to the residence appeared to be laced with the finest of marble, and the columns in front of the house were reminiscent of Roman Pillars. Each house in this exclusive enclave of Connecticut reeked of privilege.

Brian's Scott's car came to a halt. He checked himself out in the rearview mirror and combed his hair with his hands. He put his hands to his mouth and blew, not liking the smell he placed a small piece of gum in his mouth. He stepped out of his Mercedes Benz Coupe, straightened his pants then buttoned his three-piece Armani Suit. The closer he got to the front door he could feel his heart echoing in his ear. He rang the doorbell and waited.

"Right this way Sir, the lady of the house is expecting you."

He stepped in and followed her to the living room. On his way there he couldn't help but notice that the inside of the house was just as majestic as the outside.

"Would you like a cocktail Sir?"

"Yes, that would be nice, make it a double scotch."

As Brian looked around, she handed him his drink and told him to make himself comfortable then headed out the door. As soon as the maid left, he got up and strolled around the room in amazement at the quality of the furniture and decades-old mahogany fireplace. Even though he had been there before, he never really noticed it in such detail.

She stood at the top of the stairs and watched how gracefully how Brian walked across the room. With his broad shoulders and dark piercing eyes, that seemed to look through her soul. Why couldn't it just be the two of them, she thought. She knew she belonged to someone else, but she had always kept a special place in her heart for him. Before he could take another step, she said: "Hello Brian."

He turned in mid-stride then returned the greetings. "Hello, Kathlin."

The stare between the two of them lasted for what seemed like an eternity until Brian spoke.

"Kathlin, How could you, how could you do that to Ron, after he had given you the world."

She slowly descended the stairs, got closer to him then stopped. She ran her hand along the collar of his suit jacket, stared him in the eyes then walked towards the window. "I gave up everything for him Brian, everything. My degree, my life and most of all my family, they never wanted me to put my life on hold for him. My father always said, darling, I am a man, and I know men. You must always have your own first, or they will think that they own you. I can't begin to describe the look he had in his eyes, almost as if he were…disowning me. They vowed to never talk to me again, and haven't. Now look what he does,he goes and disrespects this marriage, by being with that whore, in my house, in my bed. He deserves everything he gets." She said, as she swung her long hair and walked away with the strut of a supermodel past her prime,"

"Kathlin look, he's facing a lot of time, you can't possibly want him to die in prison. Any amount of time they give him is equal to a life sentence."

"Did you know?" She asked.

"Did I know what?"

"Don't play dumb with me Brian, did you know?"

"Yes, I knew." With his head held low.

"Oh god, how could you let him touch me, knowing what he was doing?"

"Look, Kathlin, I'm sorry but you know how much he has helped me-

"Come on Brian, he treats you like shit, and you know it, but you still do everything he tells you to do. He treats you that way because he knows that you are smarter than he is, and if given the chance you will rise above him."

"Do you think it was easy to see him touching you and putting his hands all over what should be mine!"

Before he could catch what he said, and before she could get over the shock, he grabbed her by the waist and kissed her passionately. She tried to stop him, by pushing him away but felt the same level of lust shoot through her.

As Brian was getting dressed, he checked his watch. Hours had passed since he got to the house. He looked back at Kathlin, who was laid half-naked on the bed and asked. "Do they know about me?"

"No, I didn't tell them anything about you."

"Well, they said that they still have an ongoing investigation."

"So if I were you, I would lay low."

"I don't know if I can get any lower, I've got to go to work."

"Your right, for the same company whose money was stolen by your best friend, you should be alright." She said with a devilish grin.

"Tell me something, how are you getting by?"

"I have a little trust fund that Ron set up, plus you already know this is his father's house. It's been paid for, so they couldn't touch it.

"No no, I'm talking about the offshore accounts."

"There aren't any more offshore accounts. You don't seem

to understand that's what I've been trying to tell you about Ron. Someone gave him the heads up on the indictment against him, and he closed them out."

He stood over the dresser, with his face fiery red, and his fist in a ball. "So you mean to tell me that there is nothing left…nothing."

"That's one of the reasons why I did what I did."

CHAPTER 5

Prison is the craziest place in the world. Just when you think you're about to lose your mind, you adapt. Whether it's the food or the hostile environment, or the arrogance of your captors, you adapt.

Most of the stories in prison are true, but for the most part, they are overdramatized. The mental, physical and emotional stability of a prisoner, rests solely on his ability to adapt.

Ron Harper sat on the end of Eric's bed, while the old head sat on an ice cooler, watching them play chess. Ron looked at the Old head and gave him a wink of the eye as if to say watch this. It was Eric's move and his king was well protected, or so he thought. He moved his horse to say check, hoping Ron would move forward so that his queen could checkmate him. Instead, Ron slid further to the side, preventing the checkmate, which made Eric lose his composure. Before Ron made his next move, he looked at his young protégé in the eye and said.

"You know, there was an old saying that my father used to say to me."

"Oh yeah, what was that?" Eric asked.

"Oh what a tangled web we weave, when first we practice to deceive."

Eric burst out in laughter, as he looked at the Old Head. "What the fuck is that, some Shakespeare shit."

"It's just an old saying that's all you'll figure it out one day, I'm sure of it. By the way, checkmate."

Eric looked at his king and realized that it wasn't as protected as he thought.

The Old Head sat there laughing then said, "Let's go eat, It's about that time."

As they sat in the cellblocks dayroom, eating their gourmet meal, prepared by the prison's Chef, Ron said.

"This food is starting to taste better and better each day."

Eric and the Old head could not contain their laughter.

"You mean to tell me that steak and red wine is now taking a backseat to this bullshit," Eric said.

"I guess at this point, anything would taste good." The Old Head added.

"You've got that right." Ron lifted his head and mumbled through a mouth full of food.

Full from all the food they ate, and not much else to do. They sat around in the cell talking.

"How old are you anyway Old Head?" Ron asked.

"Don't worry about that, I like to keep that a secret."

"Well, you got to be older than me."

"Don't let this black and grey hair, fool you. You see I do five hundred pushups every day don't you?"

"Trying to stay fit huh?"

"That and I want to make sure I'm ready, just in case one of these young guys in here try to test me."

"Well me personally, if they tried me, I'll just have them bailed out and killed," Ron said it without any hesitation or emotion what so ever. Both the Old Head and Eric had been around for a long enough to know, that when someone makes a statement like that, they usually mean it. They just looked at each other and moved on.

For months now Ron Harper had been planning his comeback. His trial date was yet to be determined, and his bail hearing had been put off twice. Eric already had exuded confidence in his stride and was able to fit into any social setting, but knowledge of the Markets had to be essential for him to be able to interact in the financial world. Ron got a subscription to the Wall Street Journal and constantly went over his investment strategy with Eric.

Ron unfolded the paper and asked. "You ready to go over the stocks?"

"Here we go again," The Old Head said.

"How many times do we have to go over the same thing, I already know it like the back of my hand."

"Show me," Ron said.

"I already know that the S&P 500 tracks five hundred of the U.S. Stocks. The Dow Jones Industrial Average tracts the top 30 Companies, and the Nasdaq consist of Technology Stocks, like Google and Microsoft. Etc… I know the yield, the fifty-two weeks highs, and lows of each stock, how much dividends are paid for each stock every quarter. Come on baby, Put me in the game coach." Eric said, as he bobbed and weaved, and threw punches in the air, all while doing the Ali shuffle. "Oh yeah, and I'm pretty too."

"Okay," Ron said with a smile. "Well, tell me the purpose of getting into the Market."

"To buy and sell stocks."

Ron just stared at him.

"Oh," Eric said, hitting himself on the head. "Not just to buy and sell, but to make a steady profit."

"Good, now remember, I'm giving you the tools to spot what to buy, and when to buy them."

"I've heard enough." The Old Head said. "All of this stock talk is giving me a headache."

When the Old head walked out, Ron continued. "My Company has what we call a walk-on program, where stock traders compete for position. We give ten thousand dollars to each person, in an account, to see how much they can turn that into, afters two week period. That's why I've been teaching you my methods. Don't worry about doubling or tripling your money, because what goes up must come down. The Senior Executives will be monitoring you, and watching out for erratic trading. They would rather keep someone whose profits are steadily gaining, instead of a person who is all over the place, hot today and cold tomorrow, it shows no self-control. You follow me.

Eric nodded in agreement" I see what you're saying, you don't want to raise any suspicion on why I'm there."

"Correct, the more you know, the more you will fit in. Now let's go over what I need you to do."

Eric perked up this was the moment he's been waiting for. All of those nights and days they spent studying the Market, now it was time for him to hear Ron's plan.

"I have someone who is going to get you into my Company they don't know why not even my best friend Brian knows what I'm up to. All the person knows is that I'm doing you favor, because you need a job. Once you get into the company, you will have to get into my office and get on my computer. When you punch in my password, it will give you access to the company's financial accounts, which is a deep reserve. But it will not allow you to extract any money from those accounts until you break through the company's mainframe. Which I do not have the code to, because it's changed frequently.

"Don't worry about that, just leave it up to me. How much money are we talking about?" Eric asked.

"Up too two hundred million dollars."

"What?" Eric couldn't believe his ears. "Are you serious?"

Ron just nodded. "Why do you think I was so hard on you."

"I see why now. But with that much money, I doubt if it will go unnoticed."

"Listen, money is constantly coming and going, so it's going to take a minute to pinpoint. That's why I want you to take a little from each account, one or two million."

Eric lowered his head. Ron detected a hint of apprehension and kept talking.

"Eric listen, I know you could do it, I wouldn't ask you if I felt that you couldn't. I desperately want to get back at the Board, and I know that you want to help your mother, here's your chance."

When he heard his mother's name being mentioned, he lifted his head, and with a sly smile said: "Don't panic, you don't have to pull out all of your trump cards to keep me in the game."

Ron returned the smile and said. "What else could I do, it looked like I was losing you for a minute there. Listen, once you get into the company's mainframe, and extract the money, I have several accounts that I want you to disperse it to. When the money is in those accounts, I'll have someone retrieve it."

"Ron Harper! Ron Harper!" The C.O. yelled. "You got a visit, be ready in five minutes."

He brushed his teeth and combed his hair, trying to make himself look presentable.

"She comes to see you faithfully huh don't she," Eric asked.

"Whom"

"Your lady"

He shook his head from side to side then said, "You could say that."

"Ron Harper! You ready?"

He looked at the officer and said. "That don't seem like five minutes to me, but yeah I'm ready."

How in the hell am I going to get out to put this together?" Eric asked.

"Let's go, let's go." The Officer yelled.

As Ron walked out of the cellblock, he turned to Eric and said. "You have a bail hearing tomorrow morning. Playtime is over".

Eric just stood there and watched Ron as he walked away.

CHAPTER 6

Standing in the confined area of the visiting room, Ron always felt degraded. No matter how many times he went out there, he continued to have that feeling of being caged like an animal, for the world to see. Draped in brown garb, he leaned side to side and tapped his fingers on the two-inch-thick glass. Many thoughts ran through his mind, as he ground his teeth and awaited his union. The group of small holes in the middle of the glass gave slight relief to the hard grey steel that surrounded and suffocated him. Mothers, wives, sons, and daughters glowed with anticipation of seeing a loved one.

He dropped his thoughts and trained his eyes on the woman in the visiting area. She was amazing her black curly hair was rolled in a ponytail and her eyes appeared to gleam off of the light.Her smile was so radiating, that it was only matched by a child's on Christmas day. The sleek black dress that strangled her body exposed every delectable curve. He swallowed hard, cleared his throat and let out a loud sigh.

He regained his composure just in time. When she got close, they stood still exchanging affectionate smiles. Felicia Hernann lowered her head, knowing deep down inside that she could've done more, could do more. She looked up and asked.

"How are you doing in there?"

"I'm alright, I'm more concerned about you Felic, what took you so long to come and see me?"

"I was told by Brian, not to come and see you."

"I can't see why not, it's not like my wife doesn't know about us already."

"No, this has nothing to do with your wife. It's because the Government is still investigating this case."

"You tell him that I said, there's nothing to worry about. A couple of transfers here and there is all they've got. The main thing is not to panic. Kathlin can only account for the transfers in her name. She doesn't have proof of anyone else."

"Well that's good, I'll let him know. Now, when are you getting out of here?"

"I'm not sure, I'm working on that as we speak, but I'm going to need your help."

"Sure, no problem, whatever you need."

"I have this kid, that I want you to get into the walk-on program, and I want you to skip all the necessary background checks." He reached in his pocket and pulled out a small piece of paper. He unfolded it and put it up to the glass.

"She squinted her eyes and read the name. "Eric Sanders."

"Yeah that's it, give it to Joseph, He'll know what to do. Now I need you to….."

XXXX

Early the next morning, Eric was escorted from his cell block to a holding cell in the Federal Court building. He paced the large cell, which contained twenty other inmates, waiting to go to court. Some were there for bail hearings, while others would be pleading guilty or not guilty to their alleged crimes. Some would be getting sentenced, which was the worst part of passing through those dungeons.

Eric was aware of his surroundings, he noticed a man sitting on the bench with his head in his hands, unable to sit up straight. Another man stood in the corner, with peppered eyes, probably from a night of sobbing and another shook his head and pounded his fist on the wall. All in all, each face had a story to tell. He wondered what picture the other inmates drew from him and his pacing because his story was just about to begin.

"Eric Sanders you're next!" Shouted an Officer.

He stepped forward then was taken down a long corridor and escorted into the courtroom. He faced straight ahead and saw two well-dressed men sitting at the defense table.

"Eric Sanders?"

"Yes, that's me."

"How are you? My name is Joseph Cooper. I'm Rons Attorney, he directed me to represent you here today. This is my assistant Anthony Myers. Now I want you to sit back and let me do all the talking. Only speak when the judge addresses you directly, okay."

"Yeah, I understand," he said nodding his head.

"Good, I'm going to get your bail set to a reasonable amount. Now, I already spoke to your mother and she assured us the deed to the brownstone."

"I don't know about that, that's all we have." He said in a desperate voice. "I can't allow her to do that.

"Listen, I'm pulling every possible string to get your ass out of here. The Bail-bondsman is waiting right outside those doors as soon as the Judge agrees, your out."

Eric watched as people began to stand.

"All rise!" Shouted the bailiff.

"Okay, I've got a lot on my plate this morning, so let's get started."

"Well, good morning your Honor."

"Counsel," she responded with a smile.

"I'm requesting that my client's bail be reduced from five hundred thousand to fifty thousand. Your Honor, I believe my client was targeted by the Government in this instance. And that they became a little overzealous in there attempt to rid the world of evil, and deny him his rights."

"Your Honor." The Assistant U.S. Attorney said. "Mr. Sanders is a threat to the community, he was apprehended with two kilo's of cocaine-"

"It's not mine!" Eric shouted as he jumped out of his seat.

"Mr. Sanders, sit down!" The Judge shouted with equal force.

He reluctantly complied, and the U.S. Attorney continued.

"As I was saying, your Honor, not only did he get caught with illegal narcotics, he is also associated with a group of ex-offenders who call themselves Hackers inc. Now your Honor, between that and the number of drugs in his possession, I think it best to keep bail at the original amount."

"Counsel." the judge said, with a look of, come on, give me something to work with here.

"Your Honor, his mother is willing to give up her house as collateral."

"You know what." The Judge said. I've heard enough, I think that fifty thousand is sufficient enough to secure the safety of the community. Don't you think." she glanced at the U.S. Attorney to put emphasis on her sarcasm. "Young man, I expect you to be here on your next court appearance, or a warrant will be issued for your arrest. And no one, I mean no one will be able to help you, not even Mr. Cooper. Do I make myself clear?"

"Yes, your Honor."

"Okay good, let me hear the next case".

As everyone prepared for the next case on the docket, Joseph Cooper and his assistant gathered their briefcases.

"So that's it," Eric asked.

"That's it, you'll be out in a few hours. By the way, sorry to hear about your mother. No one would want to lose a loved one." Joseph said as he stared into Eric's eyes.

Eric returned the gaze, somewhat puzzled, but didn't say a word.

CHAPTER 7

When Eric stepped out of the Metropolitan Detention Center, he paused for a minute, to soak up the rays of the sun. He inhaled deeply and tasted his tongue. For some reason, the air smelled and tasted better on the outside. Everything appeared to be moving fast around him. He stood in one spot and began looking around at all the buildings as if he was a tourist.

Once the initial shock wore off, it took him no time to indulge in some of the sweeter things that life had to offer. Like choosing what he wanted to eat. He saw a vendor on the side of the curb and ordered a hot dog with everything. While he waited for his food, he focussed his attention on a young lady who walked by, revealing too much cleavage. When she turned her head, she smiled, and with his eyes glued to her butt, he yelled. "Thank you, Lord, I'm never going back to jail!" He reached for his hot dog with one hand and waited for a cab with the other.

"Where to?" The driver asked.

"Take me to 116th street."

XXXX

"When the yellow cab pulled in front of his Brownstone, he noticed all of the people outside. Some of them were sitting on their porches, and some were cleaning their cars. Kids were running back and forth trying to catch each other and multi-colored bikes were being ridden up and down the block. He stepped out of the cab and was met with an uneasy feeling, he started to wonder how his neighbors felt about him, after causing all of that commotion months earlier. As he walked up to the stairs, he could feel all eyes on him.

A neighbor, an old Jewish woman, who still had the numbers tattooed on her arm from the days at a Nazi Concentration camp in Germany, waved him down.

Damn, here it comes a million and one questions. He thought.

"Eric Listen."

"Yes, Mrs. Rosenbom." He answered in a soft tone.

"We all saw what happened to you-"

"I'm sorry for the commotion-"

"It's no need to be sorry, we don't think that was right, what was done to you."

Eric paused, not knowing how to respond. He didn't expect to hear that.

"They had no right to shoot at you like that, for nothing. Any one of us could've been killed. So if you need someone to testify for you, I will."

"Thank you." He said, looking around at all the neighbors.

"We all feel the same way." She said, spreading out her arms.

When Eric looked over her shoulders, it seemed as if the whole block was waving at him. He hugged Mrs. Rosenbom, then headed up the stairs. He tried putting his key in the door, but it swung open and the scream from his mother and sister were deafening. His sister ran and jumped in his arms.

"Lisa, Lisa." He said coughing. Your gonna squeeze the air out of me."

"Shut up boy," she said punching him on his arm and sucking her teeth.

"Come here baby, and give your mother a hug." She said, then tried to squeeze the rest of the air out of him. "I missed you so much, stand back and let me get a good look at you. You look, skinny boy. Lisa fix him a big plate."

He sat down next to his mother and rubbed his hand over the silk scarf that she had covered over her head. "You look good ma."

"Thank you, baby, your lawyers took good care of me."

"They did?" He asked with a curious expression on his face.

"Why do you look so surprised? They didn't tell you? Oh, Eric, they paid for my chemotherapy, that's why I look a little better. I still feel kind of weak, but the Doctors said that I will get stronger after a while. They want me to come in and run some more tests."

He stood up frowned, folded his arms and put one hand on his face, he stared out of the window, while he rubbed his five o'clock shadow.

"Is everything alright son?... Eric! She yelled trying to get his attention.

"Huh," he said to himself, then turned around. "I hear you Ma."

"What's on your mind son?"

"Nothing much, I'm just thinking about something."

"Oh, before I forget, your lawyer left something for you" She reached behind the couch and handed him a large yellow envelope.

He took the envelope to his room, with the food that his sister made for him. He kicked off his shoes and jumped in the bed.

After devouring the food, he stared at the envelope and wondered what was inside. He held it in his hand and measured the weight. When he held it upside down, the contents slid from one side to the other. He placed the envelope in his lap, he had no idea what could be inside. Finally, he decided to open it. He looked in his nightstand drawer, and pulled out a pair of scissors then started to cut it open. He looked inside and pulled out a stack of one hundred dollar bills, confused he ripped off the seal and started to count. By the time he was finished, he had ten thousand dollars spread across the bed.

He dug his hand inside the envelope again, and pulled out an identification card with his name and picture on it, it read ERIC SANDERS, DAY TRADER, R.H. HOLDINGS. He looked inside once more, then poured the rest of the contents on the bed. There was a cell-phone, a set of keys and a Cartier wristwatch that fell on top of a note.He grabbed the keys and unfolded the note. He glanced over it, then started to read. Eric, how are you? I hope you are enjoying your new-found freedom. Hopefully, you are loving it. By now, the suspense must be killing you, wondering what all of these items are for. Well, you need not wait any longer, just pick up your phone, push the send button, and you'll find out. He looked at the phone, then back at the note. He dropped the note reached for the phone and made the call. After a few rings, someone answered.

"Hello."

"Who is this?" Eric asked.

"Who is this?" Ron Harper answered in a joking manner. "Who do you think this is?"

"Ron! Oh shit! how the fuck did you get a cell phone in there?"

"You know how it is, all Correctional officers aren't playing by the same rules. Plus, money talks."

"I know that what I really mean is, why did you wait for me to leave before you made a move like that. Do you know how many people I could've been calling, half the world."

"Yeah I know, that's why I waited."

"What're all these items for?"

"Well, I knew you were going to need a little money in your pocket to get around."

Eric thought to himself, A little money huh.

"And the I.D. is needed to enter the building. The keys are for your new apartment on Central Park West. The key with the red tip on it will allow you to get into my office. Once you get into my office, use my password to gain access to the Company's files. If you are successful in breaking into the Company's firewalls, I want you to spread the money evenly between several accounts. When that is completed, send all nine accounts to the tenth one. Within a couple of days, the money will be accessed, and you will be fully compensated. Eric listen, make sure you don't tell anyone about what your doing"

"You don't think I'm going to be talking to people like, Hey how are you, My name is Eric Sanders, and by the way, I'm stealing two hundred million from this Company, would you like some."

Ron laughed. "Point well taken. I just want this to go off without a problem."

"There won't be any problems, don't worry. Now, what's the password?"

The password and the account numbers are on the inside of the seal, that was wrapped around the money. The watch is a gift, you can pay me back later. Oh, before I forget, you have an appointment at the Brook Brothers store on Fifth Avenue. Your first day starts tomorrow. So, until we see each other face to face, I wish you the best of luck."

Eric dropped the phone on the bed, stood up and looked outside of the window, then said to himself, what in the world have I gotten myself into.

He grabbed his car keys from on top of the dresser and walked out into the living room. He thanked his sister Lisa for getting his car back from the impound, then headed for the door.

"Eric wait!" Lisa yelled. " Three guys came by here, looking for you, while you were in jail."

He paused, turned around and said. "What?"

"Three guys stopped by here."

"What did they want? What did they say?"

"All they said was that they were just checking up on you, and wanted to know if you're alright."

"Did they say anything else?"

"No, but it was kind of strange because they kept looking

around like they didn't believe me or something. They kept saying that we'll be back."

"Was Ma here with you?"

"Yeah, we just got back from the hospital."

"Alight, I think I know who it was. I'll be back later."

CHAPTER 8

When Eric arrived at 145th and Edgecomb Ave. He pulled over at the beginning of the block. Before he could get out of his car, he was attacked by a group of hustlers, who obviously thought he wanted to buy drugs. They followed him all the way to the middle of the block, even though he was trying to get away from them. He tried to tell them that his reasons for being there weren't to get high but he kept being attacked.

"I got that good shit over here for you." a dealer said.

"Mines is better." Another yelled, then stuck out his hand and showed Eric a bunch of small white rocks.

"Back up, back up. He looks like a man who likes to smoke weed." another man added. "Whatever you want, we have it on this block, take your pick."

Trying to get to the middle of the block, was like trying to score a touchdown, but instead of dodging defenders, he was dodging dealers.

Addicts were lined up along the sidewalk, looking for the drug of their choice. Willing to pay with cash or sexual favors. Whatever the case, they had the same objective, which was to get high.

He finally reached the building, where a couple of guys were sitting on the front stoop. They looked at him, like he was crazy, except one man who knew him from high school.

"Is Beeju upstairs?" Eric asked.

"I'm not sure, hold on let me see." The dealer ran into the building, while he waited. He looked both left and right and fidgeted with his car keys. He tried to remain calm, but was unable to stand still., He was hoping that the police didn't raid the block while he was there. He could see the Judges face now, fresh out on bail, and you go right back to a drug area. You gotta be kidding me, lock his stupid ass up.

The dealer finally stuck his head out of the building, and waved his hand, giving Eric the indication to come upstairs.

On his way into the building, he thought about Beeju, a Haitian who had a reputation for violence and wondered how the meeting would go. The upstairs was crowded with beautiful women, hoping to be the next it-girl to catch a hustler's eye. When he reached the apartment door, he knocked and waited patiently. A woman answered who was half-naked. He stared her up and down. Before he could speak, a voice came from the back round.

"Let him in."

He walked in and saw Beeju sitting in a chair with two other guys.His long dreadlocks and bloodshot eyes were a constant reminder of his reputation.

"What happened to the bag, E? Beeju asked with his thick Caribbean accent.

"I got locked up, right after I got off the phone with you."

"Oh...why didn't you just say that?"

"Listen, don't send anybody to my house again, what we do is between me and you, not my family-"

"What did you say?" Beeju stood up and walked towards Eric. "I didn't hear you say that again" it appeared as if his eyes were becoming increasingly red, with each step. Eric stood silent, not because he was afraid, but because of the other two guys who were staring at him, because they had the same propensity for violence.

"Let me tell you something," he said with an angry tone, as he got closer to Eric. "You came to me, I didn't come to you. You needed my help. So I suggest that you stop talking crazy, and pay me my fucking money."

"I'm going to pay you, why do you think I'm here? Just give me a little time, I'll get it up. I'm working on something big right now."

"You know what Eric, I like you, since we go way back, and you didn't run your mouth to the police, I'll give you a couple of weeks, no more, no less."

Eric turned to leave, but before you could take a step, he was given a bit of advice.

"There is nothing that I won't do for my money E, nothing."

Eric listened carefully, then left.

Beeju watched, as he walked outside of the building. He always had a lot of respect for E, ever since high school, but business was business.

CHAPTER 9

Eric jumped in his car and headed for his appointment at a high-end tailoring shop, where they carried every name brand suit you could imagine. He weighed and judged his options and came to the conclusion that there was no turning back now, how could he, he thought. Too much was riding on him, never in a million years, would he have thought that so much would be riding on him. One wrong move could land him in jail for the rest of his life, but fuck it. What else could he do at this point?

He finally found a parking space, got out and looked around. Though he lived in New York, he didn't have a need to shop in this expensive part of Manhattan. He glanced at his reflection in the store window looked himself up and down, then brushed off his jeans and sweatshirt. He studied his Timberland boots, then lifted his head high and walked in the store.

Suits of every color were hung against the wall, different fabrics and textures played spread out on the table in the middle of the store. There were about five to six people walking around with measuring tapes around their necks, measuring the customer's necks, waist size, arm, and leg length and shoulder widths.

He walked over to the counter and spoke to an older man, with patches of grey hair and thick glasses.

"Uh, excuse me, I believe I have an appointment today."

The Old man looked up then reached under the counter and pulled out a hard covered log book. "What's your name son?"

"Sanders," he said relieved that there was such a thing as reservations to get fitted for clothes. He smirked to himself, wondering where he'd been for the last twenty years.

"Okay yes, Mr. sanders is that correct?"

"Yes, Sir."

"Alright then, follow me so that I can get your measurements."

They walked towards the middle of the floor, where a large mirror was positioned, and a rack with different styles of suit jackets. When the tailor began to take his measurements, he asked.

"Can you tell me how much all of this is going to cost?"

"Nothing for you." The old man said.

"It has been paid for already, a woman came by, picked out and paid for everything."

A strange look washed over his face. "A woman?"

The tailor looked up. "You don't know her?"

"No, I don't

"You don't?" The tailor asked inquisitively.

"No...I mean yes, yeah I know her, but how much could you really know someone, you know what I mean. I just wish I knew more about her."

"Hey, I know the feeling, sometimes you can go your whole life without really knowing someone. The more you think you know. The further away you are. Take me for instance, I've been married for forty years, and sure I know some things about my wife, a lot of things, but for the most part, you'll never really understand them. Do I love her, sure with all my heart, but you know women, can't live with them-"

"Can't live without them." Eric chimed in.

"Cheer up young man. I wish I had somebody to buy my clothes for me, I wouldn't care if I knew her or not."

Eric temporarily dozed off into space and wondered about his Wall Street transition. About how smooth or rough it was going to be. The stakes were high and the consequences severe, but people were depending on him. He knew he had to make it as smooth as possible. "I suppose your right."

"Well, we're all done here, Sir. A couple of suits shirts and ties will be ready for you shortly. The rest you can pick up tomorrow. Okay, good luck young man."

"Thank you, I have a feeling I'm going to need it." He mumbled the last part to himself.

He left the store with several bags in his hands, placed them in the trunk of his car, then jumped in now he needed to visit one of his old friends.

The opportunity placed him on the inside, something hackers rarely had the opportunity to have. Normally, you would have to try and break through a company's mainframe from the outside, which made it a bit more difficult. But now, since he was going to be on the inside, it was like putting a kid in a candy store. The more he thought about it, the more excited he became. Two hundred million at the tips of his fingers, why just take two, why not three or four that matter. Calm down Eric, he said to himself. Don't get carried away. He brushed the thought out of his mind, as he pulled up to an old meatpacking plant in the East Village and parked. It's been a long time since he's seen his friends at the computer club. By being out on bail, he knew that it wouldn't be wise to socialize with some of the City's most notable Hackers. But he had no choice, he knew that once he told them what he needed to do, they would be more than willing to assist him. The thing that most people don't realize, was that most hackers take a certain level of pride in their work. For many of them, finance is not the purpose of breaking into computer systems. Their reward comes from knowing that they achieved their goal. Basically, they like to test their knowledge and ability to do the impossible. Besides, most of the firewalls in a Company's computer system were built by hackers.

The same way an athlete prepares for the big game, or a politician prepares to run for public office, hackers do the same preparing for the big event. By being a part of this club, Eric already knew what he had to do and what he needed. But he didn't have time to sit and create a program that would help him crack the code.

He got to the door of the building and gave the secret knock. His friends looked through the peephole, then rushed to open the door.

"Hey E, what's up, man?" Peter said, greeting him with a hug, and a boyish grin.

"I'm good, what about you?"

"You know me, still fighting the forces of evil."

That was his way of describing his fight against gaining entry into a company's system.

"Still think it's you against the world huh," Eric asked.

"Who else is going to stop them from controlling us all, pretty soon they're gonna be telling us who we should buy from, how we should do it. They want to computerize every aspect of our lives, and I'm not going to stand for it! I'm going to keep fighting until my fingers are gone.

"Okay, calm down, I forgot that I can't get you started."

Peter removed his glasses, then makes believe he's blowing into a paper bag, in order to control his breathing and calm down. "Your right, sometimes I get carried away. Enough about me. What's up with you, we heard about your situation, are you sure you're alright?"

"Yeah, I'm sure."

As they walked across the room, Eric received waves and nods from different tables. Each man sat at his own table, typing away on his computer, doing god knows what.

"Eric, tell me something, why in the world would you sell drugs?"

"Don't believe-"

"Hey remember we stole all of those credit card numbers from Macy's, but you wanted to return it just hours later."

"Yeah, I remember."

You were always the most honest out of the group. What about the time-"

"Peter, listen, I would love to stand here and go down memory lane with you, but I'm onto something big, and I need to get past a numbered code."

"How do you know it's a numbered code?"

Eric stood still, thinking about what to say.

"You've got inside information, don't you? I want in."

"Look, Pete, this is a one-man show, If I'm successful, I'll take care of you. Deal."

Pete paused for a moment, then reluctantly said: "Yes, but only for you E, don't forget me."

"I've got you, that's my word."

"Do you remember what to do, when a portal opens up for you?"

"Don't insult me like that, it's like riding a bike."

He looked at Eric and said. "Don't fail me young skywalker, you represent all of us, from the moment you touch that first button."

"Yes, teacher," Eric said, then bowed. "I will not dishonor the family."

With that, their laughter filled the warehouse.

CHAPTER 10

Brian Scott was interrupted by his activities by a phone call. "Hello, He said, as he answered the phone. He quickly regained his composure, fixed himself and said. "Ron, what's going on?"

"Hey, what's up Brian, How is my old friend?"

"I'm doing well, and you, how about you?"

"As well as can be expected."

"The Company is doing well, the second-quarter earnings were up, better than the last. So the Board feels good about the ability to be able to reimburse the shareholders for their loss."

"The Loss came about, because of the Board. Instead of trying to recoup the money that was lost, they chose to turn me into the Security and Exchange Commission.

"Come on Ron, what else could they have done. If they didn't do that the whole Company would have been under investigation, you know that."

"They could've done something else, I tell you that. This Company was built on the blood sweat and tears of my father, If it wasn't for him giving them fifty-one percent stake in R.H. Holdings, where would they be?"

"You might be right, but they weren't the ones making

enormous amounts of risky investments either. The Shell Companies that were set up.For Insider trading to make larger profits on the side. Sooner or later, it was all going to come crashing down on us."

"Everyone makes a bad investment from time to time. I didn't hear any complaints when those same, so-called risky investments were paying off."

"But Ron, come on, almost half of the cash reserve gone, on a hunch, a wish."

Ron didn't have a good feeling about what he was hearing, Brian was always on his side. Never would he question his motives or business decisions. "Where's the loyalty, Brian? I haven't been gone that long Have I? Since when did you start being an advocate for the Board. If my memory serves me correctly, your name was on some of those offshore accounts."

Brian's bravado, his recent holier than thou attitude was cut in half. It was expressed by his silence on the phone. Ron changed the subject, knowing now that he had Brian's full attention. "Who did they get to replace me?"

"No one yet, but they are aggressively looking. At this point, they realize that you haven't been convicted of anything yet, so I think that they are waiting to see what happens to you at your trial. I also heard them say, that the money you lost could be considered your share of the Company."

Ron didn't bother to respond, because he knew that technically he was part owner, but financially he was ruined. "You listen to Jazz now Brian?"

Shocked, Brian said "Excuse me"

"Jazz, I heard Jazz playing in the background when you picked up the phone. You told me you hated Jazz."

Kathlin hit Brian with a pillow on the back of his head, he picked one up and threw it back at her, as he left the room. I know what I said, I decided to give it a try."

"That particular song sounds familiar, can't place it, who sings that song?"

"I don't know he answered in a nervous tone. It all sounds the same to me."

"Huh, don't worry about it, it will come to me later. Listen, when the time comes, I'm going to need you to do what we spoke about, alright."

"Yeah yeah, of course...sure no problem. Just call me when it's time."

After he hung up the phone, Brian stood still for a moment. He felt bad about the recent change of events. It wasn't his fault, he had no control over his feelings, they just got the best of him. Now he was caught between a rock and a hard place. He headed back inside the bedroom where Kathlin was waiting. When he saw her, every other thought left his mind. Lust again consumed him. She was laying across the bed in lingerie, all black, all lace, with matching high heels. When she stood up, he stared at her, he looked her up and down, and felt a combination of pleasure and shame.

XXXX

The Board of Directors at R.H.Holdings had a late afternoon meeting at their headquarters in Manhattan. Each of them with there various degrees in business, and who served on other Boards, all had a stake in this meeting. The senior member slammed a gavel bringing the meeting into order. Once everyone quieted down, the meeting got underway.

There wasn't much to be happy about, even though second-quarter earnings were up, they still had a long way to go, to recoup from the damage that Ron Harper caused.

"How's everyone today?" Asked the Senior member.

An acknowledgment of good, came from everyone in attendance.

"As you all know, profits are up, but we are going to have to make excellent investments from now on, until the end of the year, if we are going to be operating in the green."

"Well after that stunt Ron pulled on this Company, to be where we are now, I think, shows the belief that investors have in our ability to make the right investments." One member said.

"I agree, what we have to do now, is figure out where do we go from here,and stay the course." The Senior member responded. "Let's not forget that he still has forty-nine percent of this Company."

"Until he gets convicted, then the rest of those shares will go back to the Board." Another member stood up and said.

"Tomorrow, we have a bunch of new recruits coming in, hopefully, we will be able to find the newest and brightest Stock Traders in the City. Then we will be able to make our way back onto the Fortune Five Hundred list again."

"Good." One more member added to the conversation. "I feel bad about Ron, but he almost single-handedly destroyed his father's legacy. After everything his father had done for us, we had to turn him in. Thankgod Kathlin alerted us to his activity."

CHAPTER 11

Central Park West is located in one of the most Affluent sections of Manhattan, home to only the rich and famous. Apartments cost well into the millions, and Eric's was no different. It wasn't uncommon to walk down the street and run into the latest Golden Globe winner and Oscar-nominated Actors. This was where everyone with wealth wanted an apartment.

Once the cab dropped him off, he strolled into the building with confidence. The doorman greeted him while he held the door.

"Good evening Sir. Please feel free to contact me if you need anything."

"Thank you," Eric responded with a smile.

The apartment was spacious, as soon as he walked in, he noticed the twenty-foot ceilings, and handcrafted furniture that sat on top of white oak finished floors. He strolled over to the kitchen and thought about all of the meals his mother would love to cook in a place like this. The six-burner stove, two ovens and a preparation table that was fit for a chef. One day he said to himself, one day, as soon as he got his share of the money.

When he got to the master bedroom, that was it, the mattress was so thick, it seemed to swallow him up, he was no longer able to keep his eyes open, he fell into a deep sleep.

The morning came in no time, Eric felt as if he just went to sleep. After he rolled over to turn off the alarm clock, he yawned and stretched out his legs, clenched his toes and made a strong fist. He laid back to put one hand behind his head, while he rubbed his stomach and chest with the other. He still didn't believe the beauty of the apartment that he was in.

When he heard the computerized voice on the wall in the bathroom, say it's sixty-eight degrees outside, He jumped in the shower. With water pounding on his head, and steam surrounding the bathroom, he stood there motionless, as if he was a sponge soaking up every drop of water coming from the showerhead. Then I spoke aloud. "There's no turning back now baby, keep your head up champ and rise to the occasion.

He put on his robe and walked to the bedroom window. He pulled back the curtains and smiled at the sight of Central Park. New York never looked so good. It was the largest park there, and from that height, you were able to see the trees, some that were so large that it blocked his view, but he was still able to see all that it had to offer. From the joggers that followed the same decade's worn path, to the benches that were occupied by the morning readers.

He put on one of his black tailor-made suits and matching shoes, checked himself out in the mirror, then headed out the door.

As he was about to leave the building, the doorman reluctantly held the door for him.

"Thank you," Eric said.

"Is there anything you would like for me to do for you today while your gone Sir?"

"No, I'm fine,"

"Okay then, have a good day Sir," He said as he held the cab door for him.

"While the cab weaved through the morning traffic, he made a call to his mother.

"Hello"

"What's up to Lisa, how is she doing?"

"She's fine, where have you been?"

"I'm working on something right now, and it's going to take a couple of days. But I'll check in to let you know that I'm alright. Give Ma a kiss for me, and tell her that I love her."

"Eric, what do you have yourself mixed up in now?"

"I'll talk to you soon, bye" He shut off the phone before she could respond.

Little pockets of sweat began to form in the palms of his hands, and it felt as if he had a mouth full of sand, that prevented him from swallowing. The cab pulled over in front of the R.H.Holding building, in the middle of the business district. He paid the driver with a large bill and told him to keep the change, He stepped out and looked up at the building, then said to himself, let the games begin.

He checked his watch and realized that he was twenty minutes early, so he decided to go across the street for a cup of coffee, and a donut. When he swung the door open and walked inside the eatery, he caught eye contact with a beautiful woman. Who sat alone at a table near the window. They stayed glued to one another until he reached the counter. By the look on the woman's face, he could tell that she was somewhat interested, so he ordered then walked in her direction. Before she could turn around to take a peak, he was standing right behind her.

"Excuse me, is this seat taken," he asked with a smile on his face.

"No, not at all," she said, clearly taken off guard.

Her beauty was so stunning, that he found himself at a loss for words. Her jet black hair was rolled up in a bun, exposing her thin cheekbones arched eyebrows and curved nose. "Umm, do you come here often?"

She smiled and said. "From time to time."

"Well, I guess I'm going to have to get my coffee here from time to time."

"I haven't seen you around here before, where do you work?"

Eric looked at his watch, then rushed to get up, "I can't be late for my first date."

"Oh, what time is it?"

"Ten minutes to nine."

"I can't be late either." she said, "I have to check some people in this morning"

As they both rushed out the door, they didn't realize that they were both going in the same direction, until the started rushing up the stairs of the R.H.Holdings building. They paused, faced each other and at the same time said. "You work here"

"With a smile on his face, Eric stared at her and said. "Yes, and I start today."

She rejected the smile and started checking her notepad.

"What's your name?"

"He patted himself down, then pulled out his I.D. From the inside of his jacket. "Eric Sanders."

When he said his name, she turned her face away. That beautiful smile he enjoyed earlier disappeared. Only disappointment could be read, all over her face. "Hey, what's wrong?" He asked.

"Nothing," she said. "Nothing"

But by the way, she was shaking her head, he knew it was something. "I am on your list right?"

"Yes you are, are you ready to go inside?" she said slightly rolling her eyes.

She turned to walk inside the building, but he stuck out his arm to prevent her, "And your name is?"

"Felicia Hernann,"

"Now I'm ready," he said moving his hand out of the way.

The inside of the building was bustling with people, trying to get to whatever floor that they worked on. Eric looked around for people who resembled himself, then finally, at last, he saw another brown face in the crowd.

"Meet me in the last room to the right, on the fifth floor I have to check-in the other new recruits, okay."

"Alright, I'll see you there."

XXXX

Half an hour later, people were shaking hands and introducing themselves. They were talking about how good they were, and how well they were going to do. Eric joined the fray, playing his part. Only if they knew that his reasons for being there, were much more complex than they could ever imagine.

CHAPTER 12

The noise in the room died down, once Felicia entered the room. The men glanced at one another, in approval of her appearance. Before she placed the briefcase on the table, she glanced at Eric, quickly studying his deep brown eyes, and coffee skin. She turned her head and cleared her throat, then addressed the crowd.

"Gentlemen you have all been picked to participate in our entry-level program. The program will not only test your knowledge on trading but your ability to make a steady profit. Today will be the first day of your potential careers. This is a two-week course. Each of you will be given ten thousand dollars in your accounts.

You can buy and sell whatever you want, it's up to you. At the end of the course, whoever has the highest profit margins will remain, the rest will be terminated. Now, if you would go to the tenth floor, you will see your name atyour desk, your passwords will be on a piece under your keypads."

Before they had a chance to leave the room, a man walked inside.

"One-second guys." Felicia said, "This is Brian Scott, one of our senior executives."

"Good Morning guys."

"Good Morning." filled the room

"Would you like to say something, Mr. Scott?" She asked.

"Yes I would, thank you." He said, looking out at the possible next generation of the Company. "Many of you chose this profession to make money, am I right?"

"Yes, Sir" came from the crowd.

"Okay then, let'smake some money!"

The traders left the room with enthusiasm and waited for the elevators. While everyone else was involved in their own conversations, Eric looked back to see Brian Scott and Felicia Hernann in a heated discussion. When they turned to see him watching, they turned and walked away. He couldn't help but wonder what the conversation was all about.

The elevators approached the tenth floor, and everyone spilled out, it was like walking into a computer warehouse. Everyone searched for their computer, hoping to be seated next to the one that they had become acquainted with. Eric was in the far corner, near the emergency exit. They began taking their seats, searching for their passwords.

"I'm on" one reader yelled.

"Me too" yelled another.

One by one, they all had access. Eric sat at his desk and started banging away at his keyboard. He didn't pay any attention to the other traders. All he wanted to know, was what type of software he was dealing with. This would depend on how long it would take for him to reach the company's mainframe, and extract the money.

XXXX

Joseph Cooper had lunch with the U.S. Attorney and the presiding Judge in Ron Harper's fraud case. Reservations were made at a french cuisine restaurant. He was hoping to broker some type of plea deal for his client, but if a deal couldn't be reached, then maybe he could walk away with assurance for a bail reduction.

He greeted the Judge as she approached the table. "Judge, how are you?" He said pulling out her chair for her.

She sat down, put her purse on the empty chair next to them, then folded her arms. "French food huh, you must be trying to bribe me a counselor." She said with a smile.

"Bribe a Federal Judge, me, of course not. I wouldn't dare do a thing like that, but since this is your favorite food, I wanted to get this meeting off to a good start." He said winking his eye.

"Where is Mr. Goldstone?"

"I don't know, I called his office, and they said that he was on his way. You know him, he's probably off somewhere saving the world from jaywalkers and ticket scalper, I don't know."

You must've forgotten the disorderly conduct and traffic violators didn't you?"

"Here he comes now."

Sorry, I'm late, but you know me, I have to do my part to make this world a better place."

Both the Judge and Joseph was silent, they just stared at Goldstone, giving that I told you so look.

"Hello judge," Goldstone said.

"Hello." She responded, but not with the same enthusiasm she'd given to Joseph. "What do you say we order first, then get down to business."

After eating the last piece of food on their plates, and washing it down with glasses of wine, it was time to negotiate.

"So Joseph, why am I here?"Goldstone asked.

"Well, let me get right to the point, the case against my client is bogus and you know it. No jury in this City is going to convict a man on hearsay."

Goldstone turned to the judge, to study her expression. He knew a meeting like this was unethical, but he didn't get any feedback from her. She acted like everything was okay, so he responded. "I beg to differ, Joseph, in a climate like this where corporate corruption in running rampant, I'll be able to convict the mailroom clerk for delivering the wrong piece of mail.

The Judge shifted in her chair she heard enough. "It needs to sit here and go over every possible outcome of this case. The reason why we are all here is to bring about a sensible solution to your clients Delima," she said, turning to Joseph. "Now Joseph, I know that we've known each other for a very long time, but I have to agree with Richard on this one. In these days and times, the evidence could be minimal. Just last week I sentenced two brokers to twenty-five years apiece for insider trading. And if you ask me, I believe the jury on found them guilty because of the lifestyle that they lived, not for the alleged crime itself."

"Okay then, what are we talking about here?"

"I'm willing to offer twenty years, depending on the pre-sentence report. And substantial restitution of course."

"Are you out of your mind! That's a death sentence for him. I'm not even going to present that to him."

"That's the best I can do, take it or leave it."

"In that case, you can shove it."

They both stood up to leave, but was directed to sit back down by the Judge, "It appears that we have a failure to communicate, so here's what I'll do. We all agree that a lot of retirees lost value on their 401k's due to the actions of Mr. Harper, correct."

"They both nodded their heads.

"Okay then Richard, you're just going to have to prove your case to a jury, that Ron Harper in fact set up those off-shore accounts, and wired money from his own company and wired it to them. Thereby defrauding both his Board of Directors and his investors. Which in turn Joseph, you will have to prove that those transfers, if at all made, were for investment purposes only. And that your client wasn't trying to steal or defraud anyone. So, until then I'm going to guarantee a bail hearing, at which time, I will set one at a reasonable amount."

"Judge, I don't think that's fair," Goldstone said.

"Richard, I didn't ask you what you thought, don't you have a case coming in front of me tomorrow?"

He had a feeling, he knew what she was referring to, so he nervously said "Yes."

"Good, then don't get on my bad side.

When they stood up to leave, the Judge gave one final warning. "One more thing gentlemen, need I remind you that this meeting never took place."

"What Meeting?" Goldstone responded as he brushed past Joseph on his way to the door.

Joseph looked at the Judge and said. "Thank you, I thought I was gonna have to beat his ass in here."

She laughed then said. "After a meal like this, you didn't think you were going to leave here empty-handed, did you?" Then she grabbed her bag and returned the wink from earlier.

CHAPTER 13

After a long day of trading, most employees went to local bars to relax and reflect on the highs and lows of the Market. While Eric was leaving the building, he saw Felicia waiting for a cab. He walked up behind her and whispered in her ear.

"Just one drink, I promise I won't try and take advantage of you."

The sound of his voice was enough to make her reflect back to the coffee shop, where she first saw him. It's been a while since she felt that way about a man, and it felt good. She lowered her head and pondered the possibilities. Damn, she screamed to herself, why did he, have to be Eric Sanders. She worked at the Company long enough to know that business and pleasure didn't mix. Out of all the men in the City, he had to be Eric Sanders, she tried to fight the urge, but the level of lust that ran through her clogged her better judgment. She believed that she would be able to separate the two.

"Just one, what are you afraid of." He whispered again.

She tilted her head, bit her lower lip, then turned to face him, and said. "Just one, then I'm going home."

He took her to Clove's Lounge, a popular after-hours nightspot, where they served delicious food and drinks. At any given night, you were liable to see your favorite R&B Artist performing their latest hit, with one of the liveliest bands in the City. Since Eric was a regular, as soon as he walked in, he was greeted by all the waitresses.

"Hey E, where have you been?" One waitress asked while she glanced at Felic. "I haven't seen you in a while."

"I've just been chilling, you know, low key."

"Well, you need to start coming around more often. This place misses you. Wait right here while I find you a good table. As a matter of fact, have a couple of drinks at the bar on me, while you wait."

"Thanks, good looking out."

As the waitress walked away, she gave Felic one last look, and it wasn't nice.

He grabbed her hand and led her to the bar, squeezing past the usual large crowds. "What would you like?"

"I'll have whatever you're having."

"Alright, let me have two long island ice teas please."

"Coming right up." The bartender said.

He stood there, staring into Felic's eyes.

"What?" She asked, leaning back.

"Nothing much, I'm just amazed at you beauty, that's all."

"Yeah yeah yeah, I guess you are amazed at the waitress's beauty as well huh."

"What." He said with a grin. "Stop it, she's an old friend."

"Um-hum, I bet."

"The waitress returned just in time, and asked "Are you guys ready, I've got you one of the best tables in the house. Follow me."

They followed her to a table, that was a couple of passes away from the stage. Before the waitress left, Felic asked.

"Can I have another long island iced tea please?"

When the waitress left, Eric looked at Felic and said. "Just one huh."

They sat back listening to the sounds and finishing up on a small meal'

"I'm going to head to the ladies room, I'll be back in a second."

Eric took the opportunity to call Ron. He scanned the bar as he waited for Ron

To pick up the phone.

"Hello," Ron answered in a low voice.

"Yeah, it's me."

"How's it going kid?"

"I'm in."

"Good, I knew you would be alright, just remember everything I taught you, and you'll fit in perfectly. Just take it one day at a time. The art of deception is just that, an art. There are no second chances, the first time you veer off-script, all will be lost, and you will be figured out. So stay focussed."

While Ron was talking, he spotted Felicia leaving the lady's room."I'm focussed. Uh, how's the Old Head?, tell him that I said what's up, I got to go."

"All right, keep in touch and keep me posted."

Eric put his phone in his pocket, just as Felicia got close.

"Who were you talking to?" She asked.

"Nobody special."

"Nobody special huh. Well, that's none of my business anyway. We're just having drinks right?"

"You mean two drinks, don't you."

"She rolled her eye and sucked her teeth. "I don't care if you're seeing someone."

"Good, stop being nosey."

"Does this happen to you all the time?"

"What's that?"

"Don't play stupid with me, you see all of these women staring at you."

He laughed then said. "Maybe they're looking at you, who knows."

She started to feel the effects of her drinks, she licked her lips and said. "Let's give them something to look at." She led the way to the floor and could feel his eyes glued to her body. They danced in a sensual manner, to a Luther Vandross classic, that seemed to suggest they needed a room.

"I want to show you my new apartment, would you like to see it?"

She nodded in agreement, then said, "Just a tour, that's it, then I have to go home and get ready for work tomorrow."

Alright, just a tour then you can go."

They turned and headed for the door. He held felic close, while they waited outside for their cab. They watched the sidewalk full of people either coming from, or going to the Lounge. When the cab pulled up, he held the door open for her. But before they jumped in, he noticed a black BMW slowly ride by, which caused him to pause.

"What's wrong?" She asked.

"Nothing, I think I'm seeing things, that's all."

"It's probably the liquor." She pulled and his arm. "Come on let's go"

"Yeah okay," Eric said as he shook his head. "You might be right." Deep down inside he knew it wasn't the liquor.

Before they reached the apartment the passion was running wild. Inside the elevator, he couldn't keep his hands off of her. When they reached the apartment, he opened the door with one hand and searched her body with the other. He slammed the door closed behind him and forcibly turned her around, and stood behind her. He pressed up against her warm body, then started to kiss her neck. He could feel Felic grinding against him, and her moans only excited him even more. He placed his hands on her thighs pulled up her skirt and started removing her panties. At the same time, she reached behind and unzipped his pants. When she grabbed a fist full of his penis, he couldn't take it anymore. He left her panties in the middle of her thighs, pulled her hair, then penetrated her from behind. Her moans filled the apartment.

"I'm going to make you mine tonight," he said.

"Show me." It was her only response.

CHAPTER 14

The next day, Eric continued to make good investments, working off of Ron Harper's method, he increased his portfolio, by a thousand dollars. Remembering his instructions, he didn't want to get carried away with the profit margin. When he got up to leave his desk, he was bothered by Shawn pope, another trader in the program. For some reason, this trader made it his business to follow every move that Eric made. There was always one person who just couldn't mind his or her own business.

"Where are you going?"The trader asked. "If I was you, I'll keep buying and selling."

"And if I was you, I'll mind my goddamn business."

"When he stepped out of the room, he walked towards the elevators. He stepped in and took it to the top floor, where he saw various mid-level executives and secretaries. It was larger than the floor he left. He held his head up and walked around as if he belonged there, making sure not to look too much like he was lost. A large office was at the end of the floor, he wondered could that be Ron Harper's office, he stood there looking inside. He could see boxes on the couch, like either someone was moving in or they were moving out.

"Can I help you, young man?" Brian Scott asked.

Eric jumped, shocked. "Uh, no Sir, I was just looking around, wondering how it would feel to have an office of my own."

"One day, you just might have one, but until then, this floor is off-limits to new recruits."

"Oh, I didn't know, I thought it would be alright." Eric looked in the office as he spoke. "It looks like someone is packing to leave."

"Just the opposite Mr…Sanders." Brian said as he read the I.D. "Someone is unpacking to stay. We lost our C.E.O. several months ago, but in a few days we will be getting another one."

Upon hearing the news, Eric looked alittle uneasy.

"So Mr. Sanders, are you through daydreaming?"

"Yes, thank you, I need to get back to work."

When Eric turned to leave, he saw a sign that said emergency exit, right across from Ron Harper's office. "Thank you again, Mr. Scott, I didn't mean any harm."

"None took, just do your job and stay off of this floor."

"I will." He said, glancing one more time at the emergency exit.

When he got back to his desk, his curiosity got the best of him either that, or his hunches were correct. After making a few more trades, it was time for lunch.

"Hey Eric, you going to lunch? Asked the same nosey trader.

"Yeah yeah, I'm right behind you guys, I have to make up for the time I was gone. He waited a few minutes, typing away at his computer and giving the other traders enough time to leave the floor. He needed to make sure that they were all gone before he made his move. Once he felt the coast was clear, he looked up at the emergency exit next to his desk, he got up and opened it slowly, then ran up several flights. When he got to the last floor, he eased the door open, and a smile appeared on his face. He was looking directly into Ron Harper's office. Beads of sweat began to fill his forehead, and his hands became moist. He could no longer control the nerves in his body, as the sporadic jitters and shakes consumed him since it was lunchtime, he decided to wait until the floor was empty.

Everyone should be gone by now he thought, so he stuck his head out of the stairwell to see if the coast was clear. There wasn't any movement on the floor as far as he could tell, he stepped out and went straight to Ron's office. Using the red-tipped key, that was in the envelope that Ron's lawyer left for him, he went inside closed the shades, then walked over to the desk. He sat down and cut the computer on, then punched in Ron's password A TANGLED WEB, then waited patiently until it said, access granted. Now that he had access, it was time to go deep inside the Company's mainframe. He plugged in his adapter. He knew he needed to copy the information and transfer it to his laptop. Within a couple of minutes, a series of numbers popped on the screen, flipping faster than he could see them. At that moment he knew he was in. This is going to be easier than I thought he said to himself, as he sat in the chair. His head turned quickly as he heard a voice and saw a shadow go by the office. He turned off the computer and rushed out of the chair. He eased closer to the door and peeked out but no one was in sight. He pulled the door open, stepped out into the hallway, closed the door behind him, stepped out into the hallway, closed the door behind him, then went back down the Emergency Exit.

By the time he got back to his seat, he was exhausted. He sat there for a brief moment, collecting his thoughts. All he needed was time.

Across the street from the building, where Eric went to get a bit to eat, he once again saw Brian and Felic in an intense conversation, He pretended not to see them, then ordered a sandwich to go.

"Eric! Eric!" Felic yelled as she waved to get his attention.

"He tried to act like he didn't hear her until she yelled his name a third time.

"Hey, Eric!"

He looked in her direction and smiled as if he found a long lost friend.

"Eric, you remember Mr. Scott don't you?"

"Yes I remember, How could I forget." He stuck out his hand. "How are you, Sir?"

"Well Mr. Sanders, I would like to commend you on your trades so far. From what I hear, you already have posted a small profit, and it's consistent. That's what we're looking for. It shows that you are not erratic in your methods."

"Thank you, Mr. Scott, I believe that I could be a good asset to this Company. Maybe even work me up to Mid-Level Executive one say, who knows."

Brian smiled. "It's possible, all things are possible, but for now keep up the good work kid." He turned to leave, then gave Felic one last look before he walked off.

Once Brian left the eatery, Eric moved right in. "How come he stays on your case like that?"

She played coy, then said. "I don't know what you mean, what are you referring to?"

"It always appears as if he's chewing you out, that's all."

"No, it's not like that at all. It's just that he expects me to have all the answers, that's all," she responded as she lowered her head.

He detected her uneasiness and changed the subject. "All right, I hear you, I'll let that one go."

She perked back up. "Good, enough about him, how did you wake up this morning?

"If you would've stayed, then you would've known," he said his eye on hers. "I woke up holding onto a pillow."

That made her laugh, "Don't be like that, I had to go home and get ready for work."

"Work can't possibly be better than getting that morning orgasm, now can it?"

She paused, closed her eyes, then smiled. "Of course not. Listen, I have to get back to work, see you tonight?

"What kind of question is that, what do you think?"

CHAPTER 15

As he sat in front of his computer, Eric stopped trading to check on the account numbers that Ron Harper had given him. He typed in the first number that popped on the screen, it displayed zero funds. He went over each account to make sure that it would be ready to receive transactions. Each one displayed zero funds.

Eric clicked off his computer, gathered his things and headed out of the building. Damn he thought, I need to see how my mother is doing, I can't let myself get too caught up where I forget to keep in touch. He dialed her number. Anyway, this whole thing should be over with real soon. The phone rang a couple of times before his mother answered.

"Hello."

"Hey, Ma, how you doing?"

"I'm fine son, how are you?"

"I'm good."

"You know we went to the hospital today."

"What, why didn't you call me to let me know. I could've met you there."

"Well, Lisa told me that you were working on, something."

"I am Ma, this time it's big. After this everything is going to be much better for us."

"Baby you be careful now, you are already dealing with one problem."

"Don't worry, I'll be fine. What did the Doctors say?"

"Well right now it's too early to tell, we have an appointment next week."

"Make sure you tell me what day it is so that I can meet you there. Okay Ma, I love you."

"I love you too baby, be good now if you can't be good be careful."

"Alright Ma, I will."

Before Eric could get comfortable in the back seat of his cab, he saw someone duck behind a building across the street. "Wait! Wait!" he yelled to the driver with a tremendous amount of energy, making the driver peer through the rearview mirror, trying to asses Eric's state of mind.

"Is everything alright Sir?"

Silence filled the cab.

"Sir!" The driver yelled, making Eric jump. "Are you all right?"

He gave the driver a confused look, then said. "Yeah, I'm good…,I thought I saw...don't worry about it, just drive. I need to clear my head."

He wasn't drinking this time, so he knew that his mind wasn't playing tricks on him. He told the driver that he was fine, but he kept looking out the back window, trying to confirm his hunch, but he didn't see anything. The driver drove off trying to maneuver through the crowded Manhattan traffic, asking.

"Do you want me to just drive?"

When he gave it one more look, his eyes became wide and his stomach made room for his heart. For a minute he couldn't speak, he saw the same BMW five cars behind them. "Make a left!" He yelled. "Turn!, turn!"

The driver complied, then asked. "Who the hell are you trying to get away from?"

"I have no idea," Eric said when he looked back. "Just keep driving. Blend in with those other cabs in front of us."

The driver isolated himself in the middle of fifteen cars, while Eric ducked low behind the car seat.

"Do you still see a black BMW behind us? Eric asked afraid to look up.

"I think we lost him, all of these cabs must've confused him."

Eric let out a loud sigh, but he was still engulfed in fear."

"Where to?" the driver asked.

"Take me to Central Park West."

"Are you sure, now."

"Haha, very funny. You're in the wrong line of work. I'm drowning in my own sweat, and you got jokes. Yeah, I'm sure." He laid back in the cab, on his way to his apartment, he took a deep breath and exhaled. He was trying to figure out who in the world was following him, could someone know what he was doing. Could this be some type of warning for him to back off? Can't be he thought. He'd been too careful this far. Even Ron Harper's best friend Brian Scott didn't know what he was doing, so who could it be and why? Whatever the reason, he had no time to be playing Nascar with this BMW, up and down the City streets.

As the cab glided over every bump and crack in the road, he bounced around in the back seat, staring at the gleaming city lights in the dark night. He was still wracking his brain, going over every possible reason why he was being followed, then in an instant, Beeju popped in his head. How in the hell did they know where I worked at, He couldn't let them interfere in what he was doing, he had to stay ahead of them.

At least he could breathe a little easier, knowing who it was following him.

When the cab reached his building, the driver finally spoke. He was virtually silent throughout the whole ride. "Hey man, anytime you need a ride, give me a call. I'll be your personal driver, and I'll come wherever you are." He reached in his pocket and pulled out his card. Eric grabbed the card, stepped out and slammed the door.

CHAPTER 16

As Eric walked up to the door of his apartment, The smell of food brought him to life. When he opened it up he saw a table set up with two candles and a bottle of red wine The song by the Isley Brothers "I've got to have your love." filled the air. When he walked closer to the table, he read a card that sat next to the wine. Eric, I haven't felt this way in a long time, thank you. While he was reading the card, two arms wrapped around his waist.

"Uhmm, what took you so long?" Felic asked pressing her body against his. He turned around, held her in his arms and kissed her on her forehead. She stood in front of him, in one of his t-shirts, with nothing else on underneath it.

"I didn't know that you were waiting for me, if I did I would've made it my business to get here earlier."

Romantic music continued to play as they sat in his super-sized bath tube. She took the time to set up scented candles all around the bathroom before he got there. She wanted it to be a surprise. They sipped on Dom Perignon Champagne, while she laid in his arms.

"What exactly is your job description," Eric asked.

She pulled his arms around her neck and wiggled closer to him. He could sense that she needed to feel safe and secure, so he held her with a firm grip.

"I'm whatever they need me to be at the time."

"What does that mean?" He asked with a strange look on his face.

"God, I haven't felt this safe, this good in a long time." She snuggled even closer to him. "There is no particular title for my job. If I'm needed to travel outside of the State or Country with them, I go. If I have to play hostess at parties or gatherings I will. I don't have a problem with my job, people will kill for a position like mine. I have an all-access pass to some of the best restaurants and hotels around the world, and…." she looked back at him, then finished. "The best private planes."

"So I guess you are a very important person huh?"

She shrugged. "I guess you could say that, whatever they need me to be."

"For some reason, I get the impression that you are not comfortable with what you do."

"This Company has been good to me, ever since the accident."

"Accident!, what accident," He asked with concern in his voice.

With just the mention of that stressful time in her life, she started to shake and spill champagne in the tube. Eric grabbed her glass and put it to the side.

"I don't want to talk about it." She replied in a mumbled voice.

"Okay, okay, we don't have to talk about it. Just relax." He combed her hair with his hands, kissed her on the cheek, and squeezed her tight.

After a few moments of silence, she started to speak. "One night two years ago, there was a Christmas party for all of the employees at the Company, at the C.E.O.'s house. I was drinking, and I wasn't feeling well, so I left early. All I remember after that was waking up in the hospital handcuffed to the bed. A police officer was reading me my rights, and telling me that I was under arrest for murder."

"What!"

She nodded her head. "I was hysterical, a Company rep was telling me that I killed the wife of one of the Company's top Executives and his child. But I told them that, that was impossible. After numerous court appearances, I was told by the Company's lawyers, that I was off the hook when I started to question them about what happened, All they would say is that we took care of it."

"What were their names?"

"Who?" Felic asked. "The Company's Lawyers?"

"Yeah."

"Joseph Cooper..and I can't remember his brother's name."

Eric's curiosity was peaked. "What happened after that?"

"All I know is that I can see my children again and that I pray for that woman and child every day. God knows that I didn't mean to kill anyone."

"So that's why you are anything they need you to be. You feel like you owe them something. Don't you?"

She exhaled. "They've held it over my head ever since."

Eric grabbed two towels and said. "Let's get out of this water before we turn into prunes."

They laid next to each other on his king-sized mattress, warming up from the warm bath that they had together. They were holding each other like there was no tomorrow.

"Now, tell me a little bit about yourself," Felic said. "What are you caught up in?"

He paused to digest the question, wondering what she could mean. "I'm not caught up in anything, my mother is really sick and I needed a good job, to help with the bills. I hear the commissions are very high, true or false."

"True, I'm just asking because I see how hard you work, you work as if your life depended on it."

"It does, if you only knew without this job, it would be over for me." He kissed her on the forehead, then reached over and cut off the light."

CHAPTER 17

The living room was the most relaxing place in the house, this was the only place that she felt comfortable. Here she could be away from the high life and constant lies her husband use to tell her. "Oh Kathlin, I love you, you are the only one for me." Yeah right, she used to think to herself. She could see right through his bullshit. All of the time that he spent, deceiving people, he never perfected the craft with her, or maybe she felt that he had her right where he needed her to be. He probably thought that she would listen to anything he said, without question. Well, he was wrong. He was so smart, that he didn't even see that she was getting tired of the lies.

The living room was her escape mechanism, a sense of feeling safe, amidst the fairytale lifestyle she so frequently maneuvered. Here she could play her Jazz music, and sip her customary wine and temporarily drift to another place and time. That is until she received a knock at the door. She got up from her comfortable position and went to see who it was. When she looked out of the window, anger shot through her, as she said to herself. "What in the world is this bitch doing here.?"

"Mrs. Harper, open the door, I know you're in there, I need to have a word with you, it's very important."

After a few seconds of contemplating, she unlocked the door

and faced the woman who ruined her marriage. “Mrs. Hernann, what could you possibly want to talk to me about? Don’t you already have my husband?”

Felic stood still and stared at Kathlin in amazement. She’d seen her once before, at the Christmas party two years ago, but since then, she made it her business to avoid her.

Kathlin noticed the way Felic admired her, training her eye on every part of her anatomy. Look, are you just gonna stand there and undress me with your eyes, or are you going to get to the point?”

“Mrs. Harper, this is concerning Ron and the Company.”

“What does that have to do with me?”

“First off, let me apologize for my actions, I nevermeant to hurt you and I’m sorry that this ever happened.”

“You haven’t answered my question. Miss Hernann.”

“Mrs. Harper, I’ve heard through various sources, that Ron is going to be indicted on federal charges.”

“Good, he needs to be put away for a long time.”

“Mrs harper, my sources tell me that you are going to be indicted as well.”

“What, why me?”

“And I don’t think that’s right. Somehow they found offshore accounts in your name.

Kathlin was silent, as she paced back and forth, trying to figure out what to do next. She looked at Felic and asked, “Are you truly apologetic for sleeping with my husband?”

Felic stared then responded. " Why else would I be here."

Kathlin stuck out her hand and said, "Follow me." Felic took her hand and they stepped in the house. "Do you drink?"

She nodded and gave her a soft. "Yes."

As they walked towards the living room, Kathlin said. "We need to discuss the best way for me to get out of this. It just might be beneficial for both of us."

"Mrs. Harper!, Mrs. Harper!"

Kathlin shook her head and saw the maid standing in front of her.

"You must've been in deep thought Mrs. Harper, I called you several times."

"What time is it?" Kathlin asked as she sat up.

"It's late come on give me that drink." she took the glass out of Kathlin's hand then put a nice blanket on her. "I'm leaving, I'll see you tomorrow."

Kathlin laid stretched out on the couch. She knew that this ordeal would be over with soon.

CHAPTER 18

Eric awoke to the sound of his alarm clock. Before he could turn over to cut it off, Felic did it for him.the scene was much different from the night before. The warmth from scented candles we're gone, the aroma of cooked food no longer fill the air,and the lovemaking songs gave way to the morning news.

"I left the shower on for you when you're ready," she said.

when he rolled over she was opening the curtains in the room. He watched her as she walked away, then said. "Felic, come over here for a second, I need to talk to you."

From the look in his eyes, she knew that he wanted to do more than talk. " oh no, I know what's on your mind, and it's out of the question. it's getting late."

Eric smiled, then jumped up and went towards the bathroom. after a fifteen-minute shower, he walked out and saw a dark blue suit with matching shoes made out for him. he stood there thinking, now she wants to dress me huh. soon she's going to want me to be home by a certain time. women, can't live with them can't live without them. well at least I'll have somebody at the company to help me just in case something goes wrong,or I get in trouble.

she entered the room while he was getting dressed, then stood in front of him and said. “ here, let me fix this tie for you.” while she wrapped one end of the tie around the other, she fixated her eyes on his smooth face and inhale the cologne emanating from his body. “ you know what, I believe that you are going to go far in this company. What ever methods you’re using to pick your stocks, it’s a good one.”

“I had a good teacher.”

“who taught you?”

“no one in particular, just a friend of mine I spent a little time with.”

“a friend huh? must be a very smart man,” she said finishing his tie.

he is, I’m hoping to give him a hundred percent return on his investment.”

She stepped back, looked him up and down then said. “ I knew you would look good in this suit.”

in an instant, he thought about what to tell her when had told him when she was picking up his suits. irrational instincts made him grab Felic by the arm before she could walk away.

startled she said. “ hey, what’s the problem?”

“How did you know I would look good in this suit?”, he asked with curiousness in his voice.

she slowly pulled away from him, reached up and gave him a kiss. “ Because I just picked it up for you, how would I know? what’s wrong with you anyway, come here.” she put the back of her hand on his forehead. “Nope, you don’t have a fever. Must be the job. this line of work has a way of doing this to people, making them a little Restless. just relax and keep doing what you're doing, and everything will be alright."

He felt a little crazy, for even asking her that question, but then again, stranger things have happened so far. who could he believe? he took one last look in the mirror and headed for the door.

"Eric, listen, I need to make a stop, I'll meet you at the office okay."

XXXX

233rd Dyre Avenue. was in the Uptown section of the Bronx. It was considered a middle-class neighborhood period one and two-family homes crowded the area, and was divided by front Lawns and homegrown Gardens. large trees loomed over the streets below and gave Refuge from the unforgiving sun."

Every time Felic came home, it was a two-fold feeling for her. flushed with a mixture of Joy and Pain, she never knew which emotion would win her over. So much of her life was here, everything that she worked for, was for the benefit of her children. As the chauffeur driven car pulled over, she couldn't contain herself. She hopped out and ran across the street.

"Mommy! mommy!" A five-year-old little boy and afour-year-old girl ran to greet her.

"She spread her arms out as wide as she could. "oh my babies, how are you?

"Fine", they answered

she went back and forth, kissing and hugging each other one by one. "I missed you so much," she said handing him a bag full of toys. Felic looked up to see her sister at the front door.

"Kids come inside," Michelle yelled.

they turned with the look of sadness, then said. "Okay, bye mommy."

"Wait wait wait."Felic said pulling them close to her and squeezing them tight. " mommy loves you, So be good okay. They both nodded in agreement. "

"okay good, give Mommy a kiss."

After kissing their mother. They ran into the house concentrating on the toys that Felic had brought them.

"How many times I have to told you to call before you come by." Michelle said."

"Every time I call, supposedly they're never here, and I'm getting tired of it. They are mine those are my children, not yours."

"there's a reason for that, when are you going to come and be in their lives for good,not every couple of weeks."

"It's not time yet," Felic screamed.

"It's not time yet, it's not time yet. That's all I hear from you your obligation is either to your job or to them."her sister yelled pointing to the house. "You don't owe that damn company your life, do you?"

Felicia turned away with flooded eyes. "You just don't understand."

"Make me understand."

"I can't!"

"Try!"

Felicia remained silent, she wiped the tears that poured from her eyes and pulled out an envelope from a purse handed it to Michelle. "This should cover all the for a while." She turned to leave, but her sister grabbed her by the arms and hugged her.

"Felicia, I love you and those kids love you. Do whatever it is you have to do, then come back home."

"I will." She said, as she shook her head and wiped her nose.

Michele watched as Felicia walked away. An uneasy feeling consumed her, she didn't know if she would ever see Felicia again.

While the Black Limousine was driving off, they couldn't do much but share an uncertain stare. She told the driver to take her to JFK Airport, then she eased back in her seat knowing that her children deserved better than a part-time mother.

CHAPTER 19

While Eric sat at his desk, working on his computer, he noticed his phone vibrating on his desk. He picked it up and answered it. "Hello"

"Eric listen we have reservations for lunch, with a potential client. I need you to meet me at JFK, flight leaves at ten sharp"

"JFK?" He asked.

"Yes don't be late, the reservations are in Miami."

He checked his watch, to see how much time he had to get there, then jumped out of his seat and grabbed his jacket. On his way out of the office, he said. " You fellas keep up the good work I got to go."

"Yeah yeah yeah,who does this guy think he is? While the rest of us sit here and bust our asses, he's running around doing god-knows-what. I'm going to one of the senior Executives with this, the first chance I get." The nosey Trader said.

Eric ran out of the building, waved for a cab then checked his surroundings. No BMW he thought, Beeju and his crime Partners must be tired this morning."

"Where to?"The driver asked.

"I need to get there by ten."

His mind was in overdrive, trying to figure out how long it would take him to extract the money, and disperse it into the new accounts. He needed the right amount of time because there would be no Second Chances.

He reached the airport, five minutes to ten, and stepped out of the cab and ran to the front desk. " Excuse me," he said to the young lady behind the counter.

"Yes, may I help you?"

"My name is Eric Sanders, I believe I have a reservation."

"One minute Sir, let me check." She tapped a couple of keys on the computer, then said. "Yes you do Sir, Go down that Corridor to gate six."

"Thank you." He turned around and headed for the gate. When he reached the gate, there was a security guard standing there. "Uh, my name is Eric Sanders."

The guard checked the list then said. "Right this way Sir. You'll be flying on the G-5, right over there. "

He hurried towards the jet, walked up the stairs and saw Felic.

"What took you so long?" She said, smiling.

He went over to kiss her, thinking about finally joining the mile high club, but she pushed him away. "What's the problem?" He asked with a strange look on his face.

"Hello, Eric." Brian Scot said. Returning from the restroom.

Eric turned around straightened up, then said. "How are you, Sir?"

"Good, Good Mr. Sanders. Sit down and fasten your seat belt."

Eric looked at Felic, then sat down.

When the plane reached cruising altitude, they released there, seat belts, and got in relax mode.

"Ever been on a private jet before Eric?" Brian asked.

"No Sir, I haven't, but I always wanted to," Eric replied as he looked around. He wondered what was he doing there, out of all the other traders, why him?

Brian sensed Eric uneasiness, so he decided to make him feel a little more comfortable. "Eric relaxes, you must be wondering why you are here. Well, I have to tell you that your trading methods are impressive. There's only one other person that I know of who was able to continually bring in steady profits through his trades."

Eric swallowed hard, then asked. "Who was that?"

"A good friend of mine,"

"Whatever happened to this friend?"

Before Brian had a chance to answer, the stewardess walked in.

"Would you like anything to drink Sir?"

"Yes." Brian said."Bring me a scotch on the rocks." He looked at Felic, then said make that two. What about you Eric?"

"Sure I'll take one."

Good, make that three. Now getting back to your question, My friend found himself in some trouble, and he is now waiting to go to trial. Even though he was good at what he did, he let it get the best of him, and didn't want to pull back when it was time to. Eric, this is a very tricky business, today everything could be roses, then tomorrow we're all hanging on to our shirts. I'm telling you this so that you won't lose your perspective. The minute you lose your focus and things don't seem to be going your way. I don't want you to steal from the people that you are supposed to be working for, which are the shareholders. They come first without them we don't have a job."

The stewardess returned with the drinks. When Brian got his glass, he took a sip and closed his eyes. "Excellent." He said to the stewardess. "Excellent. You know Eric, it wasn't so much that he intentionally stole from the shareholders of this Company, but he knew that his investments were risky, but he still made them anyway."

"Well if he knew it was risky, why would he still make those investments?"

"For the shareholders. In his mind, he did it for them. He felt that if he could wrestle control of the Company from the Board of Directors, he could bring them a better return than they were getting at the time." Brian sighed. "One thing led to another, and he found himself in jail."

"Sounds like a shrewd businessman to me."

"Yup, shrewd and dangerous," Brian responded while looking out of the window. "Shrewd and dangerous."

When the plane landed, a black Maybach was waiting to pick them up and take them to one of the most expensive areas in Miami. The driver held the door for each of them. When Eric stepped inside, he sunk in the plush seats, then leaned back. It was the first time he was ever in a Maybach, and the first time in Miami.

As the driver crossed the Causeway Bridge, Eric took in the sights. The large Palm trees and grand Hotels made it feel more like a vacation than a business trip

The Maybach pulled into a gated community on Fisher Island, that were full of million-dollar homes, and was greeted by Antonio Smitz. “Welcome to Miami, everyone. How was your flight?”

“Pleasant,” Brian said. “Let me introduce you to my colleges. This is Eric Sanders, a soon to be a new addition to our Company.”

Eric gave Antonio a firm handshake and returned the stare. “And this is-”

“Wait a minute, this must be the lovely Miss Hernann that I have heard so much about. Pleased to meet you,” he said with a seductive glare.

“Nonsense.” Felic said, “The pleasure is all mine.”

“Well,” Antonio said as he exhaled. “Now that we are all acquainted with one another, let’s go inside follow me.”

They walked straight to the back of the house, where a large number of men and women were at different tables. Some were swimming in the pool and some were sitting around conversing. Eric found himself admiring the beautiful women that were standing alongside the pool. Before they sat down at their table. Felic gave him a hard bump on his arm, then rolled her eyes. He knew what the bump was for, but played as if he had no idea. When they sat down, the waiter started playing silverware in front of them.

“I hope you don’t mind eating out here.” Antonio said, “I figured that since it was so nice out, it wouldn’t be a problem. I have my cook prepare a seafood dish. He looked around, then motioned to one of his waiters. “Uh….bring three bottles of our finest wine, to go with this meal.”

After they enjoyed the shrimp and lobster, it was time to get down to business.

"I hope you all enjoyed your meal." Mr. Smitz asked.

"Delicious," Felic responded, and they all agreed.

"Now I've got to be honest with you, I was told that dealing with you and your Company would be a Bad Idea, due to your past problems."

"Those problems were just that, in the past," Briann said, with authority. "We have a team of new traders, as well as some of our more experienced portfolio managers."

"I just don't know how safe it would be to deal with a Company, who's C.E.O. steals from its shareholders."

"Those are just allegations, nothing has been proven."

"I understand that It's just that the people I represent like to be discrete. Do you understand? They can not be a part of any kind of investigation about where their money is coming from."

"Well as you know, we are very discrete. And I have a feeling that you have already made up your mind, so can we cut to the chase, and get down to business."

Brian was just trying his hand, he had no idea whether Mr. Smitz had made up his mind or not, he was just tired of the back and forth, but the tactic seemed to work.

"I want to invest two hundred million dollars, in the name of the Smitz Family Corp. Can you handle that?"

"Sure, that's no problem." Brian reached in his jacket pocket and handed him a card with an account number on the back.

Smitz picked up his phone, walked towards the pool, and made a call. When he finished talking, he stood there with his back facing them. After a few minutes, he received a call in return. "Yes, uh-huh, okay good." He hung up the phone, walked back towards the table, then said. "It's been sent."

Brian stood up, walked a few paces then placed a call. After a minute or two, he walked back to the table. "Everythings is clear, it's all there."

"Well, I guess this concludes our meeting."

"I believe it does."

"Oh, one more thing Mr. Scott, I was told to tell you by my associates, that if anything happens to their money, there's nothing that they won't do to get it back, nothing."

"Nothing is going to happen," Brian responded in an emphatic tone.

They shook hands then Mr. Smitz said, "I'm having a party tonight on my yacht, would you like to stay? I promise that it will have something for everyone there.

"We're going to have to pass on that, we have a lot of work to do. Thanks for the offer anyway."

On the plane ride back to New York, Brian and Felic took a nap but Eric was wide awake, he was still trying to digest what he just saw. Two hundred million, that quick-changing hands, unbelievable. He watched Felic as she slept, and thought, she wasn't even fazed by the exchange. She played her part well, she was eye candy, and nothing more, and nothing less. She basically sealed the deal. Men always want to appear rich and powerful around gorgeous women. The way she smiled, plus her physical appearance relaxed Mr. Smitz and made him feel comfortable enough to trust his money with them.

"Their flight returned by four, so they headed back to the Company. Eric bought and sold a few more stocks, just to be active at his computer, but his mind was far away from his desk.

CHAPTER 20

Late that afternoon, when everyone started filing out of the building, Eric saw an opportunity. He went through the Exit doors and ran up the stairs. Once he got to the top floor, he eased the door open and peeked through. He didn't see anyone on the floor, so he decided to take a chance, he pulled out the key with the red on it and put it in the door, but it wouldn't turn. He pulled the key out then put it back in, trying to some how-to jimmy the lock, but that wouldn't work either. The door had a new lock. Frustration set in, as he thought about breaking the door handle. He quickly changed that thought, knowing that it would draw too much attention. It would be Monday before he had another chance to try to get into Ron's office. But how?

Brian forgot his briefcase in his office, on his way out of the building, and turned back around to board the elevator. When he reached his floor, he turned the corner and saw the Emergency Exit door closing. He yelled out. "Hello!" but he didn't receive an answer. He yelled again, "Hello, who's there?" but still didn't receive an answer. He rushed to the Exit and pushed the door open. He ran down the stairwell. With each flight he came to, he opened the door and looked out on the floor. When he didn't see anyone, he continued on. He tried one last floor, and when he opened the door, he saw Eric headed towards the elevators. He found it strange that Eric would be on that floor again after he told him not to.

Brian jumped on another elevator and tried to catch him before he left the building. By the time he got downstairs. Eric was already hailing a cab.

"Eric wait!" Brian yelled running out of the building.

Eric turned to see who it was calling him, then said. "Hey, Mr. Scott I thought you were gone."

"I left something in my office, that I had to come and get. Anyway, I forgot to invite you to a party in the Hamptons this weekend."

Before Eric had a chance to answer, Brian said. "Good, I'll see you there. Felic knows where it is, he patted Eric on the back, then headed back to the building.

It's been years since Kathlin had spoken to her father. Ever since she made the decision to abandon her career and marry Ron Harper. Her attempts to reach out to him and reconcile their differences always ended with her wasting her breath and time. He refused to communicate with her, ever since she went against his best wishes. Her father was always a good judge of character, he told her that, no matter how much a snake tries to camouflage and blend into its surroundings, it was still a snake. And if given the chance, without hesitation, it will bite you. Finally, his words wrang true, she was bitten. But this time, she was determined not to be the one stepped on and walked over. She spoke to her mother one time before, whenever she decided to call, but that ended quickly. Although her mother loved her, she did not want to get in the middle of a family feud. She thought it best for everyone, is she didn't go against her husband. She knew her daughter was strong enough to take care of herself, plus her other children kept her posted on Kathlin's well being. While her brother went off to the military, her sister got a job as a reporter and worked for the Daily News Kathlin kept in close contact with both of them. Now that Ron was in jail, and she filed for divorce, she took a chance to go see her father.

When she got to the house, she pulled open the black metal gates that separated the small house from the sidewalk. She stopped to look at the same burgundy minivan, that sat in the driveway. She nervously walked around the side of the house, with each step, getting harder and harder to take. Once she got to the backyard, she saw her mother and father relaxing on lawn chairs. Everything seemed to move in slow motion, as she garnered up enough strength to speak. She cleared her throat, then spoke. " Hello Mom, Dad."

When her parents turned and saw who it was, they quickly stood up. But her father caught himself, and controlled his excitement, her mother was the only one to come over and embrace her, her father turned and started to walk in the house, until she said.

"Wait, I'm no longer with Ron, I filed for divorce."

He paused for a minute then pulled the screen door open and hurried inside, he didn't even get the chance to hear her say, I love you. All she could do was stand there and watch him walk away. She still couldn't believe that even in the middle stages of her life, she still yearned for the approval of her father.

CHAPTER 21

Kathlin sat reclined on a wicker chair in the corner of the bedroom. She had her eyes fixated on Brian as he packed for his trip to the Hamptons. She had just left her father, and now she had to put up with another man running away from her.

"Why are you so quiet? That's not like you." Brian asked.

She didn't answer him, she just looked away. He stopped everything he was doing, walked over and grabbed her hand, then squatted down and asked, "What's wrong?"

"What's wrong?, what's wrong?, you know what's wrong, I want to come with you. I've been cooped up in this house for months now, and I'm tired of it."

"Now you know we can't be seen together, not yet. People will start to talk."

"I don't care at this point, let them talk. You act like you are ashamed of our relationship."

"I'm not ashamed, I've always wanted you, and you know that. But what would people say, what would they think of me. Sleeping with my best friends wife. It wouldn't look good, now would it?"

"Oh don't tell me how people are going to think." She said as she rose from her chair, and walked away from him. Everybody knows that Ron tried to keep you beneath him."

"If it wasn't for him-"

"If it wasn't for him my ass. As a matter of fact, I believe he was jealous of you, that's why he kept you below him and would never let you advance. He knew given the opportunity, you would rise above him."

She kept drilling that into his head, every chance she got. She was trying to appeal to the ego of man and hoping he would see things her way.

"You know what, I don't want to talk about this anymore, we'll finish this conversation when I get back."

He reached for his luggage, and headed down the stairs, towards the front door. Kathlin ran and jumped in front of him.

"No Brian!" she yelled. "This conversation is not over, your treating me the same way Ron did. Like I'm nothing, just a piece of dirt to walk all over. If this is how it's going to between us, then don't come back."

Brian didn't respond, he reached for the doorknob, looked at her one last time.

CHAPTER 22

Every year around this time the Hamptons were the place to be. With its pristine beaches and multi-million dollar homes, this was the ultimate getaway. You had your choice of parties to attend and people to associate with. The lifestyles of the rich and famous were in full effect.

Eric was sprawled out on a lawn chair, while he waited for Felic to meet on the beach. He watched how the other half lived, without a care in the world, and said to himself. "Who would want to go back to a normal life after having a taste of this. Felic came walking by him, in a two-piece bathing suit that matched the sky. She didn't even notice him until he picked her up and carried her into the timid water off of the coast of the Atlantic.

As she came up for air, she wiped the water from her eyes, then splashed Eric. They frolicked in the Ocean, for the rest of the afternoon, seeing who could swim the fastest and raced each other on jet skis.

After enjoying themselves in the water, Eric sipped on his drink while Felic laid on her back, she wanted a nice tan for the party.

"Baby I have a surprise for you."

"What is it?"

"Let's get out of here, so I can show you."

‘She took Eric back to the beach house that Brian rented, to show him what the surprise was.

“Close your eyes.” She said as they walked inside.

“Okay, okay, my eyes are closed. What do you want to show me?”

She walked over to the closet and pulled out a package. She saw him trying to peek and said. “Keep your eyes closed, I see you.” As she got closer, she said, “Okay you can look now.”

When he opened his eyes, he smiled then took the package from her hands. “What is it?”

“Go ahead. Open it.”

He ripped open the package and saw an all-white silk two-piece suit.

“Do you like it ?”

I love it, It’s going to be kind of hard to keep the ladies off of me in this.” He said smiling.

“Don’t even try it,” she responded sarcastically. “I dare you to fuck with me like that, don’t make me get crazy out here.”

“Come here, you know I’m joking.”

She didn’t move, she stood still with her head tilted and her arm folded, not paying him any attention.

“Don’t make me chase you around this room, make it easy on yourself.”

She batted her eyes in a playful manner while strolling over to him when she was close enough he grabbed her. She fell in his arms and said. “Don’t play with me like that, I want to be the only one who finds it hard to keep their hands off of you."

"You know how I feel about you, loosen up." He said as he started to tickle her and chase her around the room. When he finally got her in his hands, he grabbed her by the waist and pulled her close to him.

"Uhm," Felic said, when she felt how erect he was, she instantly became moist. She reached down, and put her hands inside his pants and massaged his hard penis. Eric started to step backward until the back of his legs hit the bed. When it did, Felic pushed him onto his back, then pulled down his shorts. She used her tongue and flicked it up and down his chest and it made her even hotter as he moved with each lick. He grabbed her hair and gently guided her below his waist, which almost made him burst with pleasure when she took him inside of her mouth. Once she came up for air, she slowly guided herself on top of him and straddled him for what seemed like forever. She went for fast to slow, form slow to fast until at last, they were both reaching their desired peaks. Eric quickly sat up and placed one of Felic's peach sized breasts in his mouth, then placed both of his hands on her beautiful butt, helping to guide each thrust. She shivered as he bit down on her nipple, it caused her to dig her nails deep into his back. They climaxed together, then sat there soaking up the taste of each other tongues.

XXXX

The Lancasters were known around the world for giving the ultimate white parties. Their Mansion, which easily rented for one million dollars a month, was the talk of the town. Magazines from Vogue to Vanity fair was on hand to catch the lasting event.

Eric, Felic, and Brian reached the party, in a Company

limousine, and was treated like royalty. Felic's dress was short, exposing both her arms and legs. Her hair was flowing, and her round diamond earrings matched her diamond tennis bracelet.

When they stepped out of the limousine, Eric couldn't help but stare at the latest foreign cars, that kept pulling up to the Lancaster residence. As they walked inside, he held Felic close, with one hand on the small of her back, She smiled when she felt his hand, and said.

"I bet you can't wait to take it off can you"

"Well," Brian said. "I'm going to have to leave you two alone, there are a couple of people I need to talk to. Eric, enjoy yourself, Monday is back to work."

They let Brian go then turned and walked onto the patio. Before they could even get a chance to talk, they were interrupted by a familiar face.

"Hello, Felic." Mrs. Langcaster said.

"I'm fine, and how are you?" Felic asked with a surfaced smile.

"It's so nice to see you. Why didn't you come to the fundraiser, at the Kennedy Center lastmonth?"

"Oh, I had a lot of things that I needed to do. A lot's been going on with the Company. So I thought it best to keep a low profile until better times."

"Nonsense, they haven't gone through anything that any other company hasn't gone through. Those problems happen to everyone." After the small talk with Felic, she turned her attention toEric. "Who is this handsome young man on your arms?"

Felic smiled then answered. "This handsome young man is Eric

Sanders, he's a new recruit at the Company."

"Oh," Mrs. Langcaster said, in an accusatory tone. "Sleeping with the help are we."

Felic's blood was boiling, but she tried to contain her anger. "No it's not like that at all, we're just friends."

Mrs. Langcaster shrugged her shoulders. "If you say so, it's none of my business." She grabbed Eric by the arm and led him in her direction. " Come on Eric, let's take a walk. You don't mind if I borrow him for a minute do you?"

"Sure go right ahead," Felic said as if it wasn't a problem, but she really didn't want Mrs. Langcaster to sink her fangs into him.

When they walked away from Felic, he looked back tilted his head and shrugged his shoulders. He picked up a drink from a waitress's tray and carried it with him. They walked to the edge of the pool were she stood silent for a moment.

"Mrs. Langcaster, are you all right?"

"Sure young man, I'm fine, I always pause like that when I'm about to speak my mind...do you like this pool?"

"Yes, it's very nice, it has a unique design."

"I had it designed right after my trip to East Asia. We stayed in this little resort, where the pool was positioned perfectly to catch the rising and setting sun, the two things that are constant." She lowered her head. "I wish people were like that, you know, constant. With them, you never know what mask they are going to be wearing for the day." She raised her head and continued. "Well anyway, it inspired me so I duplicated it right here in my own home. You know Mr. Sanders, everyone is inspired by something, some by greed, others by honesty and hard work. Then you have some who are inspired by their own self-interest. You should not only be aware but be careful of that. Look around you, in this house, you have dignitaries, Leaders of fortune five hundred Companies, Hollywood Directors, and Actors. Some of the richest people in the world, but all things are not what they appear to be. Take it from me, Eric, I have first-hand knowledge of what I'm talking about, I've been around these wolves for a verylong time."

He listened intensely as she spoke and held his hand tight.

"You know, I'm usually a good judge of character, and this time is no different. From what I can tell, you appear to be pure, you don't have that deceitful eye yet. Be careful with Miss Felic over there."

He glanced in Felic's direction, then turned his head when she noticed him looking her way.

"She is not to be trusted."

Eric had a curious look on his face, not knowing whether to believe Mrs. Langcaster or not.

"I could be wrong, maybe she's changed, but in the past, she has been known to crush anyone in her path, so be careful-"

"Mrs. Langcaster." Felic cut her off, "They are looking for you inside. I told them, that I would find you."

"Well then, Mr. Sanders," she said. As she squeezed his hand. "Take care of yourself. Nice meeting you. I hope this isn't the last time we see each other."

Eric returned the squeeze, then said. "I will, thank you for the tour."

When she walked away, Felic asked. "What was that all about?

What did she say?"

"Nothing important," Eric said, with little eye contact.

She could tell, that something was said by Mrs. Langcaster that made him feel uneasy, so she slid close to him, and asked. "Did she tell you that she's on the Board of Directors, at the Company?"

He gave her a surprised look. "No, she didn't mention it."

She thought that would get his attention. "Yeah, she's one of the people responsible for sending Brian's best friend to jail." A waiter comes outside, wanting everyone's attention. "Excuse me." He said. "Can you please come inside the house, Mr., Brian Scott has a very important announcement to make. Feel free to pick up a glass of Champagne along the way."

Everyone poured into the house, one by one. Once Brian felt that he had the crowds attention, he grabbed the microphone. "First I would like to thank the Lancasters for another wonderful party."

Applause and cheers came from the crowd.

"They seem to outdo themselves every year. Secondly, I would like to take this opportunity to announce the new CEO of R.H. Holdings. She is a woman of extreme integrity. Everyone who has ever dealt with her should be familiar with her no-holds-barred attitude, and her ability to get the job done."

By now everyone was in suspense

"She is no other than Mrs. Langcaster."

Shock and adulation spread throughout the crowd. Felic was amongst the shocked. When Mrs. Langcaster stepped to the microphone, she was met with a round of applause.

"Thank you, thank you. It's my pleasure to take R.H.Holdongs to the next level of investing. As you all know, this Company was rocked with a severe scandal several months ago, Luckily it weathered the storm. I vow, not only to the shareholders but vow to the Board, that we will once again, be the envy of the investment community. Thank you."

In the midst of the smiles and congratulations, Eric knew that time was running out. He needed to get into that office before she moves in.

"Eric, let's get out of here," Felic said while she pulled on his arm and lead him in her direction. "Let's take a walk."

XXXX

On the beach, Felic couldn't keep her hair out of her face, due to the cool breeze that blew off the Atlantic. They were hand in hand walking along the sea's shore. The clear skies allowed the moon to illuminate their path, and make the sand look like crystals under their feet.

"I'm so glad we got out of there if I had to continue with this fake smile any longer, I would've turned into a statue." she stopped then gave Eric a kiss. "Listen, I may not be at this Company for much longer."

"Mrs. Langcaster and myself, we don't see eye to eye. We don't exactly have the best relationship with one another."

"Why not? What happened between the two of you?" He asked, hoping she would go into detail.

"I really don't want to get into that right now, the story is too long. Just be careful, don't let this lifestyle swallow you up and turn you into something else because it has a tendency to do just that."

"Hey, take it easy, what are you afraid of?"

"Eric listen." she said excitedly, "You haven't been here long enough to know what I'm talking about, but this shit is real, You see all of this" She spread her arms out. "The beach, the million-dollarhomes, this is how they live, twenty-four hours a day, seven days a week and they will do anything in their power to keep it, anything."

Eric didn't respond, but he heeded the warning, from both Mrs. Langcaster and Felic. For now, she felt so good in his arms, he was willing to find out which one of the two he couldn't trust.

XXXX

Early Monday morning, determined. He wanted to have those transactions completed before the end of the day.He walked to the side of the building, were the janitors normally gathered to discuss their assignments for the day. He noticed one janitor in particular, who appeared to have every key in the building on him. He walked over to him and said. "Listen, I need a favor."

The janitor looked Eric up and down and said. "A favor, what type of favor can you possibly want from me?"

"I need to get into that big office on the top floor."

"You mean Mr. Harper's office."

"Yeah, that's it, can you help me?"

"Well, that depends."

"Depends on what?"

"On why you're trying to get in there."

"I need to cross-reference some information because I made a mistake on something. If I don't correct it, I will be fired."

The janitor looked like he was well acquainted with the building, he rubbed his goatee which was filled with grey hair, then shook his head, "Do I look stupid to you young man, I've never seen you before, you must be one of those new recruits, Look I'm not trying to get into any kind of trouble. I've got a wife and a couple of college tuitions I need to pay for."

"I respect that," Eric responded. "You won't get into any kind of trouble. I promise you, no one will ever know that you let me in. I'll give you a thousand dollars if you help me."

The janitor was quiet for a few seconds. A thousand was food money, for just opening a door.

While the janitor was thinking, Eric made his move. He pulled out a stack of cash, and peeled off five one hundred dollar bills, then put it in the janitor's pocket. He looked up at Eric with bulging eyes

"Look, I don't know man."

"Don't worry, I'm going to be in and out."

Reluctantly, the janitor said. "You need to be in there when everyone leaves for lunch."

"Don't worry about me, just make sure you are there. You'll get the other five when I get in."

XXXX

While everybody in the room kept punching away at their keyboards, Eric kept glancing at his watch. It seemed like days had passed since he spoke to the janitor. He couldn't concentrate on trading any stocks, so much so that he had a loss on most of his investments. When lunch finally came, and people started to head out, he stayed at his Computer, pretending to be working hard.

"Hey Eric, stop trying to make the rest of us look bad, it's lunchtime." The nosey trader Shawn Pope said.

"You don't need any help with that, the way you look, is bad enough already."

The other trader in the room broke out in laughter, not because it was funny, but because it was true. With his face flush red, the nosey trader stormed out of the building. Once Eric knew that everyone was off of the floor, he hurried through the Emergency doors, he ran full speed to the top floor, He slowly opened the door, looked around and heard something being pushed down the hall. It was the janitor coming around the corner.

"Are you ready?" He asked.

"I'm ready." The janitor said as he stood there with his hand out, He looked at his hand, looked at Eric, then back at his hand.

"Oh shit," Eric said. "I almost forgot, here you go."

Eric handed him the other five hundred that he owed.

"Now We're talking." The janitor said. "You've got no more than twenty minutes before people start filing back in. He searched through what seemed like a hundred keys, then stopped at one and opened the door, He looked back at Eric then said. "If you get caught in there, you don't know me and I don't know you."

"Know who?" Eric responded, before walking away."

When he stepped inside, he saw pictures of Mrs. Langcaster already out on the desk, and her personal, effects emptied from the boxes. He sat down at the computer and punched in Ron's Password. TANGLED WEB, after a few minutes, he was given access. He slipped in his disk and plugged in his adapter. Everything was going to be transferred to his laptop. He checked his watch, then started typing as if his life depended on it. He allowed the disk to do its job, while he got out of his chair to look out of the window. All he saw was the janitor still cleaning, so he rushed back in front of the computer. When he checked it, he hammered the air with a clenched fist, he was in the Company's mainframe. He sat down and typed in the Company's account, and a list popped on the screen. Sweat started to trickle down his cheek, as he read the accounts.

Transit Authority Pension Fund, 97 million

Truck Drivers Assoc. 106 Million

The Nurses Union, 87 million

He scrolled through hundreds of Pensions Funds. Although Ron wanted him to transfer a couple of million from each account, Eric had mixed emotions. He didn't feel right about taking money from people's retirement accounts.

He kept searching, looking at his watch, fifteen minutes had passed, and he needed to hurry up. He came to an account which said the Smitz Family Corp., Two Hundred Million. Automatically he remembered the lunch in Miami and knew that this was a private account. So he typed the first account number that Ron gave him to send the money to, and extracted the first amount. he tapped the send key and saw forty million in the new account. He quickly sent the remaining hundred and sixty million to eight different accounts, then waited for the transaction to clear. While he was waiting, he got up one more time to look out of the office window. When he pulled back the curtains, his eyes got as wide as gulf balls. The janitor was talking to Brian Scott right in front of the office. He hurried back to the computer and saw that all the transactions were completed. Now, following Ron's instructions, he had to extract the money from all nine accounts and send them to the tenth one.

With his eyes still wide, and his heart beating faster than normal, he tried his best to maintain his composure, but he was slowly losing the battle. Within amatter of minutes, the whole Two Hundred Million was in one account.

He pulled the disk from the hard drive, yanked out the adapter, then cut off the computer and peeked out of the office window. Brian was still talking to the janitor. He stood there waiting for the right moment to leave, it was now or never. What would be better he thought. Getting caught in the office, or getting caught leaving the office. Neither was good, but he just couldn't sit around to find out. He stayed close to the door, staring out of the blinds, waiting for his chance.

XXXX

"Who told you to come up here?" Brian Asked the Janitor.

"I can't remember who it was Sir. As I said, I was told that there was a mess to be cleaned on this floor, so instead of taking my lunch break, I decided to get it out of the way."

"I think it's a little early to be cleaning this floor, so I don't care who told you to come up her. Don't ever do it again, unless someone is on this floor with you, do you understand me?"

The janitor saw Eric peeking out of the office door, so he decided to divert Brian's attention. "Yes, Sir." He said as he walked further away from the office so that Brian's back was facing the office. Once the janitor did that, Eric stepped out of the office and eased the door closed, then tipped toed to the stairwell. As the janitor walked to the elevator, Brian started turning knobs on the office doors. Just before the janitor got on the elevator, Brian checked Mrs. Langcaster's office, and the door swung open.

"Hey!" He yelled, but the janitor tried to quickly board the elevator, ignoring Brian's calls. "Hey!" He yelled again, walking fast towards the janitor. Just before the doors closed, Brian grabbed it. The janitor looked up in surprise. "Why is that door at the end of the hall open? What were you doing in there?"

"Just cleaning, I checked the trash can, but it was empty, so I just dusted. I must've forgotten to lock it back, you stopped me before I could clean the other offices."

Brian stared at the janitor, looking for eye contact, but didn't get any. "If you want to keep your job, don't ever let me catch you on this floor again, do you hear me?"

The janitor nodded as the doors closed.

CHAPTER 23

Eric took long strides down the stairs, and he was out of breath. When he opened the door to his floor, he was in for the shock of his life. The nosey trader Shawn Pope was sitting at his desk with his arms folded, staring at him.

"Where are you coming from?" asked the nosey trader.

"Where I'm coming from, none of your damn business, that's where I'm coming from." He turned his back to the other trader and slipped the disk in his jacket pocket. "You need to concentrate on yourself, and keep your mind off of me."

The trader just sat there with his arms folded, studying Eric's every move. He went out to the hallway to get something to drink He didn't realize how much he was sweating, the t-shirt under his long sleeve shirt was soaked. But at this point, nothing mattered. He took a sip of his soda, then called Ron.

"Hello"

"It's done."

"What?" Ron asked excitedly. "Oh my god, I knew you could do it, kid! Now listen, it's going to take a few days before it can be removed from the finale account. So until then, stay out of the way, stay low key and act like everything is normal. When it's time to give you your share. I'll contact you."

That shouldn't be a problem, I didn't know that it was going to be that easy, tell the Old Head that I said what's up." He shut off his phone then put some more money into the machine to get another soda. At that moment, he noticed the nosey trader on the elevator. When their eyes met, he gave Eric a sarcastic smile. In an instant, His heart began to race. "Oh no! no! no!" He screamed as he ran back to his desk, pushing people out of the way. He knew exactly what that smile was about, he yanked his jacket off of the armchair and started checking the pockets. "Damn!" He said as he ran to catch another elevator. "Get out of the way," he yelled, then reached for the buttons. He banged on them, but the one the trader was on was already near the lobby. Eric ran to the staircase barely missing people in the crowd. With each flight of stairs, he ran half the way then jumped the rest. Once he made it to the lobby, he ran outside the building and saw Shawn Pope hop into a cab. He quickly ran to the street and hailed another one. "Follow that cab, and don't lose it. The man in there stole my wallet."

"Turn here." The trader screamed at his driver." The driver complied with his request, and barely missed a pedestrian. "Someone is chasing me."

"Why? What did you do?" The driver asked.

"I have no idea." The trader answered. "I think he's crazy. Keep driving until you lose him."

"Stay on him!" Eric screamed.

"Hey buddy, I'm doing the best I can. This son of a bitch just ran a red light." With horns blaring, Eric's driver missed another car by inches. "Hey buddy, it looks like somebody is trying to catch us."

"What, why would you say that?"

With his eyes on the road, and looking through his rearview mirror. He said. "Well this black BMW has been behind us ever since we drove off."

Eric turned and gritted his teeth at the site of the BMW. "Not now Beeju, not now."

"You know this guy, the person who's following us."

"Don't worry about that, just catch that cab."

No sooner than Eric made that statement, his driver stepped on the breaks, leaving a cloud of white dust behind his car. "There's your guy, right there."

The trader jumped out and started running down the street. Eric threw his driver a one hundred dollar bill, then took off after the thief. When the Trader turned to see Eric behind him, he opened the front door of a restaurant and tan inside. He pushed down a waitress and jumped over tables while customers screamed and scrambled to get out of the way. Eric came bolting in right behind him, without paying attention. He lost all consciousness of his surroundings and was running off of sheer anger alone. Screams erupted, as people scurried to safety. The Trader ran through the kitchen, moving pot and pans out of his way. Cooks dropped trays of food, trying to escape the oncoming crash with the mad nan. He looked back one last time, to see Eric on his trail. When he tried to go through the kitchen doors, he was knocked down by a busboy coming inThis gave Eric enough time to catch up. The Trader quickly got up, but Eric was in striking distance. The trader pushed a cart in Eric's direction, which slowed him down, then ran out the back door. Into the alley. By then, he was out of breath. Before he made up his mind. On which way to go, Eric flew out of the door and rushed the trader into the dumpster. The Trader turned and struck Eric on the left side of his face, with his elbow,causing him to stumble to one knee. When the Treader tried to run, Eric lurched forward and tried to tackle him. Once he had him in his hands, he started to punch the Trader in the face.

"Where is the disk?" He yelled still punching the Trader in the face

"What disk? I don't know what you're talking about." The Trader responded with blood in his mouth.

That answer only made him receive more blows. Eric kept punching him until the Trader stopped defending himself. He reached in his pocket and retrieved the disk.

"I'm going straight to Mr. Scott when I get back to the office, and let him know what's going on."

With all the commotion going on, neither one of them saw the man that was slowly creeping up the alley.

"What's so important about that disk?" the trader asked.

Before he could go on, shots rang out, hitting him twice. Once in the neck, and once in the shoulder, sending him falling onto the ground. Eric stumbled back into the door of the restaurant, after feeling the wind from the bullets pass his face. He carefully stuck his face out, peeked down the alley, and saw a man running away. He bent down to check the Trader who wasn't moving and saw a gaping hole in his neck. He stood up, then ran to the front of the alley, and saw a black BMW speeding away.

The BMW bobbed and weaved through the mid-town traffic, making it's get away from the scene. When the occupant of the vehicle felt that he was safe, he slowed down and joined the parade of yellow cabs. When he looked down at the device on the seat, he realized the wrong person was hit. Eric was on the move.

CHAPTER 24

Ron watched as the young woman who appeared to be, barely of drinking age wait in line to see either a boyfriend or husband. The women remained calm throughout the process, they already knew what to expect, as children ran around them, and on top of them. Some of the visits ended in high notes, and some in turmoil. Regardless of the outcome, they were ready. Their smiles became silhouettes from stern faces, as they prepared to give Oscar-worthy performances. Amidst the crowd, he saw his attorney Joseph Cooper approaching the glass.

"How are you holding up in there?"

"I love it here. Who would want to be anywhere else."

"Joseph smiled then pulled out his briefcase. "Listen, Ron, I tried everything in my power to unfreeze your assets, but Judge Anderson wasn't buying it."

"Wait, most of the property that I have, I had it long before this so-called conspiracy. How can they do that?"

"Listen, the house your father left, they couldn't touch, plus Kathlin is living there anyway. Everything you continue to pay taxes on they didn't freeze. But the Condo in Miami Beach, the rental property in the Hamptons and all bank accounts were seized."

"Thank god I have something left."

"Well, there's one more thing." Joseph reached into his briefcase and pulled out a stack of papers.

"What's that?"

"Kathlin filed for divorce."

"Good, because the moment she decided to go against me, we were already divorced."

"Ron, there is no prenup remember."

Ron laughed. "Let her get her share from the government."

"It's not that simple, but since you pay me a hefty fee, I'll try and fix it."

"For a minute there, you seemed skeptical, maybe I should take back that hefty fee. It doesn't seem like it's paying off to me."

Joseph looked Ron in the eyes and said. "I've been with you a long time now, and I've done many unethical things, settled dozens of cases, and since it appears that you may have forgotten, I even made some disappear. So don't tell me your money isn't paying off. If you ask me, I think I'm underpaid."

Ron didn't say a word, He knew that the man had been with him through thick and thin. He just ran his hands through his ever-growing gray hair.

"Now even though I couldn't get your assets unfrozen, I spoke to the judge about giving you a bail hearing, so just be patient. The evidence against you is circumstantial, but as you know Kathlin is the best evidence that they have. I hope you didn't leave anything of importance that she could give to the prosecution. As of now, It's her word against ours...Oh, one more thing, I forgot to tell you, they made Alice Lancaster the new CEO of the Company.

He didn't respond, he just stared at Joseph and with all seriousness said. "I need to get out of here as soon as possible."

Joseph gathered his papers, then closed his briefcase. "I thought you liked it in there."

XXXX

On her way to R.H. Holdings, Mrs. Langcaster was prepared to whip the Company back into shape. But this would require massive layoffs and a restructuring of the Company's accounting practices. High-level bonuses, private jets, expensive meals, and Company apartments. This would all have to end.

She was laving some of her personal things brought to her office when she ran into Felic in the lobby. "I thought you would be gone by now." Mrs. Langcaster said.

Felic gave her a strong stare, then said. "I was here before you got here, and I'll be here long after you are gone."

"You think so huh? Do you really think that anyone in this Company is going to go against my word, you have been here too long." She said, with a smirk. "Today is the start of a new beginning for R.H.Holdings, which means I am ushering out the old and bringing in the new."

Felic's cockiness turned into concern, it was written all over her face, and Mrs. Langcaster knew it.

"I left strict instructions for you to be out of here before I unpacked, so what are you still doing here?"

Felic was still at a loss for words, she didn't move, she just stared at Mrs. Langcaster. If looks could kill, they would be singing her eulogy. “You bi–”

“What, bitch? Tell me something I didn’t know. She walked closer to Felic and said. “From the first time Ron brought you to the Hamptons, I knew you were no good. He was a married man for God’s sake felic, where were your morals.”

Felic maintained her composure, then smirked. “This coming from a woman who would do anything herself to get to the top. All of a sudden your morals are coming into play. Please, I see right through you, you feel threatened by my presence. When you see me, you see a reflection of what you used to be, how you used to look. And it’s a reminder to you. It says, that no matter how big you get, you’ll always remember how you got there. On your back.”

Felic turned and walked away, leaving Mrs. Langcaster standing there. She cleared her throat and adjusted her clothes, and for once was herself at a loss for words. Her life was just read by the woman she hated.

CHAPTER 25

Detective Demitrious Blane arrived on the scene to a spectacle, waiters and cooks from the restaurant were everywhere. He put his car in park and jumped out. It wasn't uncommon to see Blane draped in casual wear. By his looks and dress code, he appeared to be a mixture of both Men's Health and GQ Magazine. Due to an investment his father made in real estate forty years earlier, he was able to live off of a trust fund that was set up in his name. His parents were now spending the rest of their lives traveling the world. Their words ring loud in his ears, every time he receives a postcard from them. "You have enough money to live comfortably for the rest of your life, why do you continue to put yourself in harm's way."

Det. Blane approached an officer who appeared to be no more than twenty years old. "Why haven't you secured this area officer?"

The officer gave Blane a confused look.

"You heard me, who is the Senior Officer on the scene?"

"Hey Blane, how the hell are you? Sergeant Adams asked.

"How come the scene isn't secured, Sergeant?"

"Now wait a minute Blane, I called you down here personally, because it's something that I wanted you to see. Not to insult my men, or undermine my authority."

“Blane’s bravado was dulled by the Sergeant’s harsh response.

“Your right, your right, what do you have?”

“We already found four shell casings, here at the beginning of the alley, from a forty-five. Two shells are in the victim, and two were lodged in the wall at the end of the alley. Witnesses say that two men were running through the restaurant, one chasing the other…uh both African American.”

“Let me guess, he was being chased,” Blane said pointing to the corpse being pushed inside of the coroner’s van.

“Exactly, no one heard or saw any shots fired. My officers have done multiple interviews, and not one person has provided any substantial information. So don’t, for future references, ever disrespect me like that in front of my men.”

Blane nodded his head, “Fair enough. So, why did you call me here?”

“I remember that case you were following, the one that had you stumped.”

“You know, the one in Greenwich Ct. were those uppity rich folk lives.”

“Oh, your talking about that case concerning the car crash.”

“Bingo, that’s it.”

“What do your victims have to do with that?”

Sergeant Adams handed him the I.D. he found in the victim’s pocket. Blane read the name. SHAWN POPE, DAY TRADER, R.H.HOLDINGS. He stood still for a moment, collecting his thoughts. “You think this might have something to do with that old case?”

"I don't know, but once I saw the name, R.H.Holdings. I figured hey, why not give you a call, and see what you think about it."

"Well thanks, can you call me, and tell me what the autopsy report says."

"Will do."

Blane turned to leave, but before he got in his car, he yelled. "Hey Sarg, sorry about the misunderstanding."

Adams gave Blane a shrug of his shoulders, waved his hand and said. "Don't worry about it, I know you suit types."

XXXX

Back at his apartment, the doorman held the door for him. He saw the bruise on the side of Eric's face and asked. "Are you alright Mr. Sanders?"

"Yes, I'm fine." He responded, in an emphatic tone, as he headed towards the elevator.

"Are you sure."

"I said I was fine."

Upstairs, he entered his apartment, rushed to the freezer, and pulled out a tray of ice. He opened the kitchen drawer and spread out a dishcloth on the counter, then pored the chunks of ice onto the cloth. After covering the side of his face, he ran to the bathroom, to check out the damages in the mirror. When he moved his hand, he saw the large blue and black mark, that spread around his left eye.

Though he was upset, it was nothing compared to the fact, that a man lost his life. A knock at the door broke his thought, he didn't know whether it was the police or not, so he panicked. For a moment, he looked around as if he had some type of stolen merchandise he needed to hide. As he eased to the door, another knock startled him. When it became louder and more rapid, his accelerated heartbeat and throbbing head started to get the best of him. His hands trembled as he reached for the door to look through the peephole, but when he saw who it was, he exhaled the air that he was holding for the past few seconds, and opened up the door.

"Where were you? The other traders told me that you ran out of the building in a hurry. What happened?"

Eric sat down on the couch, and held the side of his face, with the iced rag.

"What happened to you, let me see-"

"Nothing," he said, then moved her hand out of the way.

"What do you mean nothing, let me see that." She reached for his face, then said. "Let me see, Oh my god Eric! They told me you looked upset when you ran out of the office. Now I come here and you look like you've been beaten up. Tell me what happened to you."

Eric pulled away from her and defended his ego. "I wasn't beat up, just hit hard."

"Oh, excuse me, just hit hard. I see." Felic said sarcastically.

Eric had enough. "Listen I told you it was nothing and that's exactly what it is, nothing." He got up and walked towards the bathroom. "I'm going to take a shower and clear my head."

While Eric was in the shower, his cell phone started to vibrate on the dining room table. Felic picked it up and answered.

"Hello."

Ron paused, then in a smooth voice said. "Hello Felic."

She jumped up and walked to the other side of the room, then whispered. "Ron, what have you gotten Eric into?"

"Is he there?"

"He's in the shower."

"So it's Eric huh? You two on a first name basis now."

She lowered her head. "It's not like that, he's a good person that's all, and if he's going to get hurt in the process of all of this. I'm going to tell him-"

"What? Tell him what? You seem to have forgotten that you've killed before."

Silence spread over the phone.

"I still have that information on how that case disappeared for you, and it wasn't because you were innocent. So don't threaten me, I've been keeping your ass out of jail for all of this time, so if you want me to continue, you'll do what the fuck I tell you to do."

Felic started crying. "I did everything that you asked me to do. I got him into the Company, brought the clothes for him and put him in a Company apartment. And I did all of that under the radar. All I'm saying is that it's time for innocent people to stop getting hurt."

"Listen to you, you've picked a fine time to start worrying about who does, and who doesn't get hurt. Just pass Eric the phone."

She didn't respond, she just turned and walked towards the bathroom to hand Eric the phone.

"Yeah, Who's speaking? He asked while he watched her walk out of the bathroom.

"Eric, thank god you're alright. I need you to do one more thing for me.

While Eric was on the phone, Felic paced the floor. She was tired of having that car accident held over her head and tired of being used. She needed to fight to get her life back and get away from the Company, once and for all. She wanted to tell Eric about her relationship with Ron but didn't know if she should, or how he would feel about her afterward. At this point, what other choice did she have? Ron had her life in his hands, and she needed to break free.

Eric came out of the bathroom with a towel wrapped around his waist, while he dried himself off with another. He saw Felic sitting on the couch sobbing. He walked over, sat next to her and asked. "What's wrong?"

"I can't do this anymore," she said, holding her head down.

"Do what?"

"Keep trying to act like everything is alright when it's not."

He touched the bottom of her chin with his forefinger and raised her head. He used his thumb to wipe away a tear, then looked into her eyes. Yup, it's official he thought to himself, it was no longer about sex, he was starting to have feelings for her.

CHAPTER 26

Brian was unpacking boxes in his new office. Even though he was closely associated with Ron, the Board valued his experience and his ability to turn the Company around. The office was an incentive to mark a new start for both of them. As he positioned his various degrees on the wall and personal photos on his desk, there was a knock at the door.

"Come in." He yelled

"Mr. Scott, the Board of Directors is in the conference room, requesting to see you." his secretary said.

"The Board? how come you didn't inform me that they were coming in?"

"Sir, I had no idea, no one called."

"Alright, let them know I'm on my way," he said somewhat skeptically, he wondered why they wanted to see him. Did it have to do with Ron? Did they find out about his involvement with some of those offshore accounts? He didn't know what to think or expect. What he did know, was that it was kind of strange to have the whole Board wanting to meet with you, at that time of the day.

He started to fidget with his tie, trying to keep his nerves in check, then went on his way into the valley of death. As he approached the conference room, he inhaled deeply and turned the knob. When he opened the door, he couldn't decern whether it was his fear, or his eyes, which made the Board appear to look like a pack of wolves, salivating at their mouth.

"Ah there you are Mr. Scott, come in and have a seat please." Mrs. Langcaster said.

He took a seat at the end of the table, and couldn't help but notice the somber faces on the Board members.

"I'm going to put all the formalities, and professionalism aside for the moment Brian. Now as you know Congress wanted to come in and regulate what we do. We can't have that. People are paying us to keep their shit secret, but for some reason, it's one thing after another around here."

"I'm well aware of what we do, and where the majority of our money comes from. What's with the history lesson?"

"Well Brian, it seems as if Two Hundred Million is missing from our accounts. Do you have any idea where it is?"

"What?" Brian yelled and jump out of his chair.

"The accounting department discovered it today. The transaction came from the computer in Ron's office which we all know is my new office."

"That's impossible, that office has been locked since he'd been in jail. Brian looked away, then fixed his memory on the janitor

Mr. Scott, we have to find that money, if word gets out on this, it's over for the Company. We haven't contacted the Smitz Family Corp. yet, so–"

"Oh my god.: Brian said with a placed hand over his face.

"What?" Mrs. Langcaster asked. "You look like you just saw a ghost."

Brian couldn't move he became pale white, while another Board member spoke.

"Let me truly put aside the formalities and professionalism Brian, Where the fuck is our money we want it back, or you will be joining your good friend Ron."

With all eyes on him, he couldn't say or do anything. He knew that the Smitz Family were not the type of people to play with. They practically warned him about losing their money. He reached to answer his phone, nodded, said a couple of okays, then headed for the door.

"Brian, tell me one thing. Why is Felicia Hernann still in this building." Mrs. Langacster asked before he left stepped through the door.

I"m getting together a severance package for her, she'll be gone soon. You don't want a lawsuit shoved down your throat, do you? Listen, before you contact anyone regarding this matter, let me see what I can do."

In his car, Brian tried hard to put two and two together, and go over the course of events in his mind. How could someone steal that amount of money without knowing it would be traced. He thought about the Janitor, then about the time he saw Eric standing in front of Ron's office. But he couldn't find a connection. The sounds of horns blowing, snapped him out of his thoughts, he looked up and almost missed his off-ramp. As he waited at a red light, he started to question his thoughts. Either his mind was playing tricks on him, or Ron pulled this off right under his nose, without even telling him what was going on. Ron was more brazen than he thought. But compared to what he wanted him to do now, he was actually brazen and crazy.

When he pulled up to the house, he parked in a wooded area, shut off his engine and started with his ritual. He checked himself out in the mirror, then stroked his hair with his hands. He sat in his car for a minute trying to get his nerves up, then thought all about what could go wrong.

What he had to do, wasn't written in stone, there was always the option of changing his mind. But every time the thought crossed his mind, he thought about his life, and where he would be, if not for Ron's help.

The windows in the car were fogged from his heavy breathing, and his clothes suddenly became glued to his body. He sat there and clutched the steering wheel. He knew, that it was time to go inside, but only this time, the visit would be much different. He put on his black leather gloves, then reached under the seat, and pulled out a small-caliber handgun, which he put in his pants pocket. He stepped out of the car and looked both ways before he headed towards the house. When he opened the back door, he accidentally kicked a chair in the process. The silence was broken, and the lady of the house became startled. She got up from in front of the T.V. and walked out of the living room to see what was going on. She slowly walked towards the kitchen, then called out. "Hello, who's there?" but no one answered. As she got close to the kitchen door, it flew open. She screamed then jumped back until she recognized who it was. "Oh my god, Brian!" she yelled and placed her hand on over her heart. "You scared me half to death, why didn't you just come through the front door?"

He was at a loss for words, torn between the lust that he had for this beautiful woman, and the job that he was asked to do. "We need to talk" Brian said.

In the dark kitchen, she sensed a strange tone in his voice and reached for the light. That's when she saw the chrome gun dangling from his hand. Fear consumed her but she managed to get out a light scream before she fainted and fell to the floor.

CHAPTER 27

Dressed in all black army fatigues, Eric reached over the counter and picked up a bottle of vodka. He tilted the bottle and took three or four large gulps, he slammed the bottle on the counter, then gritted his teeth.

"Baby are you sure you want to do this?"

He savored the taste of the liquor in his mouth, he grabbed her by the shoulders and said. "I"m sure, I might be a little crazy for doing this for you, but I'm sure. If this thing is going to help your situation, I don't have a problem with helping you. It's time you stop being afraid." He leaned over gave her a kiss then headed for the door.

Eric was on his way out of the building when he saw the doorman. "Damn, does thisman ever go home." He thought.

"Hey, Mr. Sanders, have a good night."

"Thank you, you do the same," Eric replied instead of saying what was really on his mind. He saw the doorman looking him up and down, as he walked out of the building. He flagged down a cab and went to 116th street.

XXXX

He had the cab pull right next to his Lexus, he paid the driver then got out. Before fetting into his own car, he wanted to check on his mother, so he went up the stairs and peeked through the window. He saw his mother and his sister laid back relaxing on the couch. They were talking to Mr. Rosneboun, the next-door neighbor. Satisfied with what he saw, he turned around and went to his car. It's been a while since he was in his car, it was a good feeling. But he had to adjust the seat just right before he got on the highway.

While he was driving, he couldn't help but think about the conversations she had with both Ron and Felic. It's said, that lightning doesn't strike the same place twice, but what about two bolts striking the same place once? He wondered why they both wanted him to break into the same place to retrieve the same envelope. Hell of a coincidence. Could it really be for the reasons that they gave him, or was it something more? Ron wanted the envelope because he said that it contained some incriminating documents, that would keep him in prison. And Felic said that it could possibly contain the reason why her case was thrown out, and finally help her break free from whatever Ron was holding over her head. There were too many things to figure out at once. But there was, one thing he had already figured out. Neither one of them would be receiving that envelope.

XXXX

Eric reached Greenwich Ct. and found Ron's house. The road leading to the front of the house was dark and narrow. He could see, how easy it would be to have an accident with an oncoming car. As he dimmed the lights, he slid his car close to the bushes around the house. A couple of lights were on in the inside, but he didn't worry because he was told that no one would be there. He squatted down then ran a few paces looking around and surveying the area. When he got to the house, he checked the front door, but it was locked. He peeked in the window, but couldn't see much, so he went around the house to the back door, he turned the knob and the door squeaked open. He opened the swinging doors, then took slow steps until he reached the bottom of the staircase. The floor felt as if it was a little wet, but he put it out of his mind. He headed upstairs to the Master bedroom.

He didn't waste any time, he went straight to the dresser and pulled out all the draws, one by one, dumping everything on the floor, and turning them over. When he got to the last bottom draw, he turned it over and unlocked a small latch, then slid off the thin piece of wood. Inside was a yellow envelope. When he took it out, a key fell to the floor. He put the key in his pocket, then put the envelope in his waistband. He ran out of the bedroom and down the stairs, but he was stopped by red footprints leading up the stairs. That's strange, he thought. He didn't notice the prints on his way up.

As he continued down the stairs, he took one step at a time, analyzing the prints. When he reached the bottom, he stepped on that same wet spot that he put out of his mind minutes earlier. He looked down, then looked back up the stairs, and in an instant, his heart started to pound. The few short seconds that he stood there, seemed like hours before he was able to move. He took slow steps, as he followed the trail of blood into the living room. The sight of the body on the floor made him back up into a large chess table and caused him to knock over its pieces. A woman was lying in a pool of blood. He pushed himself off the table and ran out of the back door.

He made it back to his car and quickly jumped in. He tried to put his key in the ignition, but his hands trembled so much, that doing so became a task. Once he got the car to start, he let out a loud sigh and drove away. When he adjusted his rearview mirror, he saw headlights behind him. Paranoia began to kick in. He sped up, but the lights got closer and closer. Before he could step on the gas harder, the car slammed into the back of him, it caused him to jerk forward and spin out of control. He wrestled with the steering wheel, but by the time the car was manageable, he was hit on the driver's side. He swerved to the left, barely missing the guardrail. He quickly regained control and smashed into the car with a fury. While the car struggled to maintain control, Eric's eyes widened when he realized it was the black BMW that was trying to run him off the road.

By now, they were doing a hundred miles per hour, whizzing past cars, and barely missing a few. Eric knew that if he wanted to get away alive, he had to outsmart the driver. So when they tried to go around the next car, Eric slowed down and got beside it. The BMW did the same, just what he wanted it to do. After a few seconds, of bumping the middle car, he looked up and veered off of the next exit, leaving the BMW in the Far left lane, surrounded by traffic. As he drove away, he made a mental note to himself, make sure you have a talk with Beeju. This shit is getting out of hand.

CHAPTER 28

Eric pulled over in front of his Brownstone and parked, he sat for a few to collect his thoughts and allow his heart to get back to normal beats per minute. “What the fuck was a dead woman doing in Ron Harper’s house?” He said to himself. He inhaled and exhaled deeply, until he nerves finally settled down, He leaned over the steering wheel, looked up and saw that the lights in the living room was still on, which meant that his mother and sister were still awake.

He grabbed the envelope from the passenger’s seat, then stepped out. He paused before taking another step, the look on his face said it all, he couldn’t say or do anything, but shake his head, The damages to his car were severe, his beloved Lexus was no longer recognizable. He placed the envelope under his shirt, then rushed up the stairs and put his key in the door. When he walked inside, he heard his mother yell out.

“Eric, where have you been?”

“I’ve been working.”

“You can’t pick up the phone, just to say hello, I’m all right. You know I worry about you.”

“Yeah I know, I was just busy that’s all.”

“Well, I hope you’re not letting that education go to waste, and start running around with those hoodlums in the street,"

"Trust me Ma, I'm running around a different kind of hoodlum, on a different street."

She failed to see the humor, as she walked to her room.

"Eric, I'm not even going to ask you about that bruise on your face. I'm afraid I don't even want to know.

Once his mother stepped into her room and closed the door, he turned to Lisa.

"So, how's she been doing?"

"She's getting better, I'll know soon if she's going to need another round of chemotherapy. Eric, what happened to your face?"

"Nothing, don't worry about it, it's nothing. I'm going to my room for a while." before he turned to leave, he stopped and gave her a hug and a kiss.

She paused. "What's that for?" Knowing that it was out of the ordinary for him.

"What, I can't show love to my own sister."

"Eric, are you sure your alright? I have a funny feeling that your not."

He laughed it off , "I'm good, don't worry, trust me."

He walked to his room, kicked off his boots and jumped in the bed. He couldn't help but notice how different it felt compared to the king-sized mattress in the apartment on Park Ave. He opened the envelope, pulled out the papers and started flipping through them. Most of the papers were account numbers, showing various transactions, times-dates-locations, and most important names. Kathlin Harper, Kathlene hicks, Ronnie Harps, ScottyBrainstone, and Felicia Hernandez. All the names either had account numbers next to them or had dashes under certain letters. Which were no doubt some sort of access code only those names would know? As he flipped through the papers, the dates went as far back as three to four years and were set up by a particular Law Firm. Cooper and Cooper.

While scanning through more of the papers, he came across a police report. He slid everything to the side and focused his attention on the document. It read. On the 24th of December Felic Hernann was foundunconscious behind the steering wheel of a vehicle. At first, it was thought that Mrs. Hernann was speeding and ran into an oncoming car, causing both cars to rear off the road, killing a woman and child. The crime scene had been initially ruled a Homicide, but Detectives couldn't find any conclusive evidence to substantiate those claims.

Upon further investigation, both cars couldn't have hit one another, because their positions would've been much different. Only one car left skid marks on the ground that night, and it came from the car that the deceased woman, Denise Bowman and her child was in. The car that Felic Hernann was in just crashed. That meant that the Executive's wife was driving extremely fast, then tried to get out of the way of the car that Mrs.Hernnan was in.

It seemed like an open and shut case until a Detective Blane noticed that the injuries suffered by Mrs. Hernann were non-existent, not so much as a scratch was on her, she should've been in much worse shape. Eric read the toxicology report which said that her blood and alcohol levels were high, and she tested positive for a high dosage of a prescribed sedative. Making it impossible to maneuver, much less drive a car. There was one last piece of paper to read, it was a statement made by a witness who was on the scene.

The witness Mrs. Angela Beset, stated that while in the upstairs room of Ron Harper's house, she heard a crash, but when she got up to look out of the window, she couldn't see anything. Eric dropped the papers in his lap then placed them back in the envelope, and stuffed them under his mattress. He couldn't wait to tell Felic what he just read. All of these years, she thought she was responsible for the deaths of two people. How could she be, when she was drugged up and drunk. Something else was going on, and by the looks of it, it was deeper than she could possibly imagine.

Before walking out of the house, he looked at his sister and told her not to worry about the damages to his car. On his way out of the door, he heard his sister calling his name

XXXX

Once the cab, that Eric was in slowed down on 145th and Edgecpomb, Eric told the driver to stop. "Listen, when I say drive, speed off, all right."

"Hey buddy, I've got a wife and kid, I'm not trying to get into any trouble."

"And I want the same thing you got one day, so don't worry."

He knew Beeju wouldn't hurt him at his place of business. When the cab stopped, four guys in front of the building stood up. "E, what's up? One of the guys asked.

"Tell Beeju to stop trying to kill me. I'll pay him in a couple of days."

The guy didn't say a word, he waited for the cab to drive away, then ran upstairs to talk to Beeju. "Yo, I just saw E, and he told me to tell you, to stop trying to kill him, that he is going to pay you in a couple of days."

"Huh," Beeju said to himself, with a strange look on his face. "I wonder why he would say that."

XXXX

Back at the apartment near Central Park, it was a relief to not see the doorman out front. At least he wouldn't have to listen to his annoying voice, that was driving him crazy. Tonight anyway. Felic was fully awake and waiting for Eric to return, so before he even had a chance to reach for the door, she pulled it open.

"Did you get it?" she asked with enthusiasm.

"Yeah I got it, but-"

"Let me see it. I want to know what it says."

"I got rid of it."

"What!, why would you do that?" she paced the floor with one hand on her hip and pulled back her hair with the other.

"You said that it might've contained some information in it, that Ron Harper was using against you, right."

Disappointment spread across her face, as she stood in silence. Before he had a chance to tell her what he read, she asked.

"Where's the key?"

Eric was shocked at the question, but he didn't show any emotion. Just a few seconds ago, she was desperate to receive the envelope, now she was asking about a key. He simply answered.

"What key?" I didn't see any key."

Once she received an answer, she quickly returned to her previous concerns. "Damn it, Eric, I needed that envelope."

CHAPTER 29

The next morning, Eric felt like an old man, experiencing pain in places, he never knew could hurt. He stumbled out of bed with sheets still attached to his legs, and almost stripped on his way to the bathroom. He looked in the mirror to see that the swelling on the side of his face was down, but the bruise was still visible. He wanted to stay home, but then he remembered what Ron said. Stay relaxed, act normal, and don't draw any attention to yourself. It was a little too late for that, he thought. But he still had to keep up his routine.

He stood at the bathroom door and stared at Felic while she slept. The sheets conforming to every curve of her body. Where's the key huh? Why was she so concerned about that damn key. But more importantly, what was it for?

The situation with Ron was getting stranger and stranger by the minute. But he knew he couldn't just pull out now, not with the way he felt about Felic, and especially not until he received his money. His emotions were beginning to clog his judgment, but he felt some sense of obligation to her, for what he did, and didn't know. There was just this look in her eyes and innocence that he couldn't get off his mind.

Felic rolled over and checked the other side of the bed with her hand, but Eric was still standing at the bathroom door.

She looked up and said. "Uhm, hey baby, why don't you come back to bed. We have time for a quickie before we got to work."

"I'm tempted, but I think we need to get there on time this morning. You know nothing is ever quick with us."

With that said, Eric turned and stepped in the shower. It wasn't long before Felic was right behind him, running her nails up and down his back, and pressing her body against his.

"All right," he said when he looked at Felic's body. "Let's at least make it as quick as possible."

When Felic and Eric's cab got to the Company, they were greeted by Detective Demetrius Blane. Who flashed his badge.

"Hello Mr. Sanders, can I have a couple of words with you?"

Eric looked in every direction, except the Detective's eyes. "Sure no problem."

Blane glanced at Felic and smiled. But, she didn't respond, she turned her head, put her shades on and walked away.

"Nice to see you to Mrs. Hernann." He said before closing the cab's door.

On their way to the building, they saw Brian Scott standing in the lobby. "Mr. Sanders I would like to see you in my office when you're finished answering the Detective's questions. Detective, I've cleared one of the conference rooms for you. It's down the hall to your left."

Blane nodded, then went in the direction of the conference room. He already questioned the new recruits, regarding Eric's association. with the deceased trader, Shawn Pope, which wasn't favorable. When they entered the room, Eric didn't know what to expect, so much has happened in such a short period of time, From getting caught with drugs to stealing two Hundred Million dollars, to being shot at, and run off the road. To top it off, he found himself standing over the dead body of not one, but two people. He tried to add up the amount of time he was facing in his head, but the numbers didn't add up. Letters were more like it, he thought. He could add that up more easily. L.I.F.E. yup life, life without parole. Even with that thought, he was determined to maintain his composure.

At this point, he had no idea what the Detective wanted with him.

Blane slowly walked around the room, trying to instill fear in Eric, and set the stage for his performance, He pulled out his note pad, got closer to Eric then put one foot on the chair.

"That's a pretty big bruise on your face, where did you get that from? Were you in a fight yesterday?"

"Eric rubbed his face, then smiled. "Of course not, fight, for what. Why would I be in a fight? I don't have any problems with anyone."

"So, how did you get that bruise?"

"I was doing some work around the house, and accidentally hit my head on the table."

Oh okay, I noticed it when you stepped out of the cab with Miss Hernann. What were you doing yesterday at around one-two o'clock?"

Since he wasn't prepared for the question, he had to think for a couple of seconds. I had to take care of something important."

"What was that?"

"My mother is very sick, and I needed to see her."

"Would she verify that?" Blane asked as he wrote in his pad.

"Yeah, why wouldn't she?"

"Is that why you were so anxious to leave this building yesterday?"

"Anxious, I wouldn't say that I just don't like disappointing her."

"Oh okay." Blane was becoming visibly frustrated. " So you mean to tell me, knocking people down and running them over doesn't constitute being anxious?

"Look, I don't know who would say a thing like that, but I don't remember doing all of that. Was I in a hurry, yes, but knocking people down and all of that other stuff, I don't know what to tell you? Somebody is being a little overdramatic."

Blane kicked the chair he had his foot on, away from him then said. "Do you think this is some kind of game? I spoke with several people who told me that they saw you running and that it appeared as if you were chasing someone."

"I don't know, you tell me."

Feeling a little heat, Eric responded defensively. "Why in the world wouldI be chasing someone?"

"I don't know, you tell me."

"Well, I wasn't, what's with all the questions anyway?"

"Do you know Shawn Pope?"

Eric made a gesture with his face like he was trying to remember. "The name sounds familiar, but."

"I don't see why you don't know him, he was a trader right here on this floor."

"Nope, don't know him," he said shaking his head.

"Hum, that's not what I heard. Some of the other traders said that you two didn't get along. Almost like he was jealous of you or something."

"I don't know him, Detective." He was starting to become annoyed at the questioning.

"No you don't know him, here let me show you a picture of him." he slammed a photo of Shawn Pope on the table in front of him, then waited for a reaction. But Eric remained calm.

"The man is dead, and you think I-"

"Did you?" Blane screamed and put his face directly in front of ERic's

"You have the wrong man Detective, I'm no killer. I don't know what the other traders are talking about, I never had any problems with this guy." He pushed the photo back in Blane's direction, then asked. "Are we done here? I have a lot of work to do."

Blane stood in his signature stance, legs spread apart with both hands on his hips, as if he was ready for war. Then said, "For now, If I have any further questions, where would I be able to reach you?"

"I'm here every day."

"No no, I mean other than here."

"3750 Central Park West. apartment 8-B."

“Blane closed his note pad. “Thank you for your time, Mr. Sanders, I’ll be in touch.”

Eric was so much in a hurry to get out of that conference room, that he forgot his identification card, which Blane conveniently slid off the table and put in his pocket.”

XXXX

Eric waited near a window in the hallway and watched as Detective Blane left the building. He wondered how long it was going to take before he started talking to cab drivers. It wouldn’t take a rocket scientist to figure out, that if he was chasing Shawn Pope. And he ended up dead ten to fifteen blocks away, they had to get there somehow. It didn’t take long for his question to be answered, Blane was standing in front of the building trying to get the attention of the cab driver.

“Mr. Sanders, in my office now!” Brian yelled.

As he turned to walk away, he felt like a caged animal. All eyes were on him.

CHAPTER 30

Outside, Blane was seeking out cab drivers, who may have seen Eric chasing the victim. Since he was shot fifteen blocks away, he knew that most Wall Street workers took either cabs or the train to work. So he started with the row of cabs, that sat in front of the building.

"Excuse me, Sir," Blane said to the overweight gentleman, who was dressed down, in a short-sleeve pullover shirt. Worn out jeans and jogging sneakers. "Can I have a few minutes of your time?"

"Sure, no problem." the driver said, then stepped completely out of the cab.

I"m looking for someone, who may have seen these two men in their cabs yesterday. I believe around twelve or one o'clock." He passed the driver the photo and flashed he badge.

The driver reached for the photos. "Sure, I know these guys, we drive them around all the time. One was killed yesterday wasn't he?"

"Yes, he was, this guy right here." Blane pointed to Shawn Pope. "And I'm trying to find out by who."

The driver stared at the photo, scratching and shaking his head. Tough one to swallow here could've been one of my own sons. You think the other guy did it?"

"I don't know, can you help me?"

He looked around then yelled. "Hey, Dialo!"

A short man with thick wool hair, and wearing a permanent frown on his face, stopped in the middle of his conversation and answered in his African accent. "Yeah what's up, what do you want?"

The other driver waved him over. Once Dialo got closer, the driver asked." didn'tyou tell me yesterday, that you were driving so fast, that you almost crashed."

Dialo gave the driver a look as if to say. Yeah, I told you, not so you could tell someone else. "Who are you?" He asked Blane.

When Blane flipped his badge, that was all he needed to see. He turned and ran right into the middle of the street, with total disregard for the oncoming traffic. A car swerved to miss him, and he almost hit another. Blane was on his trail yelling stop, but that wasn't enough to make Dialo slow down. He was pushing people out of the way, trying to make it to the subway across the street. Barely making it without getting hit, he ran down the stairs, and along with the platform, trying to duck and hide behind people waiting for the next train. When Blane made it to the platform, screams could be heard throughout the station, as people started to scatter from the sight of his gun. He pointed left then right, right then left, trying to find Dialo. As the train pulled into the station, Blane spotted Dialo hiding behind a pole, towards the end of the platform. As the train doors opened, Blane waited for him to make his move, but Dialo stayed glued to the pole. Blane stood behind another pole with his hand on the trigger. When he heard the train conductor say watch your step, he made Dialo think he was getting on the train to look for him. But as soon as the doors were about to close, he jumped off, catching Dialo as he tried to get away.

"Don't move!" Blane yelled and pointed his gun in Dialo's direction. "Let me see your hands!"

Dialo threw his hands to the sky, bowed his head then dropped to his knees.

Handcuffed to a bench on the platform, Blane started to question Dialo.

"Why did you run from me?" I just needed to ask you some questions."

With his head still down, he said. "Because I don't want to go back to my Country."

"What, your country. I'm not...you thought I was from immigration?"

"You're not from-"

"Listen, Blane said breathing heavy. "You had someone in your car yesterday when you were speeding. Just tell me what I want to know, and I'll let you go."

Dialo raised his head as if the weight of the world was off of his shoulders.

"Now which of these men did you have in your car?" Blane showed him the pictures.

"That one," he said, pointing to Eric's picture.

"Good, now what did he say?"

"All he said was to follow the cab that was in front of us. Because the guy in there stole his wallet."

Blane waited a few seconds, then said. "Go ahead, keep talking."

"That was basically it..oh, then I told him about the other car that was following us."

Blane stopped writing and looked up. "Another car?"

"Yeah, a black BMW. I told him, that from the time we pulled off, it was behind us."

"Did he say or do anything?"

"Yeah, he looked back then said, Not now Beeju. Like he was annoyed or something."

"He must've known who it was then." Blane kept writing in his pad. "What happened next?"

"When the cab stopped, the guy that we were following, jumped out and ran into a restaurant that guy." Dialo nodded towards Eric's picture. Gave me a hundred dollar bill, then got out and ran after him."

By this time, the Transit Authorities were on the scene, wanting to know if Blane needed assistance. He told them that he was all right, and had the situation under control.

"Okay, stand up." Blane took off the cuffs. "You see how easy that was. Now I don't want you to say anything to that guy in the picture when you see him. If you stay out of my way, I'll stay out of yours, here's my card, call me if you can remember anything else. Deal?"

"Deal." Diablo nodded his head while he rubbed his wrist.

"One other thing before I let you go. What did the BMW do when you stopped?"

"It waited for a second, then drove off around the block."

"Did you get a look at the driver?"

"No, not really, but I glanced, and when I did, I could tell that the driver was black.

XXXX

The slam of Brian Scott's door vibrated throughout the hallway. As he stood in front of Eric he asked. " What kind of trouble are you bringing into this Company?"

"I don't have any idea what you're talking about Sir"

"Don't play dumb with me, why out of all the people in this building to question, he would pick you."

"He's right Eric said to himself, It wasn't looking good for the home team. He had to think of something that made sense and would be believable. "I asked him that same question, why me? But he said that he spoke to several people, and they gave him my name. They told him that I had a disagreement with Shawn Pope, but I don't know where all of this is coming from. I never said two words to the man since we've been here.'

"Listen, Mr. Sanders, this Company is already under the microscope. We don't need any more Detectives snooping around here, from any agency. Hopefully, they will find Shawn Pope's killer, and then move on. Until then, I suggest that you keep a low profile If you want to continue to work here at this Company. Is that clear, Mr. Sanders."

"Loud and clear Sir."

He stood up to leave, but before he could make it to the door, Brian's secretary called on his speakerphone.

He pressed the button then answered. “Yes.”

“Sir, you have a call on line one, a gentleman by the name of Mr. Smitz.”

“Fear instantly appeared on both of their faces.

Brian looked up. “Mr. Sanders, I said that you can go.”

Eric left the offices but he had a feeling that Mr. Smitz knew his money was gone.

“How did it go?” Felic asked as he stepped out of the office.

“Well I didn’t get fired, so I’m alright for now.”

“No, I mean with Detective Blane.”

He wanted to know what happened to Shawn Pope, I told him that whatever happened to him, has nothing to do with me, so he’s just wasting his time.”

“Can you believe it, I just heard about it myself, from a couple of people who were talking about it in the lobby,”

“Oh yeah, probably the same ones who put that Detective on me. Listen, I’ve got some things that I need to do, I’ll see you later.” He said, then turned and walked away.

“Okay, I’ll see you later. Try not to let this stress you out. I’m sure this is nothing but Idle chit chat.

He went back to his desk and sat down, but before he could turn on his computer, he noticed a small package sitting on his desk. When he picked it up, it said, to Eric Sanders and it had no return address. The package was flat and able to bend. He ripped it open and pulled out a stack of pictures that was covered by a small piece of paper. A smile appeared on his face, thinking that

Felic had sent him some enticing pictures of herself. That Idea was quickly thrown out of his head, once the note was removed. His smile turned into shock, as he flipped through each picture of himself standing over a woman covered in blood. As he stared at the pictures, his heart started to race, sending him into panic mode. He stuffed the pictures back inside the envelope, then unfolded the note and read it. I know what you did, if you don't send the two hundred million that you stole from the Company to this account, I will send these photos to the police. You have twenty-four hours, to make your decision. He lowered the note, then looked around at the other traders, to see if anyone was watching him. But everyone kept working. No one looked in his direction. They all knew that Eric was chasing Shawn Pope the day before, so they kept their distance.

He got up to run to the bathroom and stuffed the photos in his pocket. On his way there, he saw Brian and Felic in the hallway talking. Because of the look on Eric's face, Felic asked.

"Eric, what's wrong, are you all right?"

"Nothing, I'm fine." He responded as he entered the bathroom, He rushed to the sink and splashed water on his face. He looked in the mirror and searched for the answers to a thousand questions, but none made any sense. How could something that started out so simple, turn into a fucking mission impossible? The door swung open, and Felic walked in.

"Eric, what's wrong?"

"Look, I told you that I was all right, stop asking me what's wrong."

She walked closer to him and tried to touch his face, but he moved her hands away, turned and walked out of the door. He knew that he needed to retrieve that money, Or spend the rest of his life in prison. He went to his desk and typed in his password, in order to gain access to his laptop. Once he was in, he tried to gain access to the last account that he sent the money to, but when he punched it up, it read, access denied. He went back over each account one by one, thinking that he might have made a mistake, but he didn't. Each account number popped up, so did it's destinations. When he typed in the last account, again it said access denied. A few seconds later, it read, password needed to gain entry. "Password!" He shouted as he banged on the computer. "You've got to be kidding me."

Finally, he got the attention he was looking for, as every trader on the floor stopped what they were doing, and focussed their eyes in his direction.

CHAPTER 31

When he arrived at3750 Central Park West, Detective Blane walked up to the doorman and asked about Eric Sanders. He couldn't help but notice the doorman's eagerness to provide information, once Eric's name was mentioned. In his line of work, he knew that wasn't a good thing. Because when someone didn't like you, there was always a chance that the would say and do almost anything to get you in trouble. Especially when it came to the police.

He pulled the picture out of the doorman's hand, then asked.

"So how long have Mr. Sanders been living here?"

"No more than a week, or maybe two at the most."

"Have you noticed anything strange about him lately."

"Well....yesterday when he got back, he had a large bruise on the side of his face."

"Are you sure he didn't have it the day before? Maybe you missed it."

"I'm sure it wasn't there. As a matter of fact, I asked him about it. I wanted to knowif he was alright."

"What did he say?"

"He said that he was all right, but he seemed to be pretty aggravated bymy questions."

"I wonder why Blane thought to himself. By now, he was beginning to get aggravated by the doorman as well, and it's only been ten minutes. The doorman was amixture between Danny DeVito and Joe Peshi. The only thing he was missing, was the humor. He was more annoying than anything else. "Okay, thank you for your time...Uh, is there anything else you would like to add? Maybe you forgot something."

"Well, I was still here when he got back last night."

He now had Blane's undivided attention.

"Okay and," Blane said with a strange look.

Normally, he dresses professionally, but last night, he was dressed in black army fatigues and black boots. I've never seen him dress like that before, I thought that was strange." the doorman said noticing Blanes agitation

While Blane wrote in his notepad, he received a call from Detective Neal, a veteran of the force, with only a year left until his retirement. He stopped writing and answered his phone. After a minute, he said. "You've got to be kidding me. Alright, I'm on my way." He thanked the doorman, then headed for his car. "Neal take this down."

"Hold on, let me find a pen. Okay, shoot."

"Eric Sanders, you got it?"

"Got it."

"I need to know everything you have on this guy."

"I've got my own work to do Blane."

"Yeah yeah, I know you do, but I'm not talking about filing reports, I'm talking about good old fashion Detective work. I know you want to go back to that. Do this and drinks are on me."

"You know what I like right?"

"Yeah, I know, you and Jack Daniels are on a first-name basis."

Blane shut off his phone and was about to get into his car until he looked up and saw the doorman still staring at him. "So, if you see anything out of the ordinary, give me a call."

"I will Detective. I always wondered how that guy was able to afford this place."

Blane stopped and gave the doorman a disgusting look, but decided not to dignify the statement with a response.

While in his car, on his way to Connecticut, he now knew that Eric had lied to him about his whereabouts and his affiliation with Shawn Pope. He wanted to secure a warrant for his arrest and get another killer off the streets, but he needed a motive. Why would he want to kill Shawn Pope, only a week into his job? Did Pope catch him in the middle of another crime, or was it just rage. Blane shook his head, as he parked next to a blue and white police car. He needed to focus his attention on something else at the moment, so he temporarily put Eric Sanders out of his mind.

As he sat there, in the driveway of this expensive home, he watched the commotion, and the various law enforcement divisions scurry to take claim of the crime scene. He wondered, will they, be left with a cold case, or will this time, justice prevail.

Thoughts of the past popped in his head, bad memories of a crime left unsolved, two innocent people who lost their lives, and for what. God only knows. He squeezed the steering wheel, leaned his head back and promised himself that this time, no rock will be left unturned, no lead, not followed up on, and every victim will be vindicated by the prosecution.

As he got out of his car, gave him a jolt of excitement. He showed his badge to the officers on the scene, then was greeted at the door by an old friend.

"Blane, how you been doing? It's been a long time."

"I'm good Jim, how are you? Blane said looking around and extending his hand. He met Sergent Jim Kesler a couple of years ago during the car crash investigation. He was a man who appeared to be older than his years, with reddish-brown hair and goatee to match. "Am I going to be alright, remember what happened last time I was here, and all that jurisdictional shit that stood in my way."

"Don't worry about that, I called you up here. Seems like old times huh."

"Or better yet, bad memories," Blane responded with all seriousness. "What've you got?"

"Well, the maid called 911 when she came into work today, I have an officer interviewing her now. Follow me."

They went inside the house and walked over to the bottom of the staircase, Where he showed Blane a puddle of blood.

"Is this where it happened?"

"No, I don't think so." Sergeant Kesler said, walking around to the living room, where more blood was on the floor. "I believe something took place in this room. You see how the blood is smeared on the floor. Like something was dragged towards the door. Come on, follow me."

Blane looked around the room, and nodded in agreement to what Kesler said, then followed him up the stairs, where Detectives were taking pictures of bloody footprints. When they walked into the master bedroom, Blane paused, only one place in the room was ransacked.

"Looks like they were looking for something specific," Blane said.

"You better bet it," Kesler replied.

All the draws in the dresser were pulled out, emptied and thrown to the floor. Blane put on a latex glove, and held up each draw one by one, until he stopped at a draw that had a thin piece of wood, and slid off the back of it. He held it up while looking at Sergeant Kesler. "Well, they must've found what they were looking for. Now tell me, where is the body, and what do you think was the cause of death?"

"That's the thing, Blane, there isn't a body."

Blane stopped in mid-motion and gave Kesler a questionable look. "I don't understand, I thought you told me you had a-"

"Potential Homicide. I know what I said."

"But why would you tell me that, if you don't have a body?"

"For three reasons, One because of the amount of blood that we just saw. Two, because we have tried several places to reach her and was unsuccessful. And three, Ron Harper will be going to trial soon." He leaned closer, then said. "And his wife was supposed to be the lead witness against him.'

Blane stood still with his hands on his hips and looked around the room. He was trying to make sense of what he was just told.

"Now do you see why I called you."

"You think he had his wife killed?"

"It's the only logical thing that I could think of"

A young officer came into the room with his findings, interrupting Blanes and Kesler's conversation. When the officer began to speak, Blane's jaw dropped.

"Repeat that, please. "Blane asked.

The young officer looked at the surprise on Blane's face then repeated what he had said. "A witness said that she saw a black BMW parked down the road, and saw what appeared to be a Blackman jumping into it and speeding off.

Blane had a puzzled look on his face.

"Why is that so important?" Kesler asked.

"It's just that I'm investigating another murder, and the guy who is the suspect, in that case, a witness said that he was being chased by a black man in a black BMW."

"Just might be a coincidence, no?

"I might be inclined to agree with you if it wasn't for one thing."

"What's that?"

"Both the victim and the suspect work at Ron Harpers investment firm.

Sergeant Kesler scratched his head, looked to the ground then said. " Blane, what the hell is going on around here?"

"I don't know, but I'm glad you called me. This is bigger than I thought."

The young officer stood silent, listening to both of them talk. He didn't know whether he should continue or not, until they glanced at him, giving him the indication to go on ."Oh, okay." The officer said. "I was waiting for you to..anyway, once the witness told me about the BMW I decided to call the department to see if highway patrol pulled over a speeding car, fitting the description. But what I got was reports of numerous people calling in saying that two cars were trying to run each other off the road." He glanced at his notes. "Uh, a black BMW and a white Lexus."

As the officer spoke, Blane was writing every word in his notepad.

"Also the maid said that she comes to work every day this time, and Mrs. Harper is always here to let her in."

"Okay officer, good job." the Sergeant said. "Good job.

While Kesler spoke to his officer, Blane walked towards the window, still writing in his pad. He stopped for a minute and pulled back the curtains. He watched as the displaced cars and squadron of men roamed the premises. Some with dogs, and others with large flashlights. He took a good look at the narrow winding road, and for a minute was lost in his thoughts. Images of the crash crossed his mind.

"Blane!" Kesler yelled. My officer wants to show us something."

They followed the young officer to the back of the house, where he showed them a door that had a lock on it.

"The maid was never allowed in this room." the officer said while opening it up. "When I broke it open, this is what I found." He opened the door displaying a room full of flat panel screens, which kept surveillance of the entire house. Inside and out. “It appears to be disabled, but I reported it to the forensic department. Maybe they will be able to retrieve footage of the incident.”

“My god” Detective Blane said. “Whoever is involved in this, had to know about the cameras. Jim, I’ve got to go. Thanks for the heads up. I knowhow jurisdictional this could get, so I appreciate it.”

“Hey, with me, we’re all after the same thing. When the forensics and lab technicians process their findings, I’ll give you a call.”

“Thanks, and if I find anything of interest to you, I’ll do the same.

CHAPTER 32

After circling the block twice, the driver waited for its passenger's instructions.

"Stop here, I need you to wait for me, about five or ten minutes at the most. Here's fifty dollars, don't leave, I'll be back."

"Don't take longer than that, or I'm gone."

Eric hopped out of his cab and ran through the yard of a family friend, which led directly into the backyard of his Brownstone. When he entered the house, both his mother and sister were about his behavior. Because he never entered the house through the back door.

"Eric, are you alright?" His mother asked with a demanding voice.

"Ma, I'm alright. I'm just in a hurry that's all." He ran to his room, lifted the mattress and grabbed the envelope that he got from Ron's house. He picked up his lap-top computer, then ran back out of the room. "Listen, if a Detective comes by-"

"Detective!" His mother yelled. "Why would a Detective come by here?"

"Don't worry Ma, if he comes by, just tell him that I was here with you yesterday, around one or two O'clock. Okay, I love you, bye."

He ran out of the backdoor, and back to the cab. As it drove off, he surveyed the area and noticed that the BMW hasn't followed him since he spoke to Beeju. That was a good thing. Dealing with that was a headache of itself. How was he suppose to pay him the money he owed him when he had to send the money to a new account. He felt as if he let his friend Ron Harper down, but at the same time, he didn't want to go to jail for murder.

He slumped in the back seat, going over the contents of the yellow envelope. For some reason, besides the name, Kathlin Harper, there were other names on the account that was familiar to him. But he couldn't place it. No matter how hard he tried to wreck his brain, it wouldn't come to him. "the same thing," He told the driver. "I'll be back in a minute, don't leave."

The doorman in front of Eric's building was busy taking care of another tenant. Thank god he thought, as he put the paper's back into the envelope, and rushed up the stairs back to his apartment.

He tried to open his door, but his keys fell to the floor. His nerves haven't been the same since the moment he stepped foot in Ron Harper's office. And put on his computer. When he bent over to pick up the keys, he focussed on the key that he found in Ron's house. With everything that had been going on, it slipped his mind. He had no idea what it was for. Once in the apartment, he ran in the bedroom and stuffed the envelope behind the dresser draw.

Back downstairs he prayed he could walk past the doorman without being noticed and without anything being said. No such luck, he felt like he was in a dance club and was given a shout out by the D.J.

"Hey, Mr. Sanders what time will you be coming back?" The obnoxious doorman said.

Eric cringed at the sound of the doorman's voice. He ignored him and hopped in the cab. "Wall Street please," He asked the driver. He looked around, but there was still no sight of the BMW. Good he thought, Beeju must've got his message. On the short ride to the R.H. Holding's building, Eric tried to unscramble the puzzle in his mind. There were too many things that just didn't add up, nothing made sense. The more he thought about it, the more confusing it became. Both Ron and Felic sent him to retrieve the same envelope from the same house, on the same night. They both told him that there wouldn't be anyone in the house, either one of them lied, or they just didn't know for sure. As of now, he had to watch everyone around him.

Before he entered the building he paused. For some reason the, R.H. Holding's sign stood out to him. It caught his attention, but he didn't know why. After a few seconds, he walked inside. As he walked to his desk, he looked at each trader in the eye, trying to see if he could find the extortionist, but no one was paying him any attention. When he sat down at his desk, he was welcomed by another envelope. He opened it up and saw more pictures of himself near Kathlin Harper's body.

He went through numerous attempts, to figure out the password to the account, which held the two hundred million but was unsuccessful. He sat back in his chair frustrated, he knew that tomorrow would be the last day to transfer money to the new account. Or the photos would be sent to the police.

CHAPTER 33

On the way back from Ron's harper's house, Detective Blane made a call to the department. He needed to know what information was gathered on Eric Sanders.

"Hello, Homicide division." Detective Neal answered.

"Yeah, tell me that you've got something good."

"Real good. That Sander's guy, he was locked up a few months ago."

"Locked up, for what?

"For possession of cocaine."

"Get the hell out of here, he's a criminal. How in the world is he working on Wall Street?"

The phone fell silent for a few seconds, then they both broke out in laughter.

"Yeah I know, stupid question. That's were most of the criminals are. What I meant to say was-"

"How did a Wall Street firm hire him, Knowing about his crime?"

"Exactly."

"That's a good question. It says here that he was represented and bailed out by a prestigious law firm, Cooper and Cooper."

Cooper and Cooper huh, I see that all the king's men are still around."

"You think you've got something to connect this kid, with the death of that trader Shawn Pope."

"I believe so, and it's opened a pandora's box of crimes. Listen, Ron Harper is in prison waiting to go to trial. Call the Metropolitan Detention Center, and try to find a connection to Eric Sanders. Then get a search warrant to search his apartment. The address is 3750 Central Park West, Apartment 8-B."

"What about the address on this arrest warrant?"

"What is it?"

"275, 116th street and Lenox Ave."

"This must be his mother's address." He thought to himself.

"You want me to send a car over there?"

"No, that's alright. I think I know who lives there. Make sure you call me back with that information.

"Sure. no problem boss."

"I don't mean it like that, Please call me back..oh, one more thing I interviewed a cab driver, who said that while Eric Sanders was a passenger in his car, he asked him to chase the victim Shawn Pope, who was in another cab."

"Are you serious?"

"No joke, then he said another care was following him. Have you ever heard of the name Beeju before?"

"Beeju, yeah, I've heard that name before. Supposedly, he's one of the biggest drug dealers in Harlem. I have a good friend in Narcotics, who is always speaking about this Beeju character, and this war on drugs bullshit. But says that they can never catch him because no one would ever testify against him, Why you ask?" what does that have to do with this case?"

"It's not important, the name was just thrown at me, that's all."

"Alright, I'll call you as soon as I can. Be careful."

Blane changed course and headed for Harlem. He started to think like the doorman in Eric's building, but his reasons were much different than the doorman's. He wondered how this young guy from Harlem, go from possession to prison to Wall street, in a matter of months. He just couldn't see it.

Blane parked his car, then took time to admire the vintage Brownstones on the block, and the excellent condition they were in. He checked his notepad, looked at the number on the house, then headed up the stairs and rang the bell.

"Who is it?" a female voice screamed from the inside.

"My name is Detective Blane ma'am. I would like to have a word with you, concerning Eric."

"Lisa peeked out of the door, then said. "Let me see your badge."

As he reached in his jacket to pull out his badge, another question came from behind the door.

"What's this about?" she asked.

"I would like to ask a few questions, that's all."

He stepped back as he heard the locks being removed. She

opened the door and said. "Come in Detective, how can we help you?"

When the door opened, he was in awe at Lisa's appearance. Her complexion was flawless. She had her hair cut in a Hally Berry style, but her hue was much darker, lips fuller. And her brown eyes matched the roundness of her face perfectly. He was at a temporary loss of words. He cleared his throat. "Uh,...Like I was saying, I would like to ask some questions about Eric. Is he your-"

"Brother, yes he's my brother. Come in the living room, would you like something to drink?"

"No, I'm fine, thank you."

When they walked inside the living room, he saw a woman who appeared to be sick, lying on the couch.

"Why are you here Detective? Eric's mother asked. "Is my son in any kind of trouble?"

"At this point, I don't know. I'm trying to make sure he's not." Blane said scooting to the edge of his seat. "Was Eric with you yesterday, between twelve and one?"

"Yes he was," she answered without hesitation, eyes fixated on his.

He stared back and without blinking asked. "Are you sure Mrs. Sanders?"

"Detective." She said, reaching out to touch his hand. "When other kids were in the streets, Eric was in here, studying. He is a very bright young man, and I'm not just saying that because he's my son. After he graduated with top honors from his high school.

He started getting offers from companies such as Microsoft, and Google. But he didn't want to leave me here in my condition. Once my Cancer got worse he started to worry more about me, more so than focus on himself.

Lisa stood to the side, with her arms folded, and listened to the conversation. As Blane spoke, she stared at his cleaned shaved head, and thinly sharp goatee.

Eric's mother squeezed the Detective's hand and said. Whatever it is, please keep my son safe."

"I'll try my best," he said as he got up to leave.

Lisa didn't say a word, she just glanced as Blane walked out of the door.

When he left the Brownstone, he could feel the love that was in that house. The look that Eric's mother gave him, he knew was genuine. It wasn't just a mother protecting her son. He hoped that there was a reasonable explanation for Eric's involvement in this nightmare., That is until he passed a white Lexus with scraps and dents on the driver's side. As he got closer to the car, he noticed that there were traces of black paint on the car, he flipped through his pad, then tapped a page with his finger. Then he went over the notes that he took while he was in Connecticut, about a black BMW and a white Lexus trying to run each other off the riad. He walked around to the back of the car and called in the license plate number. He wanted to know who the car was registered to. He had a hunch, but he wanted to make sure.

In less than a minute, the information came back, it was registered to Eric Sanders. He called the police impound and told them to come and pick up the vehicle.

Before he got into his car, he looked up to see Eric's mother watching him through the window, with her hands in the prayer position, and he could read her lips clearly saying. Please help my son.

XXXX

"Don't worry Ma," Lisa said as she held her mother's trembling body close. You know that Eric knows how to take care of himself."

"I know that, but I don't want to lose him to the streets, or the prison system. He's smart, but sometimes you can be too smart for your own good."

"Do you want me to call his lawyer, to see what's going on with him?"

"Yeah, that's a good idea, do that."

Lisa dialed the number to Joseph Cooper and was put on hold. It wasn't long before someone answered.

"Hello, Mrs. Sander's what, seems to be the problem, my secretary said that it was urgent."

"Well, I think my brother is in some kind of trouble."

"Why would you say that?"

"Lately he's been acting kind of strange, and a Detective just left here, asking all types of questions about him."

"What kinds of questions specifically?"

"He wanted to know where Eric was yesterday around one or two O'clock."

"What's the Detective's name?"

"Uh....Blane, Demitrius Blane."

Joseph Cooper was silent for a second, then said. "Okay, I'll look into it, then get back to you. Don't forget, If you need anything, don't hesitate to call me. It won't be a problem, alright."

"All right, I will. Thank you, bye-bye." Lisa hung up the phone and stood next to her mother. "Ma, he said he's going to look into it."

Mrs. Sander's didn't respond to what Lisa said, she just kept staring outside the window. When Lisa focussed her attention on what her mother was looking at, she realized why she didn't respond. Eric's car was being towed by the New York Ploce Department.

CHAPTER 34

In the hallway, Brian paced nervously. He didn't pay any attention to the onlookers and those that walked passed him. He was preoccupied with other things, like finding out a way to get the Smitz Family back their money. It was either his ass on the line, or somebody else's, and he was going to make sure that it wasn't his.

Felic saw Brian pacing the hallway, and asked. "Brian, what's wrong? What are you so nervous about?"

Brian stopped in mid-stride, looked at her, then said. "You can't be serious, can you. You want to know what I'm nervous about. Let me see, Ron is in jail, people are dying, who are either loosely associated or directly associated with this Company, money is missing, again. And as if that wasn't enough, Detective Blane is on the trail, that's what I'm nervous about!"

"Don't yell at me like that, it's not my fault that damn Detective is snooping around here again."

"It's not?, I think it is."

"Listen, Ron asked me to do a favor for him, that's it. That's all I did."

"A favor Brian said with a smirk. "That's what he always says. A favor, next thing you know, you're in too deep. He's had both of us on strings for years now, while he used this Company as his own personal playground. Ever since you came to work here, you've done whatever he told you to do, no questions asked."

"I know, I know." She said with her head down. "But you have too, and you have to admit, he's gotten me out of a tough situation. You think it's easy to walk around knowing that you killed someone Brian, a child at that. I have lived with that guilt every day, and if it wasn't for him, I'll be in jail rightnow."

Brian glanced at her, then changed the subject. He didn't want to talk about that night, because it haunted him as well. She gave him a strange look when he quickly changed the subject, she recognized that he didn't want to go there.

"Felic look, Ron has taken care of me, my entire adult life, but he's still a piece of shit. I know that, but I guess I was caught up in this lifestyle to ever let it affect me." He laughed, then continued. "Did you know, in college, he beat up two guys for me, I'll never forget it. They were harassing me right there in the school cafeteria, I mean the man didn't need any help. There I was." He said becoming theatrical. "Holding back the crowd. I didn't even throw a punch. After that, even the Fraternity brothers left me alone."

In a more somber tone, she said. "That's fine, but somewhere along the lines, he started using things like that against you."

"Maybe your right." He responded. "Maybe your right. All I know is that soon, the Smitz Family is going to send someone out here, and I don't know what I'm going to tell them."

Felic vaguely heard him, she was concentrating on people coming in and out of the conference room. "What did you say, Brian, I didn't hear you?"

“Nothing, It’s not important. What’s going on in the conference room?” He asked as they both stepped out into the hallway.

When they got closer to the conference room, they saw the widescreen plasma, that was turned on to the news.

XXXX

Detective Blane was on his way back to the department when his phone rang. He reached on the dashboard and picked it up. “Yeah Blane, what’s up?”

“Blane, I’ve got the warrant, it took me some doing, but I got it done.”

“Good, I’ll meet you there.”

Blane had the warrant, but something wasn’t right. He normally had a good feeling when he was onto a suspect, and couldn’t wait to put the cuffs on them. This time, he felt a little uneasy and thought that Eric was in way over his head.

There wasn’t any sign of Detective Neal when he pulled up to Eric’s building, so he sat and waited patiently until the sight of a waving hand caught his attention. It was the doorman. Blane inhaled, then exhaled loudly, as he got out of his car. Thank god Detective Neal was pulling up at the same time. He didn’t want to talk to the doorman any longer than he had to.

“We need to get into Eric Sander’s apartment,” Blane said to the doorman. “Do youhave the keys?”

“No, I don’t but the buildings supervisor does. Let me see if I can find him.”

The doorman ran into the building as if he was apart of some joint task force. Blane had to yell out.

"Good, we'll wait for you in front of his apartment."

Blane checked the warrant, while Neal looked up and down the hallway. It appeared that he never forgot his training in the Academy. It teaches you to survey the area because it could mean the difference between life and death. That and the fact that he was almost a twenty-year veteran, it was a part of his instinct.

"Told you I had to jump through hoops to get this signed, didn't I. They told me to tell you, that you better find something."

"Find something huh, I don't even know if I have the right person," Blane responded with a skeptical look on his face.

Detective Neal didn't have a chance to respond, because the supervisor was getting off the elevator, with the doorman on his heels. When he opened Eric's apartment, they walked inside.

"That's far enough," Blane said holding the doorman back.

"Well, if you Detectives need me, I'll be in my office."

"I promise you, that nothing will be destroyed," Blane responded with the same sarcasm.

"What's with the doorman? He seems to be a very annoying guy." Neal said.

"You noticed that quick huh?"

They had a warrant to search Eric's apartment for possible weapons, anything else would be fruits of the poisonous tree. Making it hard to challenge the validity of the search in court.

Blane checked the living room, while Neal searched the

kitchen. They wanted to find the weapon that killed Shawn Pope, but nothing came up.

"Nothing in the kitchen, but a few leftovers. What about in there?"

"Same in here, nothing."

They headed for the bedroom. Where they split up. Neal checked the dresser while Blane checked the bathroom

Neal opened up each draw. He slid the clothes side to side, but nothing was there. When he tried to close the last draw he searched, it wouldn't close, something was blocking it from going all the way in. He pulled the draw out, then put his hand in the back of it, to see what was preventing it from closing. He pulled out a yellow envelope. Blane was coming out of the bathroom when he saw Neal holding the envelope.

"What do you have?" Blane asked.

"Looks like bank accounts and a police report on

Felic Hernann."

"What! Blane said in surprise, let me see that." He scanned through the paper, then said to himself. "What the hell was Sander's doing with these?"

"Excuse me.' The doorman said as he walked into the bedroom with a garbage bag in his hand.

Blane turned around furious. "Didn't I tell you not to come in here!"

"Yes, but-"

"But what! You are interfering with this investigation. Do you want to go to jail?"

Nervously he spoke. "No, I just wanted to give you this bag, Eric Sanders threw it out this morning." he held out the bag. "But I saved it."

"Oh..okay, thank you." he reached for the bag. "Now you can go." When the doorman left, he took the bad and set it on top of the bed. Inside were a pair of army fatigues and a pair of black timberland boots. The same clothes that the doorman said he saw Eric Sanders in when he left the night before. He turned the shoes over, but couldn't detect whether blood was ever on the bottom of them or not.

"Neal, I need you to take this to the forensic lab immediately and see if they could find any trace evidence on these items."

"I'm on it." Detective Neral said, putting everything back in the bag.

"Then I want you to call Sergeant Jim Kesler, of the Connecticut Police

Department. To cross-reference their finding with ours."

"No problem," Neal said, on his way out of the bedroom. "I need it before the end of the day."

"Oh, I almost forgot to tell you, so much was going on. Eric Sander's and Ron Harper were housed in the same cell block at the Detention Center."

CHAPTER 35

Eric was still hard at work, trying to break through the firewalls that Ron set up, and figure out his password. Ron went to great lengths to keep someone out of that account, Eric wondered why, and was it him, that he was trying to keep out. Whatever the case was, he did an excellent job.

He still thought about keeping the money in the account, then getting his cut later, but he knew that meant becoming a fugitive.

While he contemplated what to do. He heard a lot of commotion in the hallway. When he got up to see what was going on, people were talking about what they heard on the News. He rushed to the conference room and saw more traders and executives watching the news. The newscaster was speaking about the wife of a high powered executive who was missing and presumed dead. Eric started to get nervous when he saw News cameras in front of Ron's house.

Sergeant Jim Kesler was preparing to give a press conference.

"At this time," Kesler said. "There is an ongoing investigation into the possible murder of Kathlin Harper. The perpetrator or perpetrators appeared to have been looking for something specific. Because only one area of the house was searched. So if anyone has any information regarding the whereabouts of Mrs. Harper, please notify the Connecticut Police Department. Homicide Division."

"Sergeant Kesler, do you have any idea of who it is that your looking for at t his point?" One reporter asked.

"No not at this time, there are some things that I am not at liberty to discuss. But oncemore information starts to come in, I can begin to share with you, what we know and what we don't know."

"Sergeant, isn't it true that Mrs. Harper was the lead witness in the criminal trial of her husband Ron Harper. And that she was about to testify against him." Another reporter asked.

"Yes, that's correct. But there isn't any indication that Mr. Harper is involved in any way, either directly or indirectly."

"Mr. Kesler, Sergeant Kesler!" A reporter jumped in. "It's been rumored reports that there were large amounts of blood found at the scene, is that true, and if so. Is that why your ruling this a possible Homicide?"

Kesler stared at the podium for a second, then said, "No further questions at this time."

"Well, there you have it." The Newscaster said. If channel seven receives any other information, we will report it immediately. Again, here is the picture of Kathlin Harper, if you have seen this woman or know of anyone who has, please contact your local police."

Eric felt his heart fall to his stomach when he saw Kathlin's picture, he became so light-headed that he stumbled back, knocking over a pot of warm coffee.

"Eric, are you alright? Felic asked as everyone in the room turned to face him.

With a shallow look on his face, he said. "Yeah yeah, I'm

alright, I just need a little water, that's all."

While everyone in the room kept talking, Brian watched as Eric and Felic spoke.

"What made you become so uneasy?" Felic asked.

He didn't respond, he just sipped his water.

"Talk to me Eric, you're making me nervous. "What's going on?"

Clearly shaken by what he saw on T.V., he wouldn't answer.

She stared in his face, then back at the T.V. where the News was showing Mrs. Haprer's picture, over and over again. After a few seconds, she got the answer to her own question. "Oh my god Eric, you killed her."

"I didn't kill anybody." He responded after he put his hand over her mouth. He pulled her to the side. " "Keep your voice down. She was already dead when I got there."

"Why didn't you just turn around and leave?"

Because you said that you needed that envelope. Plus I didn't see her until I was on my way out of the house."

"Oh Eric." she sighed and lowered her head. "Why didn't you tell me what happened? This doesn't look good."

"Doesn't look good, for who? I'm the one who was in that house."

"Eric, you don't understand." She paced back and forth. "People are going to start talking."

"All right people, that's enough neither one of us can be of any help at this point. Let's get back to work." Brian said."

Eric had a feeling, he knew what she was talking about, so he leaned closer to Felic and whispered. "Don't worry, I told you that I destroyed the envelope. There won't be a connection to me and that house."

XXXX

"This is the picture of Kathlin Harper if you know anything about the whereabouts of this woman, please contact the Connecticut Police Department at once. Your identity will remain a secret. Or call into the channel seven stations. Now for other News.

Everyone in the cell block looked at Ron Harper. The block was saturated with snitches and other poor bastards that would do anything to get back on the streets. He turned from the T.V. once the reporter switched to other News. He shook his head and felt the high beams on the back of his neck, as he walked to his cell. He didn't know whether to jump for joy or sit and mourn. The passing of his wife was bittersweet, he thought about the good times and the bad. All in all, he actually loved her in spite of his cheating and voracious love for money. Somewhere along the way, devotion to wife and family was given a back seat, he needed to get out of jail, before one of these poor bastards that he was around, started getting funny idea's. He heard it all before, if he stayed any longer, the prosecution would have a new witness against him. He could see it now, the prosecution talking to the jury, giving his closing arguments. Ladies and Gentlemen, you have to believe this man, He just told you under oath, that Ron Harper told him while they were in prison, he wanted his wife killed. Because she was the only one that could testify against him in this trial. Mr. Harper not only told him that he needed her killed, he told him that he needed to find someone that would do the job. Yup, that's all it would take. He said to himself, and he would be spending the rest of his life in prison. Come on Joseph, he murmured under his breath, time is running out I need to get out of here.

CHAPTER 36

Detective Neal took the clothes that were found in Eric's apartment, downtown to the Forensic Lab. He wanted to see if any blood could be found on the boots and fatigues, that could be matched with Kathlin Harper's. When he stepped inside the lab, there were three people working at different stations. They were using the latest technology to uncover trace evidence left at the crime scene. He looked in the back of the lab and saw Denise Palmer, the lab leading technician. He walked over to where she was working and dropped the bag on the counter.

She stopped what she was doing, and in a calm voice asked. "What is this Detective, can't you see that I'm busy."

"Yes, I can see that, but I desperately need your help."

She grabbed the bag, then said. "There are procedures to follow, you know."

"I know but this is part of an ongoing investigation, and this evidence could be the deciding factor in pursuing an arrest warrant or not."

"Detective, I have a ton of other evidence to process as well, what makes this-"

"I realize that, and I'm not trying to say that one crime is more important than the other. But what I have in that bag, I believe is the proof that we need to lock up the killer, of that woman who has been missing in Connecticut."

"Connecticut, isn't that a little bit outside of your jurisdiction Detective?"

"It's a long story, and it's one that I don't want to get into right now. Look, I need you."

"Listen to you, as if you have a choice." She said, standing there with her hand on her hip. "Tell me the short version."

"Okay listen, you heard about the woman right."

"Uh-huh, the wife of that high powered investment broker right..uh"

"Ron Harper."

"Yeah, Ron Harper." The News said that she was just missing and presumed dead. You think she is actually dead?"

He just stared at her, then said. "Look, I need you."

She let out a loud sigh and reached for the bag, she took the pants out of the bag and spread them out on the counter. Then she put the boots beside them. "How do you know that blood is even on these items?"

"We're not sure, that's why I'm here to find out."

She sprayed luminol on both the pants and boots, then placed it under a florescent bulb, to see if it had possible traces of blood. When the spots lit up, she said. "Yup its Blood."

"I knew it," Neal said with emphasis. "I need you to extract the DNA so that we can cross-reference with evidence found at the scene. Thank you, thank you. I would offer to take you to dinner if you weren't married."

"Don't let that stop you, detective. My husband and I can always use a free meal. Plus it would be good to take your wife out to a nice restaurant."

"A good restaurant, who said anything about that, I said dinner. That could mean anywhere."

He walked over to the side, to call Sergeant Jim Kesler and tell him about his findings and ask if they could meet so that they could cross-reference their information. After a few minutes on the phone, Kesler agreed. They decided to meet before the day ended.

XXXX

By now, Eric was tired, he tried all afternoon to break into the last account, but couldn't get through. He decided to go home and clear his head. He went outside and waved for a cab. Once the cab stopped, he got in, but before he could fully close the door, Felic came running out of the building. She swung her arms wildly as she tried to get Eric's attention. When she saw Eric pause, she ran up to the cab and pulled the door.

"Felic, listen to me, I'm working on something, and I've got to get it done."

"Eric please, I don't want to be alone tonight."

He stared at Felic for a few seconds, then pushed the door open. "Get in," he said as he slid to the side.

"Where to?" the driver asked.

"Uh, drop us off at the coffee shop on fifty-ninth," Eric said.

The ride was quiet, Eric focused his attention on the work ahead. He could see from the corner of his eye, that Felic wanted to speak and break the silence, but she fought the urge to do so. He had a few questions that he needed to ask her, but tonight wasn't the night. He was more concerned with breaking Ron's password.

When they got to the coffee shop, they took a seat at the counter. Eric turned on his computer and went to work.

"Can I help you?" A waitress asked.

"Yes give me an espresso. What about you Eric?"

He didn't respond, his eyes were glued to the computer screen.

"Bring him the same thing," Felic said. "Thank you." When the waitress walked away, she turned to Eric. "What are you working on?" She asked as she glanced at the computer.

He ignored her and kept typing.

"Looks like you are trying to break some type of code. What is it a code too?"

He stopped what he was doing, and faced Felic. Tired of the questions, he said. "Its a code to the Smitz Family account."

She gave him a strange look but didn't speak because she saw the waitress approaching.

"I stole-"

"Here are your expressos." The waitress said, cutting Eric off. "Enjoy."

"I stole it." He said.

"You what?" She responded, while she pulled on his jacket and leaned closer. "You stole it?"

He looked at her calmly and repeated himself. "I stole it."

Felic was quiet for a few seconds, then chuckled. "Yeah right, you didn't...are you serious?"

He focussed on the screen in front of him and kept typing.

She leaned closer and waited for a response, but she didn't receive any.

"You are joking, right? Eric, tell me that you are joking."

"I've never beenmore serious in my life."

"Oh my god Eric, didn't I tell you that these are not the type of people that you want to play with. Why did you steal their money in the first place?"

"It doesn't matter why, the only thing that matters now, is that someone found out. Now they are blackmailing me onto sending the money to a new account."

"Blackmailing you, with what?"

"Pictures of me in Ron Harper's house, standing over Kathlin Harper's dead body."He gritted his teeth. "Why didn't you tell me that she would be there?"

"I told you that no one would be there remember. How could I have known that she would still be there? I thought all of Ron's assets were frozen."

He frowned his face but didn't look in her direction.

"The Company has an automatic system built into its mainframe to trace any large transactions that take place. She said, after taking a sip of her espresso. "You had to know that."

"I knew that....Damn!"

"What, what is it?"

"I'm not going to be able to break this code without a password. I've tried everything, and I have by tomorrow to do it."

He picked up his cup to take a sip of his coffee, and it shattered in his hand. The hot coffee splattered on his hand and in on parts of his face, as he pushed Felic and threw himself to the floor.

A man in a hooded sweatshirt kept firing in their direction. He hit chairs and everything else that was left on the counter. Customers screamed and tumbled over one another, as they tried to rush out of the side entrance.

The shooter concentrated on Eric but didn't anticipate the waitress jumping up from behind the counter. Without hesitation, she splashed a pot of coffee in his face.

The pain was so unbearable, that he dropped the gun and reached for his face. When the waitress saw the gun fall from his hand, she ran from behind the counter and smashed the glass pot over his head. That caused him to buckle and fall to his knees. Then she ran out of the door behind Eric and Felic.

As they ran away, Felic frantically asked "Eric, who was that shooting at us?"

"I can't say for sure." He responded, just as frantic, but I have an idea."

CHAPTER 37

Felic was shaken and trembled with fear. Eric held her close in his arm, while they were in the elevator going to his apartment.

"Eric, you need to figure out that code, and send that money to whoever you need to send it to, She said, with her head still leaning on his shoulders. "Whoever it is sending you those photos, appears to be deadly serious."

"I don't think they had anything to do with what just happened. Why would they try to kill me, when they need me to get that money for them." He said, shaking his head. "Your right though. This is getting to a level where I never thought it would reach."

When they stepped off the elevator, he noticed a piece of paper sticking out of his door. He pulled it out and scanned over the documents. It was a copy of the search warrant. He rushed to open the apartment door and ran straight to his bedroom, but it was too late, the yellow envelope was gone. When Felic came into the room, he was sitting on the bed, staring straight ahead.

"Eric, what the hell is going on?"

"That Detective was here, searching the place."

"Don't tell me that he already suspects you of murder."

"You might want to put an s on that, you mean murders"

"Murder's?"

"Yeah, Shawn Pope, and Kathlin Harper."

I don't understand, how could he possibly suspect you of Kathlin's death so soon?"

"I dont have an idea, I was in and out. "I know I didn't leave any evidence behind.

XXXX

Blane couldn't believe the hand that fate had dealt him. On his desk sat evidence that could solve a new crime, and evidence that could re-open an old one. He read through each page from the envelope that was found in Eric's apartment. And was in deep thought when his phone rang.

"Yeah, Detective Blane, Homicide Division-"

"Blane, it's a match!"

"What?" He said, leaning up from his reclined position.

"It's a match. After I left you, I went straight to the forensic lab and had Denise check the evidence.

"Who?

"Denise Palmer, she's the head technician at the lab."

"Okay go on."

"Anyway, she found blood in between the ridges under the soles of the boots. And blood splatters on the legs of the black fatigues. So I did what you said, and called Sergeant Jim Kesler."

"I take it he was happy to hear from you."

"Was he, he said that the blood in Ron Harper's house was indeed Kathlin's. They verified it through a strand of hair they took from her hairbrush. That's' when I told him that I needed to meet with him so that I could cross-reference some evidence that we found in Eric Sander's apartment. Once there-"

"It matched perfectly to Kathlin's DNA."

"Yup, black fibers from the fatigues, were found in the blood at the scene as well. Blane, he was there, the evidence doesn't lie. We got him."

Blane didn't respond, the words echoing true in his ear.

"Blane!, Blane!"

"Yeah, I'm here, I was just thinking about something, that's all."

"You don't seem to be too excited about the findings. What's the problem?"

"I know, I know, it's nothing. It's just that... I think our perp is being set up some kind of way, that's all."

"Blane come on. You're not going soft on me are you?"

"No, I'm serious, follow me for a second. This has been on my mind for a while now. First of all, what is a guy, who got caught with two Kilos of cocaine, doing in a billion-dollar company? I spent close to an hour with his mother and sister, they appear to be decent people. Something just doesn't add up."

"Blane, the world is full of criminals who have good families. What does that have to do-"

"Follow me for a minute. The mother has Cancer, she lied for him, then again, what mother wouldn't. But as I held her hand and looked in her eye, I knew something wasn't right."

"Right, what's right? All I know is that there are two people dead, In which he was directly, or indirectly involved. We need to bringhim in."

"Neal, you've been on the force for a long time. Do you think somebody like him is going to take his time and get rid of a body."

"Maybe we have a conspiracy to murder, and we're missing a few players."

"What about this Beeju character?"

"I don't know, but I don't think so. He doesn't seem the type to get involved with things outside of his territory. That's one of the reasons why the narcotics squad can't catch him."

"Yeah, you might be right. It doesn't make much sense. I'm just shooting shit in the air."

Blane look, I know you. I'm withwhatever you say..hey, you did say that Microsoft and Google offered him a job, didn't you?"

"That's what his mother told me."

"Maybe Ron Harper wanted him in his Company, to do something to it's Computers. I don't know, just call me tomorrow, and let me know if you want me to draw up a warrant for his arrest."

As soon as Detective Neal hung up, Blane slammed his fist on the desk and whispered with emphasis. "That's it, that's it."

XXXX

"Flight 497 to JFK should be arriving shortly. Please return to your seats, and fasten your seat belts. Thank you." The stewardess said in a calm voice.

They sat in first class, three men in black suits. They were contacted to retrieve the Smitz Family money. By looking at them, you could tell that there weren't going to be any games played. The stewardess couldn't even get a smile out of the three. And she was one of the pretty ones. They denied the food, and complimentary champagne.

Once at the terminal, one of the men made a phone call.

"Hello," Ther person on the other end of the phone said.

"Yes, we have just arrived at the airport, what would you like us to do?"

"It's late, get some rest. First thing in the morning, pay a visit to Mr. Brian Scott at the R.H.Holding building on Wall Street. Start with him, and let's see where it takes us."

"All right, I'll keep you posted."

"Remember, do all that you have to do, to retrieve that money. Do you understand?"

Nodding his head, he said. "I understand."

CHAPTER 38

Brian sat at the kitchen table in his condo, he was finishing the last of his medium-rare steak. It was prepared for him just the way he likes it.

'I can't get enough of your cooking." Brian said. "It's almost better than-"

"Than what?" She asked as she threw the table cloth at him, cutting off his sentence.

"You know what I mean, then your, uh...desert,"

She slowly walked over to the table and grabbed his plate.

"I don't think I'm going to serve you any desert. You might not be able to handle it, after everything you just ate."

Brian laughed, you're sure about that?"

"I'm positive, it's too sweet for you."

He smiled then changed the subject. "You would never guess who was at the Company today."

"Who"

"Remember that Detective from the crash at Ron's place a couple of years ago. The one that just wouldn't let it die."

"Blane?"

"Exactly, that's him."

"What was he snooping around for, this time?"

"Well. one of our new traders was killed a couple of days ago. And he wanted to question another trader in connection with his death."

"Hum, if I can remember correctly, Blane is no fool. You need to be very careful with him."

"Why should I, he's investigating a murder, not me. At this point, no one knows that either one of us was involved with those offshore accounts."

"I'm starting to have second thoughts. You don't need him to start becoming suspicious about that."

"Don't worry, everything is going to work out fine. Nothing is going to happen to me."

"This is getting out of hand, maybe we should–"

"Listen, sit tight. There's no need to get hysterical on me. Just calm down, he's not even thinking about us."

XXXX

The morning air was crisp, so he decided to leave his window open, on the drive to Westchester County. After staying up half the night reading the information found in Eric's apartment. He tried to put two and two together, but it wasn't adding up to four. He couldn't seem to get something off his mind. Why wasn't the sole witness in this case sought after by the district attorney's office?

The reading of the toxicology report itself should've raised a few eyebrows.

He left Bellevue Psychiatric Hospital, after trying to talk to the Executive whose wife and child were killed. But he was no closer to the truth than he was before. The whole thing was becoming more and more complicated by the minute. Why would a high paying Executive, whose earning six figures one day, be in a psychiatric ward the next? It didn't make any sense. Though natural to grieve for the loss of a loved one, going full-blown crazy is another thing. He knew he needed to get to the bottom of it.

Luckily he got a lead on the eyewitness in the case. Somehow she was allowed to leave the scene of the crime, without giving a place of residence. At least the officer who was interviewing her had sense enough to take down her name. Ms. Angela Beset, which Blane traced through a credit card transaction.

He pulled up to the one-family home that was surrounded by a small yard. It was separated from the sidewalk by a short iron gate. He pushed past the gate, then bent down to pat the small dog, that came to greet him. Before he could ring the bell, a man opened the door dressed in sweats.

"Hey, can I help you?"

"Yes, I'm looking for Miss Beset."

"You mean Redford, Angela Redford. Beset is her maiden name. What's the problem?"

"I would like to ask her a few questions."

"Why? Who are you?" her husband asked in an uneasy demeanor.

"Oh, excuse me. My name is Blane." He pulled out his badge.

"Detective Blane."

Angela's husband stared at the badge, then asked. "Is she in some kind of trouble?"

"No, not at all. I would just like to speak to her for a few minutes, that's all."

When he turned to call her, she was already standing at the door.

"It's okay honey, let him in. You go for your morning run. I'll be alright."

He looked at her, then back at Blane. I don't know, are you sure?"

"I'm sure I'll be fine," she said, then gave him a kiss and rubbed his back. "I'm fine."

"All right, I love you."

"Blane you said, right?" he asked before he reluctantly walked away.

"Yeah, Blane."

"Come in Detective," she said as she bent over to pick up her two-year-old son. "Can I get you, something Detective?"

"No I'm fine, thank you. I wanted to ask you a few questions, about the night of December twenty-fourth. And go over some of the things that you said in your interview."

She squeezed her son tight. "What questions Detective?"

"Well for starters. Why did you give your maiden name when you were questioned by the police, at Ron Harpers mansion?"

“I had to, I didn’t want my real name to end up in print.”

“Why?” He asked with an inquisitive look.”

She paused, then rocked her son. “When I was in that upstairs bedroom, I wasn’t withmy husband.”

Blane cleared his throat. “Who were you with?”

Tears began to build up in her eyes, as she said. “Jeff.”

Blane wrote the name in his note pad. “Jeff, who’s that?”

“Jeff Bowman.”

“Jeff Bowman! “ He responded with excitement, while he leaned off the couch. “The Executive whose wife and child was killed that night.”

“Yes,” She said unable to control her tears.

He was not expecting the new revelation.

“Can you imagine how much of a burden I’ve carried around with me. All of those years. The infidelity, trying to convince myself, that it wasn’t my fault.”

“It wasn’t your fault.”

“It was!, if I wasn’t with jeff, maybe he could’ve saved his family.”

“There wasn’t anything anyone of you could’ve done, to save their lives. But what you could do now, is help me catch the person or persons who did commit this crime. I’m not here to judge you, we all make mistakes. Now walk me through the course of events that night.”

“I already told everything to some lawyers who were there that night."

"Lawyer's, what were their names?"

"One was a guy by the name of Joseph Cooper, and I can't remember the other one. They told me what to say to the officer. They said that if I tell the officer what I really heard and saw, I would be all over the News. I just couldn't humiliate my husband like that."

Blane lowered his head.

"I was thinking about my family Detective, don't you understand."

"Your family is alive Mrs. Redford! Yours is alive!" Blane jumped up from the couch. "I have a statement with your name on it, saying that you couldn't see anything from your vantage point, because of the trees."

She continued to sob.

"Mrs. Redford, I was recently in Mr. Harper's home, in a room that gave me the same view. Not only was I able to see the winding road, but I was also able to see the crash site."

The tears kept coming. All she could do is rock her son while Blane spoke.

"You gave your statement on the twenty-fourth of December. There weren't any leaves on those trees. You were able to see clearly what happened, now tell me the truth."

"Guilt and shame were written all over her face. When she looked up to speak. "Like I said I was in an upstairs bedroom when I heard the crash. At first, I wasn't going to pay it any attention. Then I heard another crash."

"Another one?"

"Yes, I got up to look out the window, and I saw…" she paused and stared into space. "I saw a man carrying a woman to a car."

"To a car?" Blane asked, confused. "Are you sure he was carrying her to a car, not from, a car?"

"Yes, I mean...maybe, I don't know. To one of the crashed ones. He was walking towards the wooded area."

"Okay, can you tell me who this man was?"

She turned her back to him.

"Ma'am!" he said forcefully. "If something ever happened to you and your son, wouldn't you want the truth to come out."

"Yes, but…" she paused, and continued bouncing her son. Part of his t-shirt was soaked with her tears. She knew very well that these weren't the type of people to play with. For years now she's been wrestling with her secret, patiently waiting for this day to come. Now it was finally here, she had no idea that she would be this afraid.

"Mrs. Beset," Blane yelled again.

With Bloodshot eyes and trembling with fear, she turned and said. "Ron Harper!, it was Ron Harper!"

CHAPTER 39

Not too many traders were in at the R.H.Holdings buildings, at this time of the morning. Except for the customary kiss asses. Those who thought, by coming in early and leaving late, would help them climb the corporate ladder. Wrong. Little did they know, that it didn't matter how hard you worked, or how long you worked. The only thing that mattered to the Executives, was how much money they made for the Company. You could kiss all the asses you want, but without a large profit margin, you will be a distant memory.

As the Janitors started making their way into the side entrance. The coffee and donut shops began to open up. One, in particular, was greeted by three men.

"Do you mind if we have a seat until things are ready?" asked one of the men.

"Sure, no problem." the shop's manager said. "What are you guys, Russian. I've never seen you around before."

The three men ignored her, as they strolled inside and took a seat.

They ordered coffee sat quietly and glanced from time to time, at the building across the street. Once they saw heavy traffic pick up at the Company, they got up to leave. One of the men put fifty dollars on the table, before they left, then nodded at the waitress on the way out. The manager tapped a pen in her hand and watched as they crossed the street.

"That's a strange bunch right there.' she said to her co-worker.

Detective Blane pulled in front of the R.H. Holdings building and hurried out of his car. His thoughts were racing, as he ran up the steps in front of the building. There were just too many coincidences, so he wanted to make sure he put everything in its proper perspective. Just when he thought one way, his leads led him in a whole different direction. Funny, he found himself back where he started from. Before he entered the building, he was bumped into by a large man.

"Excuse me," Blane said, but the man kept walking accompanied by two other men.

They appeared to be just as much in a hurry as he was. They were now walking side by side, down the hallway, making their way to the elevator. When the doors opened, they stepped inside. Blane stood to the back, with one or two other passengers, and stayed focused on the men, their stance and demeanor. It reminded him of ex-military or professional hitmen. By the way, their clothes were tailored, he knew that they were concealing weapons. And not selling girl scout cookies. When the doors opened, the three men stood, looking around, they didn't know exactly which way to go. Detective Blane exited the elevator and bumped into the same man that bumped into him earlier. This time, he didn't say a word. Their eyes caught each other, for what seemed like forever. Then he walked directly towards Brian Scott's office. He passed the secretary's desk without speaking, then reached for the door.

"One minute Sir, you can't just-"

Her words went on deaf ears, as he barged in.

Brian hung up the phone. "Good morning Detective, what can I do for you?"

"Exactly what is going on at this Company Mr. Scott?"

Brian stood up and buttoned his jacket. "What do you mean what's going on?"

"Don't play dumb with me."

"I swear, I have no idea what is it your talking about."

"Okay then, should I start with the car crash of Diana Bowman, and her young son."

Brian swallowed hard, and that self-assured confidence quickly faded away. "I don't have anything to do with that. I believe it was declared an accident. If I can remember correctly."

"What about all the other strange things that have been going on around here? One of your employees murdered. Ron Harper's wife missing, and I just got off the elevator with three men, who look dead serious about something. It looks like they're headed this way."

When Brian pulled back the curtains and looked out of the office windows, fear engulfed him. He knew that those men were representatives of the Smitz Family Corp.

He stepped back, unbuttoned his jacket, and sat on his desk. Blane pulled back the curtains and took a glance. "Uh-huh, that's who I'm talking about right there. So either you want to tell me what's going on, or deal with them."

The three men walked up to Brian's secretary, and one asked. "Is Brian Scott in?"

"Do you have an appointment?"

They remained silent. But by the looks on their faces, she wasn't going to receive an answer.

She pushed a button on her phone then spoke to Brian. "Sir there are three men out there wishing to speak with you. What would you like for me to tell them." She looked at the man while Brian spoke. "Okay, I hear you. I'll let them know. He told me to tell you that he'll be with you shortly. Have a seat."

Patience wasn't one of their strong suits. That's not what they were hired for, they were hired for results. But as they scanned the office floor, there were too many people around not to comply with the secretary's request. They reluctantly sat down, not wanting to draw too much attention to themselves. Something they threw out of the window a long time ago.

After a few minutes had passed, the door to Brian's office opened. The three men stood up and walked in Brian's office, instantly the two men who had twice earlier bumped into each other, locked eyes. Neither would break the stare. Blane studied the man's partially combed hair, sharpened nose, and sunken cheeks. All while continuing to look in their eyes. Finally, he swung open his jacket. He put his hands on his hips and finally displayed his badge and firearm. For a split second, it was like watching Doc Holiday and Ringo in Tombstone. The man, whose stare was as deadly as a Hawk, looked at Blane's waist, then back at him.

Brian broke the standoff, by saying. " "Right this way Gentlemen."

Hawkeyes gave Blane a quick smirk, then walked inside Brian's office.

"Where is the family's money, Mr. Scott."

"Wrong answer Mr. Scott."

"We are trying to trace the transaction."

"Wrong again Mr. Scott. I have to tell you. I was told to do everything in my power to retrieve that money. Do you understand that."

One of the men flipped open his laptop computer, while Hawkeyes spoke.

"Now all you have to do is send themoney to this account-"

"Wait, I...I can't just send you Two Hundred Million dollars. It just doesn't work that way. As I said, our Company is conducting an investigation and working on some of those leads. It's going to take some time, you're just going to have to bear withme for a little while."

"Hawkeyes took a few steps towards Brian, then said. "I really don't think you understand me. There isn't a Detective or policeman in this city that will be able to protect you if we do not get our money back. So I suggest that you start telling me something."

Brian stumbled over a chair, while he was backing up. "Okay, okay, wait a minute. I have an idea where you could start looking.

Outside, the three men were about to get into their car until Hawkeyes happened to see Blane exit the building. He waited to catch the Detective's attention before he stepped inside.

Blane was on the phone and had a sudden feeling of being watched. When he turned, he saw one of the three men lighting a cigarette.

Hawkeyes looked up, blew a puff of smoke in the air, then flung open his jacket. He was proudly displaying, his badge and firearm, a bulletproof vest and a semi-automatic weapon.

CHAPTER 40

"Blane, Blane!"

"Yeah."

"That's Smitz Family Corp. right?"

He lowered his hand as he studied the car, and it's occupants. He watched them drive off and knew, that wouldn't be the last time, that they would meet.

"Blane!" Detective Neal yelled through the phone, a few more times.

"Yeah", I hear you, go ahead."

"What's going on"

"Nothing, nothing. Just get that information to me as soon as you can."

"What about the arrest warrant for Sander's."

"Not just yet, I'll let you know."

"Well, you better let me know soon before Sergeant Jim Kesler puts one out on him."

"What do you mean?"

"Blane, remember those bloody footprints leading up to Ron harper's bedroom."

"Yeah, I remember."

"Well, they match perfectly to the boots we found at Sander's apartment. That along with all the other evidence. He says it's his duty to pursue any and all leads."

"He's right, I've got no room to argue there. So tell him that we'll be bringing him in shortly."

"Shortly? I think you're getting a little too emotionally involved with this kid. Now, Blane, I'm a team player, but all of your suspicions and hunches would serve the public best if this kid was behind bars. Once we get him there, then you can go on your crusade to prove his innocence."

"I know, your right. I just have a feeling, work with me."

Detective Neal let out a loud sigh. "All right, whatever you say."

"Good, if it doesn't pan out. Then we'll pick him up and arrest him tomorrow."

Blane weighed and judged his next course of action, he realized that time was running out. He didn't want to overplay his hand, but he had to give both Felic and Eric the opportunity to fill in the blanks. Since he was alone, he had to play both good and bad cop.

XXXX

Living the high life, was all Joseph Cooper wanted to do. Ever since he was a child, coming up from modest means, he was one of four children who were all the spitting images of their father. So much so, that he dreaded the day his hair would start to fall out. One of the few things in life, he couldn't control. His parents worked hard, to keep a roof over their heads. But barely had enough to put food on the table. His father clocked shifts in the meatpacking district, And his mother worked in-home care services, caring for the elderly. They rarely enjoyed the sweeter things that life had to offer. But with hard work, he and his brother made it through Law School. They promised themselves, that they would never do without.

Being the Senior partner at one of the largest Law Firms in the New York Metropolitan area was beginning to take a toll on him. Over thirty years of service, he gave, defending some of the worst people in the City. Political scumbags, and drug dealers who felt they were above the law. And often had the capital to make such a statement a reality. Each time the Law was violated. Whether it was married businessmen being associated with underage prostitution. Or dealing drugs within a hundred feet of a school. It wasn't a problem. Just call Joseph Cooper, and he'll roll out the red carpet. You will be treated like royalty. He started to have second thoughts. To hell with the rest of them, and how they plan to make amends with their maker. He took account of his own life and wondered if he had a chance at salvation. Would he be forgiven for all of his transgressions, or would he have to pay with his own life

He thought about how the rich and powerful were able to pay for their freedom, while the less fortunate filled up the prisons and jails. Many of whom were innocent and shouldn't have been there in the first place.

It was all about an obsession at this point, an urge to win. To show himself that the skills he learned in Law school, could even set the guilty free. But this was it, he promised himself, as he pulled in the garage of the Federal building. This was it.

CHAPTER 41

"Ron, you gonna make a move or what?"

"Patience young man patience. I'm working on checkmating you, you just want to push-pieces. The game is much more strategic than that."

Ron Harper!, Ron Harper!" the correctional officer yelled. "Get dressed."

Ron stood up. This is going to have to wait until I get back. Study the board, and try to stop what I'm about to do to you."

Before he was finished washing his hands and face, he heard his name being called again.

"Ron Harper!, are you ready?"

"I guess I'm going to have to be," Ron replied. " Thanks for giving me enough time to get myself together."

While the officer was putting the cuffs on Ron, he watched as his young adversary studied the board. Before he walked out, he yelled at him. "Remember while you study the board. All things are not what they appear to be."

The young man he was playing, just sat there staring at the board. Ron's words going through one ear and out the other.

XXXX

As they walked down the hallway, Ron asked. "Where are we going?"

The officer gave him a strange look because every inmate in the system waited for a day like this. "You don't know?"

"Nope, not at all."

"You have a bail hearing this morning."

Inside the holding cell at the Metropolitan Detention Center, Ron couldn't stop thinking about the outcome of the hearing. About the disappearance of his wife, and if that would be a factor in the judge's decision, In allowing him to post bail.

He hoped not, He thought about what would be his first order of business. There was so much to do in such a short period of time. His plan couldn't have worked out sweeter. He would have liked to see the expression of the board members' faces when they found out that money was missing from their accounts. There's no better joy than betting back at those who screwed you.

"Ron!, Ron!"

He snapped out of his daze and rushed over to his lawyer.

"How's it going, old friend? I've got us a bail hearing in front of an understanding judge. You get me." He said while giving Ron a wink.

Oh okay, I follow you." Ron replied with a smile on his face.

"So just sit tight until your name is called." Cooper turned, and went back out of the door, to wait for the hearing to begin.

Ron found himself pacing the same floor that he paced several months earlier.A lot had taken place since his absence, he didn't have a clue. One thing he did know for sure or thought he knew, was that he was two hundred million dollars richer, and about to leave the country. All he needed to do was make the necessary arrangements to have it withdrawn.

"Mr. Harper are you ready?" the C.O. asked.

He released a breath of heavy air. " As ready as I'm ever going to be."

When he walked into the courtroom, it was much different than before. There weren't any crowds or so-called friends in attendance. The fanfare from when he was first in the courtroom had faded away. It seemed as if there was no one interested in the Powerful Ron Harper. He stood at the defense table unshaven and humbled. When the judge walked in, she asked. "Are both parties ready?"

XXXX

"FELIC HERNANN REPORT TO THE CONFERENCE ROOM", A voice yelled over the intercom. Eric heard the announcement but kept concentrating on his thoughts. Time was running out and with each passing hour, the outcome was becoming more and more uncertain.

"Mr, Sanders," Brian yelled.

Eric got up and walked to the hallway. "Yes, Mr. Scott, how can I help you?"

"Detective Blane is in the conference room. He said he would like to have a word with you."

"Here we go again," he said to himself, as he put everything out of his mind and took control of his nerves.

When he got to the conference room, he could see Blane holding a yellow envelope. He put his game face on and went inside.

"Eric, how are you? Have a seat."

He grabbed the first chair he put his hands on and sat down. "I'm fine Detective,how are you?"

"I'm not so good Eric. Now, I've been doing this for a long time. And I have never given someone so much benefit of the doubt. Especially in a case like this, where the evidence is so overwhelming. I normally arrest them and let the jury decide. But for some reason, I think that you are being set up. I haven't figured out every little detail yet...but it just doesn't add up. Would you like to fill in the blanks for me." He said, throwing the envelope at Eric.

Eric looked at the envelope, then back at Blane.

"You do know where I found it, don't you?"

Eric didn't say a word.

"Look, Eric, I see people go to jail with less evidence than this. Ii can have a warrant down here in twenty minutes, but I choose not to. A choice that may soon be out of my hands. I need for you to tell me what the hell is going on around here."

Eric lowered his head.

"Whatever trouble you've got yourself into, I can help."

Eric tried staring at Blane, but couldn't maintain eye contact. He looked around the room instead. "How can I tell you something that I don't know anything about."

A loud noise echoed throughout the room, as Blane slammed his fist on the table. "Do I look like a fool to you?"

Eric jumped, finally showing some emotion. "No, you don't."

"Then talk to me, if you are innocent. I am the only one that can help you."

At that moment, Felic came walking in. she glanced at Eric, then at Blane. "You wanted to see me, Detective?

"Yes, have a seat." And with all seriousness in his voice, he said. " I want to know what is going on around here, and I want to know right now."

She showed just a bit of apprehension then responded. "I don't have the slightest idea, what you are talking about."

"Idea?", he inhaled deeply, then turned his back to them. He put his hand on his forehead and took a few steps.

Both Eric and Felic took that opportunity to look at one another. Nothing was said, but the intensity of the stare spoke in volumes. Blane kept walking, he decided to give them a couple of minutes to think. They had to know that it would be better to talk to him. Instead of digging themselves in a deeper hole.

Felic looked at the yellow envelope on the table but said to herself. Can't be.

Blane spurn around then said. " Eric, did you know that Miss Hernann is having an affair with Ron Harper?"

"Was," she said with emphasis, "Was."

"Oh excuse me, was having an affair with him."

Eric bit down on his teeth but maintained his composure. If that was said to extract a negative response, He didn't bite.

"What does that have to do withme?"

The room became plush with tension. Blane knew he added fuel to the fire.

"Well, I've got to tell you. It doesn't look good for you.

Follow me for a minute. Ron Harper goes to jail, right. His wife who is testifying against him is missing and presumed dead."

Eric shifted around in his chair, while Blane spoke and he recognized it. The pressure was starting to mount.

Now you're running around with his mistress. People aren't stupid Eric, certainly not me. All anyone has to do is put two and two together, and-"

"And what!, Look I already told you that I don't have anything to do with her death or anything else around here." He stood up realizing he was about to lose control. "Can I go now?"

Blane stared at him, then cool calm and collectively said. "Sure you can go, but don't go too far. I haven't figured out whether I'm going to arrest you or not. For the murder of Shawn Pope, among other things." He didn't want to push Eric over the edge. He knew from his experience in dealing with suspects, that you only take them to the edge. Don't get them to hate you, or you won't get any information in the future.

On his way out, Eric had that look on his face, He knew Blane was right, it didn't look good for him.

Inside the conference room, Felic sat with her legs crossed. She glowed with the beauty of Cleopatra. Even a seasoned Detective like himself couldn't fight the seductive pose of this Queen. She was well aware of the effect she had on men and used it as often as she could. Whenever she wanted to divert the attention from thing to another, she revealed the vivacious curves of her body. As she bent over to fix the buckle on her shoe, her cleavage was revealed. Which was perfect in its presentation. When she looked up at him, eye contact was impossible, he was elsewhere.

"Detective," she said, in a sexy but accusing voice.

He quickly straightened his tie and jacket. Then he regained control of the situation, with one statement. He cleared his throat and said. "Let's talk about the car crash from a few years back, on December twenty-fourth."

She twisted her hips, threw her hair back with her hands, then tightened the shirt around her cleavage. She sat back with arms folded, then responded. " You already know about that case. What's there to talk about.

"The police report says that when you woke up in the hospital, you couldn't remember a thing. I believe that, but can you tell me that last thing you remember from the party?"

She took a deep breath, then exhaled. "Well, that night, I remember that I was on my way to the lady's room. When I got to the top of the stairs, I noticed Ron's bedroom door was cracked open. So I peaked in an saw him and Brian Scott arguing with Mr. Bowman. An Executive at the Company whose wife and whose child was..." she stopped and lowered her head.

"If you want to take a minute, we can?"

"No," She said. Shaking her head. "I'm all right."

"Did you hear what the argument was about?"

"Not exactly, but by the looks of it, they were trying to pressure him into doing something, because Jeff was shaking his head, and started to yell. He was saying I'm not going to do it, over and over again-"

"That's it, that's all you could make out?"

"That's it, I couldn't understand anything else that was being said. After that, everything pretty much went blank."

Blane knew there was more, so he continued to push. "What is it with you and this Company? What are you protecting them from?"

"Protecting them! protecting them!" she yelled and shifted to the edge of her seat. "They've been protecting me."

"Protecting you, He heard enough. He picked up the envelope and slammed it in front of her. "In that envelope, is proof of your innocence. They haven't been protecting you from anything."

She stared at the envelope, then sucked on both sides of her cheeks. She didn't know what to expect. Eric must've lied to me she said to herself. Plus, by the way, Blane was talking, she didn't know if she wanted to see what was in it. "What's inside," she asked.

A bunch of names and account numbers. But most importantly, a statement from a witness, who was in the house that night. That differs from what they are saying now."

Both of Felic's hands trembled, as she reached for the envelope. For years now, she been made to fear the unbearable, and think the unthinkable about herself. She had no idea, that the freedom to her dimly lit past, rested in her hands. She carefully opened the envelope and scanned through the papers.

Blane sat back and waited for her reaction. When she got to the police toxicology report, she started to read what Blane was talking about. Her eyes widened and her jaws dropped.

Blane nodded his head to her reaction. "How in the world could you get behind the wheel of that car, much less drive it?"

She was still speechless, he figured he had her right where he wanted her now. He moved in and played the rest of his hand.

For years now, they lead you to believe that you took the lives of two people, one of which, was a child. The view up wasn't for you. The cover-up was for them. And the fact that they or somebody that they're trying to protect committed cold-blooded murder. So, what are you going to do?" Continue to bear the burden for the actions of someone else. Or are you going to tell me what in the hell is going on around here?"

She clutched the envelope with both hands and didn't respond. She let a few minutes go by before she calmly said. "I told you everything I know Detective."

Blane sat back in his chair. He knew that even if he wasn't closer to the truth, all he had to do was wait. Things were beginning to crumble in paradise.

"Can I go now, Detective?"

"You can go." He said, but as Felic got up to walk out of the room, he yelled. " "You don't owe these people anything Miss Hernann, nothing."

After she left the conference room, she hurried down the hall. She turned the corner, then leaned on the wall. She could no longer contain herself, as her emotions got the best of her. She stood there and wondered, how could Ron after all of this time, use her like that. Making her think she killed a child, knowing how she felt about her own children. All the things that she did for him, crossed her mind. Stupid, stupid, stupid. She mumbled as she hit the wall.

All of these years, she was nothing but loyal to the Company, and this is how they repaid her for it. Having her think she was repaying a debt. The love that she had for Ron Harper was fading into pure hatred. Maybe she could go back to a normal life, and forget about the money and exclusive lifestyle. It all sounded good, she played it over and over again in her head. It was too late.

CHAPTER 42

Eric had a million things running through his mind. Even if he did extract the money for the account, how did he know that the person sending him photos would destroy the copies? The evidence against him was mounting anyway. It wasn't like Blane would need any more help, to lock him up, and throw away the key. Then he thought, they can't even find Kathlin's body, whoever killed her got rid of it. No body, no crime, right. Even he watched enough cold case files to know that. The pictures are just that, pictures. He should be able to explain that.

"Shouldn't he?"

He fixated his attention on the name that was on the accounts in the envelope. Then he remembered that each account had a dash under certain letters. Which was no doubt meant to mean something? All hackers knew that codes weren't just in numbers it could be in letters as well. Or both. He tapped his fingers on the desk, then suddenly stopped. A strange look appeared on his face. Then he jumped up.

Something compelled him to run outside. When he got to the front of the building, he stood there and focussed his eyes on the name R.H.Holdings, and stared at the R.and H. He folded his arms, lowered his head, and scratched his chin. For amoment, it seemed as if he was the only one standing on the sidewalk. Just him and the concrete fixtures. Everything and everyone appeared to move in slow motion, as he looked at the title on the building. Still confused he yelled to himself, come on! then in an instant, it came to him. He looked at the name on the building one last time, then ran back inside.

Hit with a bolt of energy, he ran back to his desk and was greeted by another package. He picked it up and tossed it right into the trash can next to his desk. It was no time for that, not when he was close to his goal. He cut on his computer and went straight to his files. He punched in all of the account numbers, and one by one a destination appeared for each. He didn't see any dashes under the letters, but he didn't give up. He typed in rapid motion, lining up the destinations of each account, nothing made any sense. He knew the answer lied in front of him, but time was running out. He wanted to get this nightmare over with as soon as possible.

As he stared at the screen in front of him, an idea popped in his head. He typed in the destinations of each of the accounts in the order that money was sent.

CANADA

OSAKA JAPAN

SPAIN

THAILAND

AUSTRALIA

ROME

ITALY

CUBA

ASIA

He stared at the different Countries and tried his best to figure out the encrypted code. With sweat drowning his forehead, and his brain about to fry, it seemed as if the clouds parted and the heavens opened up. He saw what he thought was the password to the tenth account. He typed in Canada then put a dash under the first letter, then Osaka Japan, and Spain. Then Thailand, next he typed in Australia, Rome, Italy. Finally Cuba and Asia.

After putting dashes under the first letter of each Country, he typed out what it spelled. COSTA RICA. He punched the enter tab, with his eyes closed, when he opened them, he sat motionless as he watched the screen blinking. It read, access granted.

He took a napkin and dried his forehead. He remembered how Ron always spoke about getting away to a Central American Country, with its inexpensive lifestyle and favorable tax laws.

He started to type in the new account number so that when the time was right he could switch the money. But his phone rang. He reached to answer it, then said. "Hello"

"Eric, it's Lisa"

"What's wrong?" he asked, fearing the worst.

"Ma is in the hospital, I think she has to go through another round of chemotherapy."

"What hospital are you in?"

"We're in Jacobi Medical Center."

"All right, I'm on my way." He grabbed his jacket and ran to catch the elevator. When the door opened, he ran into Felic.

"Eric, where are you going so fast?"

He stepped around her. "I have to take care of something, I'll see you later."

"Eric wait. She yelled as the doors were about to close. "Did you figure out the password yet?"

He held out his arm to prevent the door from closing, then whispered in her ear. "Yeah, but I didn't send a dime yet."

"Why not, what are you waiting for? You don't have much time left."

"I know, but right now, I have to go."

She reached out her hand and stared into his brown eyes. She glanced at his chiseled face and ran her hand over his hairline, which was just days earlier, sharper than a razor. "Eric, I'm sorry for not telling you about my affair with Ron."

He pulled her closer to him, then gave her a passionate kiss. "Don't worry about it, that was then, and this is now. We'll talk about it later."

XXXX

When he checked Eric's computer, there wasn't any trace of what he was working on. Not a clue to the trouble he found himself tangled in. All of this needed to come to an end before more people lose their lives

A check of the draws revealed nothing, except folders and office supplies. Scattered pieces of paper sat alongside on empty soda can, and a half-eaten sandwich.

Still searching around the desk, he noticed a small package in the trash can, next to Eric's chair. The contents in the package were flat and able to bend. When they opened it, pictures of Eric standing over the body of Kathlin Harper was exposed. They looked over their shoulders to make sure no one was looking, then read the small note that was attached. "You will be in jail soon if you do not transfer the money to this account. He put the photos back into the envelope, then walked out into the hallway.

"Hello Detective, I see your still here. I thought you left." Felic said, after bumping into Blane.

"I needed to check something out since I can't get any cooperation out of you."

While he held the small package in his hand, he reached for his cell phone, then turned his back. " Yeah, go ahead,"

"Blane I've got that info you wanted on the Smitz Family Corp. Listen, they are a legitimate business entity. But Florida authorities say that they are suspected of laundering money for some high-level dealers in the Florida area, I'm talking tens of millions of dollars. Blane you still there?"

"Yeah, I'm listening, go ahead."

"From what I was told, they keep their hands clean, by using third and fourth parties to handle their business. They also use top the line assassins, to take care of things they feel are out of control."

"I can believe that. I think I had a run-in with some of their people earlier."

"What!" Neal yelled through the phone."

"It wasn't a physical run-in with them, just a staring contest, but I'll tell you this, they weren't afraid when I showed them my badge and gun. Infact, they laughed. One of them even showed me his bulletproof vest and a semi-automatic weapon."

"Well, that's enough for me. I'm going to assemble a team, and keep them on call just in case."

"That's a good idea. It looks like it's going to get a lot worse before it's all over with." Without being conscious of Felic still standing there, he continued to speak. "Listen I was searching Eric Sander's desk and I found pictures of him standing over what appears to be the dead body of Kathlin Harper. And it had a note attached, warning him to send the money to a new account. Or he will be going to jail."

"What money?"

"Oh, I forgot to tell you. Two Hundred Million dollars is missing from the Companies accounts, and I think Sanders stole it."

"How did-"

"I don't know how, but I have a feeling why. I believe he did it for someone else. Remember what you said before you hung up last night."

"Uh...one, minute, let me...., yeah, I remember. You talking about when I said that since Eric is good with computers, maybe Ron Harper wanted him to do something for him."

"Exactly, that's what I believe happened. Now somehow, somebody found out, and is blackmailing him."

"While Blane spoke on the phone, Felic focused in on every word that he was saying.

"Well, at least we have him at the scene of the crime," Neal said.

After a slight pause, Blane responded. "Your right, but-."

"No buts, we need to put this thing to rest. Put a warrant out on him, and bring him in before somebody else gets killed."

“Okay do it. I’ll call you later. He turned to leave, then looked at Felic and said. “Tell Eric to turn himself in, before something happens to him.” Then he headed out the building.

He got in his car and closed the door. But before driving off, he replayed the series of events, over in his mind. He looked at the photos one more time. He flipped through each of them, one by one. Something caught his attention, in the photo, Eric appeared to be startled by the body of Kathlin Harper. If he killed her, why would he be startled by what he’s done? Blane thought. Something wasn’t right, it was time to pay Ron Harper a visit.

CHAPTER 43

As he made his way through the hospital. Eric rushed to the reception desk. He tried to get the attention of a nurse who was on the phone. “Excuse me,” he said.

She held up one finger, then finished the last of her conversation. After about, half a minute, she spoke. “Yes, how can I help you?”

“My mother is here, being checked out. Can you tell me where to find her?”

“Sure, what is her name?”

“Sanders, Mrs. Lori Sanders

“One second, let me check.”

He leaned on the computer, and couldn’t help but to smell the death and disinfectant, that filled the air. A lone security guard stood off to the side, glued in one position. Quiet he thought, as he looked around. The deafening silence consumed the hallways. And the uncertainty on people’s faces mirrored his own.

“Mr. Sanders, your mother is on the third floor. When you get off the elevator. Make a left, and go to the middle of the hallway.”

“Thank you,” he said as he rushed from the front desk. When he got to the third floor, he saw his sister leaving the soda machine, and called out her name. "Lees!"

She turned, then reached out to hug him.

"How's Ma?"

Her doctor said that she might need to go through another round of treatment. He thinks her Cancer is back."

Eric put his arm around his sister, as they walked to the room where their mother was resting. He peeked in the room and watched her as she laid on the bed. A little salt and pepper hair was starting to come back. She lost most of it going through her first round of chemo. But she didn't let that stop her from feeling confident about herself. She always said, that if that woman from good morning America, Robin Roberts can wear her hair that short after chemo. And look good in front of millions, then so can I. She was right.

She felt a slight breeze coming through the door when Eric opened it and looked up. "Come over here and give me a hug boy," she said forcing a smile.

"Hey, Ma, how you feeling?"

"I've been better, but you know me. Strong as an ox."

"Yeah, I know. Did they tell you anything yet?"

"Well, they did some blood test, and said I could go home until they are ready,"

"Here comes the Doctor now," Lisa said.

"Hello Mrs. Sanders, how are you feeling? The Doctor asked.

As well as to be expected Doc." She responded sitting up.

"How are you Doc?" Eric asked with his hand extended.

"Okay Doc, give it to me straight, what's the damage?"

"Well, for now, let's just wait to get the blood test back, before we jump to any conclusions. Then we can work from there. But by the symptoms, I think...I don't know for sure. I believe that you're starting to show signs, that your tumor is returning. But like I said, I don't know for sure. I've seen this happen before, and it was just a scare. So I'll call you in a few days, and let you know what steps we should take next. Okay.'

"All right Doc." Mrs. Sanders said. "We'll be awaiting your call."

When Lisa and her mother walked out of the room, Eric pulled the Doctor by the arm. "Is she going to beat this thing or what Doc?"

"I believe that she can, she's strong."

He shook the Doctor's hand, then turned to leave.

"Uh, Mr. Sanders, who will be taking care of the financial aspect of her treatment, if she needs it?"

Eric looked away and drifted off. He knew without a doubt, that he would rather rot in prison than let his mother die.

XXXX

The Detention Center was packed, with people going through the receiving process. After being put on standby for a while, Detective Blane finally got the attention of a Correctional officer.

"Yes, can we help you?"

"Yes, thank you. I would like to speak to one of your prisoners,

It's very important, his name is Ron Harper."

"Sorry Detective, but visiting hours are over. You will have to come back in the morning."

"Listen Blane said forcibly, as he hit the table with his hand. It's a matter of life and death, I need to-"

"Did you say, Ron Harper?" Another officer asked. Overhearing the conversation.

"Yes I did," Blane responded.

"I thought you did, he got bailed out this morning, sorry you missed him."

"Damn, can you tell me who bailed him out?"

"Yes, it says here, that he was bonded out by the international bonding group."

Blane shook his head and said to himself. "Of course he was." Blane knew all too well who owned that bonding company. Somehow Joseph Cooper was able to pull off the impossible.

He got back in his car and headed for the Homicide Division, and tried to rationalize the fact that Ron Harper was allowed to post bail. Especially when his wife was missing.

Inside a trendy loft on the upper east side of Manhattan. Ebony oaked floors and Ivory paint set a classic color scheme, that spread throughout the open space. The air that circulated from the quiet ceiling fan, gave no indication of its presence, in the barely furnished apartment. It held only the bare essentials. A lonely plush sofa sat in the center of the floor, across from a large screen plasma. The dining area possessed a small table with chairs. And a king-sized bed cornered the bedroom with two matching dressers. The place was barely used, Felic was just about as much of a stranger in it, as the people she occasionally had over. She preferred the services of luxury hotels. Plus she wanted, no, she needed a place that would be sacred to her. A place to get away from it all, without the stress of her job. And more importantly the stress of Ron. He initially brought the place for her, so that they could carry out their affair. That was until she told him that she only wanted to see him in hotels. He agreed, what else could he do, he was infatuated, and she knew it.

Felic stepped out of the shower, with a towel wrapped around her hair, and one loosely wrapped around her body. She froze and allowed her ears to guide her intuition, she swore she heard a noise. She slowly walked out of the bathroom, then yelled. "Whose there?" No one responded, but she still didn't feel right, something was wrong. When she cut the lights on in the living room, she screamed and squeezed the towel that was wrapped around her. Her suspicions were correct. Ron was sitting on the couch.

"What's wrong?" he asked. "You don't seem to be too happy to see me."

Felic continued to tighten the towel around her body. "How did you get out?"

"It's no need to concern yourself with that, did you do everything I asked you to do?"

"Yes," she said, shivering from the light air that circulated from the ceiling fan.

"Good everything will be over in a couple of days. I want you to go to work tomorrow and put in for your vacation and meet me–"

"I'm already on a vacation, a permanent one."

"What do you mean by that?"

"Mrs. Langcaster terminated me."

"Terminated you, how?"

"She's the new C.E.O. of the company."

Ron stood up and smiled. "Well, I can't do anything about that. Everything is going according to plan, I'll see you soon." he turned and walked out of the door, without so much as a second look.

Felic thought that was strange, usually, he would be filled with passion and desire for her. Though she no longer wanted him, the fact that he didn't even try to touch her made her wondered why.

CHAPTER 44

While they sat across the street from the Brownstone, two blue and white cars pulled up. Neither one of them budged, they became permanent fixtures in their seats and took deep breaths. Now wasn't the time to get into it with the police, not until they had their chance to get their message across. The officers got out, but no one was home. They finally left, after sitting a few minutes in front of the house. The men in the car across the street had no doubt that they would soon return.

When a cab pulled in front of the Brownstone, Hawkeyes and his men snapped into attention. They noticed a young man and two women exiting the cab. When they started to walk toward the house, Hawkeyes said."That's him, let's go." they got out of their care, and walked in the family's direction. "Eric Sander's?" Hawkeyes asked.

Eric hesitated and looked at the three men. "Yeah, that's me, who wants to know?"

"Uh...I was wondering if he could have a word with you."

"About what?"

"Don't worry, we're not the police."

Eric didn't know if that was a good thing or not.

"We would just like to talk to you for a minute."

He looked at his family and said. "I'm all right, you can go inside."

"Are you sure Eric?" His mother said.

"I'm sure, go inside, I'll be right behind you."

Once Eric's family walked into the house, Hawkeyes spoke.

"Listen, Eric, your name came up during our investigation."

"Investigation, I thought you said that you weren't the police.

"We'renot, we represent the Smitz Family Corp. And we would like for you to return the money you stole from their account."

Eric gave them the poker face and tried not to show any emotion. "Sorry but you guys have the wrong person. Someone is lying to you. I-"

"Look, Mr. Sanders, we can do this the easy way, or we can do it the hard way. I don't have time for the games, I normally have a short temper. I promise you all we want is the money returned, in full, and no one will be hurt."

"Eric kept up the poker face. "Look, I'm telling you, somebody fed you false information."

Hawkeyes saw that the young man wanted to play with his life, so he handed him a card with an account number on the back. "You know what Mr. Sander's, I'm going to give you a couple of hours to think about it. On the back of the card is an account number. Use it, or I can promise you, you're going to wish that we were the police."

He took one last look at the other two men who were with

Hawkeyes, then walked up the stairs. When he walked inside the house, he was flooded with a million questions. He tried to assure them that everything was all right, but deep down inside, he knew it wasn't. He sat down and threw his head against the back of the couch. Lisa stood near the window, and his mother sat beside him. She put her his hands in hers and looked him in the eyes.

"Baby...you know your whole life, you tried to help other people. I can remember when that bully in high school wouldn't leave people alone, remember that?"

He laughed and said. "Yeah, I remember."

"What did you do?"

'He gave a faint smile.

"You had to be the one that beat him up. You helped the other kids, but who got suspended. You did. What about the time somebody was robbing old people in the neighborhood. You took it upon yourself to sit outside all night, to make sure it stopped. Now don't get me wrong, I admire you and love you, but at what point are you going to say. I need to start looking out for myself."

He tried to speak, but she put a finger over his lips.

"Whatever trouble you got yourself into, to help me, baby, it's not worth it."

"Ma, I wouldn't be able to live with myself, if I don't do everything in my power to help you."

"My son, I wouldn't be able to live knowing that you wouldn't be here with us. Do you understand that?"

"I understand."

"There goes that damn BMW again," Lisa said.

Eric jumped up. “BMW, what color?’

“Black.”

By the time he got out of his seat and made it to the window, it was gone. “How many times have you seen it?”

“It passed through here a couple of times. It even parked across the street, until people started to notice it.”

While he reached in his pocket to grab his cell, he leaned outside the window to give it a second look. “Hello”

“Eric meet me on the corner of 73rd. I think I know who is trying to blackmail you.”

XXXX

Muggy was the word to best describe the Homicide Division at the N.Y.P.D. Every year around this time, it became harder and harder to breathe. The last time a budget was given to re-renovate the office, to give it more ventilation they received new chairs and better fans instead. There was really no one to blame because the office use to be a storage room, for old case files. But ever since the Homicide crimes began to increase, the Department needed to use it for office space, To accommodate more Detectives.

Both, Detectives Neal and Blane, sat at their desk opposite one another. They were going over evidence from four murders, Two of which were cold cases, and two were not more than a couple of days old.

Neal started in his customary way, pencil in one ear, eyeglasses on, shirt sleeves rolled up, peering over documents. He looked more like a college professor than a Detective. Blane was already in his mode, He was reclined in his chair, hands folded behind his head, rocking back and forth.

"At it again huh fellas."Another Detective said as he walked by.

After a couple of minutes, Blane said. "All right, what've we got?"

"Well," Neal said, pushing the folder to the side. "With the new developments concerning the car crash and the sworn statement from Angela Redford, that actually seals this one. That alone should put Ron Harper away for life. All we have to do is get this information to the prosecutor's office."

"Okay," Blane said, then stood up. "NowI know that Eric Sanders is our primary suspect in these other crimes, but humor me for a minute. Like we've said before, here's this kid, who specializes in computers right,"

"Uh-huh."

"For the life of me, I can't understand why he would be dealing drugs...that's another story within itself. But he goes to prison right, where he runs into that maniac C.E.O. of ours. They talk,then come up with a place to steal two hundred million from his own Company-"

"Now you see, that doesn't make any sense. Why would he steal from himself? Eric had to do this on his own."

"I can't agree with that."

"Sure, look at it. He probably gave Ron Harper a sob story about his mother's condition. Ron got him out, gets him a job at his company, and this is how the kid repays him. Once Sanders is there, he uses whatever information Harper gave him, and stole that money on his own."

"From what I was told, that's one of the reasons why he has locked up anyway, for stealing from his own Company," Blane said, then sat back down and leaned back in his chair,

"Okay, what about the day trader Shawn Pope, you think he was on to Sanders. He was spotted chasing him right?"

"Doesn't mean he killed him."

Neal paused, gave Blane a sharp look, then took a sip of his coffee. Then in a calm voice, he said. "Your right."

Blane notices the look, then responded, "Yeah, Shawn Pope was probably on to something. I don't know, but it had to be something serious, to make him chase him into the alley. Check this out, the casings were found near the entrance of the alley. Remember now, witnesses said that he was chasing Pope, First in a cab, then through the restaurant, then into the alley. If he killed him, why didn't he just shoot him right there? You mean to tell me that he waited to get to the front of the alley, then turned around and shot him."

Neal checked his notes, raised his eyebrow, then nodded in agreement.

"Of course not. How many people you know, when they're being chased, just stop, as if there is no place else to go. Our victim stopped once he reached that alley Because he had enough. And was going to confront Sanders. But when he turned to face him, he was shot by someone else, who was at the other end of the alley. Look at the entry wounds."

"Neal stared at the photos. "They're on the right side of his body, The spent rounds that were lodged in the wall behind them, is a testament to the fact, that they were shot from a distance."

"All right, if someone else shot him, who do you think it could be? And more importantly, why?"

"Now that's where I'm lost," Blane said. "I have an idea of who it could be."

Detective Neal pulled out the picture of Eric standing next to Kathlin's body, from the yellow envelope, and slammed them on the desk. "What about these Blane! Do you have and explanation for these? How in the world is he going to get around that?"

"If you look closely at the pictures, it appears as if he's surprised by the body."

"Hum..he looks like someone who is admiring his work to me," Neal said with a smirk.

"Come on man, look at them again, and tell me what you see.'

Neal studied the photos again, then said. "He's holding a yellow envelope in his hand."

"Thank you, do you mean to tell me that he killed her. He went to look for the envelope, then came back and stood over her body. No one is that stupid."

"No, but it's consistent with the evidence,"

"What do you mean?"

"The bloody footprints heading up the stairs. Proves something happened to her before he went up toretrieve that envelope."

Blane sat silently. He knew Detective Neal made a good point.

CHAPTER 45

Felic stood at the corner of 73rd and checked her watch. It seemed like she'd been standing there, waiting forever. She turned her head at each passing car and wondered what was taking Eric so long. She leaned on the side of the building, and denied the advances of a gentleman that walked by, "Sorry but I'm waiting for my husband."

"He's a lucky man, have a good night." The stranger said before walking away.

She rolled her eyes, and looks to the sky, once the man left. She couldn't count the number of times, she had to reject unwanted advances, from both men and women. The looks that God gave her was both a gift and a curse.

She paced back and forth, in a frantic mode, then glanced at her watch once more. She removed a strand of hair from her face, then folded her arms and mumbled under her breath. "Come on Eric, what's taking you so long?"

At that moment, a cab was approaching at a slow pace.

Felic viewed the cab with uncertainty, as it pulled over, then she recognized Eric's face. When he stepped out of the cab, she greeted him.

"What took you so long?"

"I had to take care of something with my family, before-"

"Follow me." She said, as she pulled on his hand and guided him towards the building.

"Where are we going? You told me that you knew who was blackmailing me."

"We're going to Brian Scott's apartment. I think he's the one doing it."

Mr. Scott, why would he-"

"Hello Miss Hernann." the doorman said when they entered the building.

"Hey...it's been a long time, how're the kids?"

"Fine, thank you, There getting big, and giving the wife hell at the same time."

"I can imagine." She said laughing. I'm going to go upstairs and wait for Mr. Scott. We have a new client, that we need to go over some things with. Okay?"

"Sure, do you need me to let you in. Or do you still have your key?"

"I still have my key, thank you."

The doorman scanned Eric up and down with suspicion, as they walked over to the elevator.

"See you later," Felic said once they were the elevator, with a smile that reduced his apprehension.

"What is it with these doormen? Eric said.

"What do you mean?"

"Don't pay me any attention, I'm just thinking out loud, that's all. What makes you think Mr. Scott is the one doing this to me?"

"I have a feeling that's all, I could be wrong."

When Felic opened the door to Brian's apartment, they eased inside, being cautious with every step. Personally, Eric was amazed. It appeared as if he spent every last dime he had to furnish his apartment. Below him were Persian rugs, and above him were golden chandeliers. The paintings were from the finest artist, past and present, and porcelain vases sat on wooden mantles. The light in the living room was dim, but he was still trying to make out the couch. He was staring at it as if he wasn't sure of something.

"Yeah, it's Burberry," Felic assured him.

Just when Felic satisfied his curiosity, he turned his head and looked up the stairs. He felt like he was being watched. But no one was there.

"What's wrong?"

"Nothing, I just had a feeling, that's all.'

"Listen, Brians's office is right over here. You check the cabinets, and I'll check the desk. We don't have to much time. We need to hurry up."

Eric opened the file cabinet and started searching each file one by one. But he couldn't find any photos.

Felic pulled open his desk drawer, pushing the contents, from one side to another. "I know it's here," she said to herself, moving at a frantic pace. But she couldn't find a thing.

Eric walked over to Felic, then stopped in mid-stride. He locked his eyes on a small stack of envelopes on the dresser. "Your right, it's Mr. Scott." He said with his heart pounding. He reached over the desk and grabbed a stack in his hand. "These are the ones he was sending me."

She looked up for a brief moment, then continued to feel under the desk. She moved her hand from one side to the other. "I think I got something" She bent her head down lower for a better look. She stretched her hand back further. Then touched something that was taped to the desk. She stretched a little further, then yelled. "Got it."

She pulled out the same small envelope that Eric was holding in his hand. She stood up and ripped it open. Photos of Eric was inside, along with another note.

He snatched the envelope from her hand and stood there with his anger building.

"Eric we have to go, we have to get out of here!"

He didn't pay any attention to her, it was as if he was in another world, consumed by the blood that was boiling inside of him.

Eric let's go!" She yelled again, but this time reaching for his arm.

That seemed to bring him back to reality.

"Brian will be here any minute now."

As the started to walk towards the door, he paused, "How did you know that he was blackmailing me?"

"Eric, there is no time for this, we have to go.

He grabbed her by both arms, cutting her speech. "Then asked. How did you know?"

She pulled away from him, then said. “Detective Blane had a small envelope in his hand, that he found somewhere in the area where you work. I recognized Brian’s handwritingon it, then I heard him on the phone, telling another Detective about the photos.”

He smacked himself in the forehead, then remembered that he threw the last package in the trash. “Damn, I forgot about that, how stupid could I be? Let’ get out of here”

On their way out of the door, neither one of them noticed the pair of eyes watching them from the top of the stairs.

CHAPTER 46

Joseph Cooper and Ron Harper sipped on aged brandy in one of the offices at his Law firm. Ron sat with his feet crossed, on top of Joseph's desk. He splashed the intoxicant around in his mouth, he wanted to savor every drop of his newfound freedom. After a loud gulp, he raised his glass into the air to admire its contents. "Home sweet home." he said, "Home Sweet home."

The plaques that lined the mantel on the wall, was a testament to the Law Firm's success. Joseph's office always amazed Ron. He stared at the picture of the States Senators and other public officials. His Law Firm ability to win high profile cases, both criminal and political, made his, the most sought after Firm in the City. And one of the most prominent men in the socialite circle.

"Well, this time tomorrow, I should be on my way to Costa Rica," Ron said.

"So that's it huh, no coming back?" Joseph asked.

"Nope, no coming back.:

"Your starting to doubt the skills I see."

"Actually, I believe in your ability to get an acquittal. But for me, I think I have overstayed my welcome. I already have a villa picked out. where I will spend some of my days, and it ain't gonna hurt being two hundred million dollars richer, I tell you that." He said as he threw his glass up, toasting his success.

"Minus my cut of course." Joseph responded as politely as possible."

"Of course, of course," Ron said, clearing his throat in the process. "Give it a couple of days, then check your account, I got you. You will be pleased."

"Let me ask you a question Ron, Where is all of that money that your father left you?"

"He didn't respond, he just kept taking sips of his brandy.

"You spent it all, all of it?"

"Hey, I would be the first to admit, I was out of control. I made some risky investments." He shrugged. But hey, that's the name of the game. You win some, you lose some. Now I could've recouped most of the money that I lost if they were patient. But to strip me of my role as C.E.O. and take everything, my stake in the Company. I just couldn't sit back and let it end that way, Nope uh uh." He said shaking his head. "So I gave myself an early retirement, with a great severance package."

"When was the last time you talked to that kid Eric Sanders. You know his sister called me and said that Detective Blane was questioning him."

"Fuck Blane. I haven't talked to Eric in a while. Let me call him. He doesn't even know I'm home yet."

XXXX

Eric and Felic walked at a fast pace, down the sidewalk. They were trying their best to get as far away as possible, from Brian's apartment building. Besides the occasional glance at one another, they barely spoke. Eric slowed his pace, then reached in his pocket for his phone. "Hello...Hey!, what's up? He said turning his back to Felicia.

"Eric I'm out. You haven't called me in a while, is everything all right?"

Listen, a lot has been going on since I transferred that money."

Ron's smile turned into a frown, as he put his Brandy on the desk and sat up. He cleared his throat then asked. "Eric, what's the problem?"

"I ran into a little trouble with this guy at the Company."

"Who, what's his name?"

"Brian Scott."

Brian, what does he have to do with anything?"

"He's been blackmailing me."

"Brian, with what?"

"With pictures of me standing over the body of your dead wife."

"Huh, how is that possible?"

"I promise you that I didn't kill her-"

"I don't understand, why is he blackmailing you?"

"The money I stole from your Company."

The only sound Eric heard was the call being ended.

XXXX

Detective Blane paced the floor, going back and forth with Detective Neal. they were trying to make sense out of the mounds of evidence, cluttering their desks. Each had come to their own conclusion. Blane felt that Eric was being set up, while Neal held sided with the facts. As Blane paced the floor, He paused suddenly, he took one last look at his desk, then grabbed his jacket.

"Blane wait, where are you going?"

"I just thought of something, I'll be back."

Neal got up grabbed his jacket and said. "Shit!, I've come this far, there's no need to turn backnow."

Blane stopped him and reminded him of his retirement, but Neal wasn't paying that any attention He was determined to go.

"All right listen, play the background, and let me do all the talking."

"You got it, your the boss."

"You plan on telling me what's going on. Where are we going?"

"To see Brian Scott."

Neal turned his head in Blane's direction.

"It was right in front of us all the whole time. In order for Sanders to get into that Company. Somebody had to get him in. who else knew about the missing money? Besides the Board Members, and more importantly. Who else would have known about the surveillance system in Ron's house? Somebody killed those people, but it wasn't Eric Sander's."

CHAPTER 47

The three men who represented the Smitz family, sat in the back of a small restaurant, in the east village. As usual, they were all silent. Each was in their own thoughts, focusing on the task ahead. They had been there before, on the hunt, following the money trail. Nine times out of ten they were successful. The times they weren't, one of them was able to detect the obstacles early on and bring it to the other's attention.

One of them broke the silence, by tapping his fork on the table, the other two immediately gave their undivided attention. "I don't know about this one gentleman, it doesn't feel right to me."

Nodding his head in agreement, one of the other men said, "He's right,normally we would've been done by now, and splitting the profits."

Hawkeyes dropped his fork in his food then said. "You've got to have patience. This is the biggest score we've ever had. Bigger than we could've possibly imagined, and you're worried about not feeling right. What's there to feel right about, when we stand to make five million apiece."

They each started to shift around in their chairs. Then one replied.

"Whatever you say. We've been following you this long, it's no need to stop now."

"All right then. She wants us to go to Brian Scott's apartment next."

XXXX

Ron Harper waited for the right moment to enter the building. He didn't want to be seen by the doorman, who knew him so well. He stood across the street until he noticed an elderly woman about to go in. It was now or never. He ran across the street, then walked up to her, just before she was about to go inside.

"Excuse me, Ma'am, let me help you with your bag."

She stared him up and down, gave him a skeptical look, but didn't feel threatened. "Do you live here son?"

No Ma'am, I want to surprise my brother, I just got in from out of town. Between work and the family, we barely have time for one another. I can't wait to see the smile on his face when he sees me. He's going to be so happy."

"Aw, that's so sweet, Come on, I'll let you in with me."

He reached for her bag, and walked with his head down, right past the doorman, on to the elevator.

He let himself into the apartment, with a key that Brian had given him and Felic a year ago. Whenever he went out of town for a few weeks, he wanted one of them to go by and check on the place. Instead, they often threw lavish parties, entertaining past and future clients.

Ron walked through the front door, and mistakenly let it slam shut behind him. He paused and waited to see if anyone was there, but the silence remained. He wrapped a handkerchief around his hand, then took out a bottle of Bacardi from the liquor cabinet, and placed it on the bar. He lifted a small glass with the same handkerchief, poured himself a drink, then sat on the Burberry couch. He sat back and waited for Brian, in a cool calm and collective manner.

Upstairs in the apartment, the demeanor was much different. A woman sat on the bed in panic mode, wondering what would be her next move. She knew that she would be the last person in the world, that he would want to see. And she intended on keeping it that way.

When Brian walked through the front door and laid his briefcase on the table. He had an uneasy feeling. He proceeded with caution. When he saw it was Ron, he said. "Hey." with a mixture of concern and urgency. What are you doing here?"

"You don't seem to happy to see me, Brian, I wonder why."

" What I mean is, why didn't you call me, I could've picked you up."

Ron rose from the couch and stuck out his hand to greet his old friend. "I just got out this morning, and I didn't want to make a big deal about it. You know what I mean."

"Yeah, I understand."

As the longtime friends spoke, she listened, still uncertain of what she should do.

"I saw the news before I got out of prison...hey, what did you do with the body?"

"I buried it right there on the property?"

"Good job, I knew I could depend on you. Now let me tell you what I've been working on. I got someone in the Company to steal two hundred million from its accounts"

"What?" Brian said. Acting surprised as if he didn't know."

"That's right, a hundred for you and a hundred for me," Ron said with a large smile on his face.

Brian let out a loud sigh, he felt like a fool for even thinking Ron would hold out on him. He became relaxed and started to laugh. He sat down and let his head fall in his hands. "Ron, you're not going to believe this, but-"

His speech was interrupted, by a thin piece of wire, that was being wrapped around his neck. He never saw Ron easing behind him. Instincts threw his hands to his neck, but it was too late, Ron was too strong for him. Brian kicked his feet, and smashed the glass table in front of him, sending fragments of glass everywhere.

While Ron was strangling Brian, the woman tipped toed down the stairs. She was barely able to breathe. She didn't want to take a chance on her own life. She consciously made the decision to sneak past the commotion and make her way to the front door. If she could just get to the hallway, she would be able to make it from there. When she reached the bottom of the stairs, she was temporarily paralyzed by what she saw. But the fear of being seen far outweighed anything else. She reached the door, and like Ron minutes earlier, mistakenly let it slam shut behind her.

Ron turned around shocked but didn't move until Brian wasn't breathing. By the time he ran out to the hallway, the elevator was reaching the first floor. He ran back to the apartment, pulled back the curtains and saw someone running out of the building, hailing a cab. He could see the person looking up, watching him, as he watched them.

As the cab drove off, he heard police sirens, then saw a car with flashing lights pull up. Two men jumped out and ran into the building. Ron turned and started to wipe down everything he thought he touched. When he stepped out of the apartment, he wrapped his handkerchief around the doorknob and closed the door. He ran to the stairwell, then waited to see if he could hear anyone coming up. When he didn't, he headed down the stairs.

XXXX

The Detectives stepped off the elevator and checked the numbers on the apartment doors.

"Here it is right here," Neal said. Apartment 7-B right?

Yeah, that's it"

They got closer and knocked on the door.

"Brian Scott, open the door, it's the police!"

Blane checked the doorknob and found that it was open, he looked at Neal. They drew their weapons and entered the apartment with caution. They advanced closer and closer until they reached the living room. There they saw Brain slumped over on the chair. Neal searched the apartment while Blane checked for a pulse. Brian's body was warm and still. Blane reached for his radio.

"This is Detective Blane, send an ambulance to 1017, east 73rd street."

"The rest of the apartment is secure," Neal said. "Just a few minutes earlier, and we might've run right into the person who did this. I'll be downstairs, waiting for the for forensics."

As Blane walked through the apartment, he noticed that Brian's office was searched. Papers were thrown everywhere, and cabinet draws were left open. As he got close to Brian's desk, he observed a stack of envelopes, that was the same kind he found in Eric's trash can. He shifted through the stack and saw that a couple, already had Eric's name printed out on them. He dropped the envelopes and on the desk, then turned and walked out of the apartment.

Downstairs Neal called out to Blane. When he caught his attention, he waved him over. "Blane listen to me, the doorman said that Miss Hernann was here earlier with a black guy who he never saw before."

Blane nodded his head. "I think that they somehow figured out that it was Brian Scott who was sending him those pictures. I found envelopes on his desk, addressed to Eric."

Neal was stoned faced. "You still believe your guy is innocent?"

Blane looked around, lowered his head, then reached for his radio a second time. "I want an A.P.B. out on Eric Sanders, Ron Harper, and Felic Hernann...They are all wanted for murder."

CHAPTER 48

When their car turned the Corner of 72nd, they were met with a surprise. Blue and white lights were bouncing off of the brick building, and squad cars barricaded the streets. E.M.T. workers were putting someone in an ambulance, who was covered in a white sheet, and there were about four or five cars in front of them, being held up by an officer. It was too late to try and back up now, it would only draw attention to themselves, so they sat and waited patiently.

By now, more cars began piling up behind them, and a familiar face popped out of the building.

Detective Blane held a notepad in his hand, as he talked to another officer. The three Albanians kept there eyes focussed on him, while the officer who was directing the traffic, allowed it to ease up. The windows were fogged from their heavy breathing and the adrenaline that flowed inside of them made them feel nervous.

Blane was preoccupied with the dramatic change of events, that he couldn't give the officer his undivided attention. Could it be, he had Eric all wrong, and he was the killer of all those people. It was now too many coincidences, for him not to start thinking otherwise. First Shawn Pope, then Kathlin Harper, now Brian Scott. The only one who was holding out hope for Eric was now the same person who couldn't wait to get his hands on him.

His thoughts were interrupted again by a feeling telling him to look up. A man in a passing car, who looked a lot like the one he had a staredown with, in front of Brian Scott's office, was lighting a cigarette.

Once Hawkeyes inhaled and blew out the smoke, he stared at Detective Blane, then flicked the ashes on the ground.

Blane stopped and office in mid-sentence and walked towards the street. He needed to get a closer look. In an instant, they both reached for the weapons. Blane was able to get off a few rounds hitting the car and shattering the window, but Hawkeyes semi-automatic was too strong, Blane had to duck for cover. At least fifty rounds or more was sprayed from the vehicle. Bullets hit the ambulance, squad cars, and the apartment buildings windows. When the firing stopped., Blane jumped up and started to run behind the car. He emptied his gun but was useless, they were too far away to get a clear shot.

The driver sped off, leaving two dead officers and half dozen other wounded.

When Blane returned to the scene, he yelled. "Is everyone alright?"

No one said a word, all he saw was E.M.T. workers trying to pump life back into someone on the ground. As he walked over to see who it was, other officers held him back.

"What's going on, get off of me." He yelled and struggled to get free.

"Blane, don't go over there." And the officer said 'Let them work."

"That's when he sawDetective Neal stretched out on the

sidewalk. He tried, but couldn't tussle with the tears, they got the best of him.

He leaned against a squad car, and watched as his friend being put in the ambulance,it sent a burst of emotions through his body. For him, the scene was a familiar one, Watching family and friends going hysterical over the death of a loved one. Though he took the oath to preserve and protect, by putting his life on the lines daily. Being on the other end of the spectrum was agonizing.

"Sir," A young officer said. "The sergeant told me to tell you, to come to the station. He wants to speak with you."

"Tell him you didn't see me Blane responded, then turned to talk to another Detective.

"Yeah Blane, what's up?" The Detective asked.

"Neal told me, that he had a team assembled, just in case we needed them."

"Yeah he did, they are still awaiting the call. Whenever your ready, they're ready. Everybody is gonna want a piece of those assholes.

"Okay good, I have a feeling that the night is young."

Without a specific destination, they roamed the streets of Manhattan, still silent. Eric was focussing on his dilemma. How did he know that Brian Scott didn't have copies at another location, and if so, who would be trying to blackmail him next?

"Now what?" Felic asked, breaking the silence.

"I don't know yet, let's just sit for a minute."

They leaned against a parked car, and he rested his computer on the hood.

"I can't believe Mr. Scott was the one doing this to me. He must've been the one who killed Mrs. Harper."

Felic leaned on the car without uttering a word.

After a few more seconds of silence, he leaned off of the car and patted himself down. He reached on the side of his jacket pulled out his phone and said "Hello"

"Eric!" Lisa yelled in a hysterical voice. "That BMW is in front of the house again."

He didn't respond, he cut off his phone, jumped up and stopped the first cab that he saw. He handed the driver a hundred dollar bill, then said. 'I need you to get to 116th street as fast as you can." Before the could even get their doors closed, the driver sped off.

"Eric, what's going on?"

"I think somebody is trying to hurt my family."

"Who?"

"This guy...I owe him some money."

"For what Eric?"

"It's a long story, I'll tell you about it later. He opened up his laptop and punched in a few keys. He wanted to make sure he still had access to the money. He pulled out a card, and placed it on the corner of the screen, then sat there fighting two opposing forces in his mind. Should he send the money to Hawkeyes, or should he leave it where it was, and pay Beeju the money he owed him. The whole thing couldn't be over with soon enough, he thought. An announcement on the radio refocussed his attention.

A WALL STREET EXECUTIVE HAS JUST BEEN KILLED IN HIS APARTMENT. POLICE DO NOT HAVE A MOTIVE

AT THIS TIME BUT ARE SEEKING TWO PEOPLE OF INTEREST AT THIS POINT, A MALE AND FEMALE, WHO MAY OR MAY NOT HAVE HAD CONTACT WITH HIM EARLIER THIS EVENING. WE WILL PROVIDE YOU WITH MORE INFORMATION AS IT COMES IN.

The driver looked through the rearview mirror and noticed the reaction on his passenger's face, as they started to whisper to one another. When the cab neared the corner of 116th street, an explosion was heard. It was so loud and powerful, that it shook the ground, shattered windows and sent a plume of smoke into the air

Eric's eyes widened when he saw the flames coming from his house. Without thinking, he closed the computer, jumped out of the cab, and ran in the direction of the flames. He was being pushed by an increase in adrenalin and heroism. He ran, jumping over debris. The reality of not being able to get into the house didn't hit him until he got to the first step. A second explosion and a burst of flames threw him onto his back.

"Eric!" Felic yelled she ran in his direction, dodging some of the residents in the street, and even pushed some of them out of the way. By the time she made it to hin, he was already struggling to get on his feet. He was visibly shaken and emotionally distraught.

"Why!" He yelled out, watching his house go up in flames.

"Eric!, we have to get out of here," Felic said as the sounds of fire trucks and police cars could be heard approaching. "Maybe they weren't even in there, you don't know."

All reasoning was gone, anger consumed every inch of his flesh. There was only one thing on his mind. Beeju.

"Eric, are you alright." Mrs. Rosenboun asked, with tears pouring from her eyes.

“I’m alright,” he answered with an empty stare. “I’m looking.... do you know if-”

Two police cars broke his speech and made him look in that direction.

“Eric, we have to go! Felic yelled again.

He took the laptop from Felic and gave it to Mrs. Rosenboun. “Hold this computer for me until I come back.”

She grabbed the computer, but before he could go she said. “Eric wait, your mother and sis-”

“I got to go Mrs. Rosenboun.” He said nervously looking around. “I’ll be back.”

Both he and Felic disappeared into the crowd. Too many police cars were on the scene, and he knew that they would be looking for them. He wasn’t going back to jail until he got his hands on Beeju,

CHAPTER 49

When Eric reached Edgecomb Avenue, the smell of cocaine hugged his nose, and the addicts were playing their usual positions. Death was on his mind, he never thought about killing a man before, until now. He walked straight past the addicts and headed to the building where Beeju was standing. He balled up his fist and focussed every bit of his attention on Beeju, then charged. A man who was in the crowd noticed Eric running towards them, and yelled.

"Who the fuck is that?"

He made the rest of the guys in the crowd look up, then reached for their weapons. But there was no need to fire a single shot. Eric was tackled to the ground before he even got close to Beeju.

"Why the fuck did you blow up my house?" Eric screamed. "I said I would pay you."

"What the hell are you talking about? I didn't do anything to your house."

"I know it was you. My family didn't have anything to do with our deal." He said, as he shed and uncontrollably amount of tears, and tried to break free.

"Go find out what the fuck he's talking about," Beeju whispered to one of his lieutenants, then turned to face Eric. "Pick his ass up."

"I know what you did. You think I'm stupid, you had your men following me in a black BMW for weeks now."

"I haven't had anyone following you, I don't even own a black BMW. you think I need somebody to follow you, for thirty thousand dollars. I make more way more than that in a day."

Eric lowered his head, then wondered who could've been following him. It didn't take long for him to find out. As shots were fired at him from a black BMW. Two of Beeju's men were hit. Eric ran for cover, as some of the other dealers returned fire. The BMW was showered with bullets, causing it to jump a curb and crash into a building. Once the BMW stopped, Beeju and his men approached the car with their guns drawn. Smoke from the engine rose from the hood. One of the men slowly opened the passenger's side door and found an older man slumped over the steering wheel.

"What's this?" then the man said reaching for a device on the passenger's seat, a red light was beeping on the screen. "You E, come over here and check this out."

When Eric got closer to the car, he had the shock of his life. The man in the driver's seat was the Old Head, the guy he became cool with while he was in prison with Ron.

"Why in the world would the Old head be trying to killme?" He thought out loud.

"He must've been following you through this device. " Beeju said, showing it to Eric. "It's a tracking device, the closer you came to the car, the faster it blinked. You must have something on you, allowing it to track you."

Eric patted himself down, then took a glance at his watch. He quickly popped the clasp and pulled it off. When he threw the watch, the red dot on the screen moved.

One of Beeju men came back and whispered something in his ear.

"Alright, good, I want this car moved to another area before a hundred officers start crawling around here. "Who was that guy? You looked at him as if you knew him."

"A guy I was locked up with, he's a nobody."

"Oh yeah, then why was he trying to kill you?"

"Man I don't know. I'm trying to figure that out right now."

As he sat on the curb, he ran a few things threw his mind. The Old Head he thought. Huh, what does he have to do with this? Then he remembered that Joseph Cooper was the one who left him the package with the watch inside. He lowered his head, then suddenly it came to him. He jumped up and thanked Beeju for saving his life, then said. "I promise, I got you, I'll get you your money soon. I got to go."

"Yo E, what kind of trouble are you mixed up in?" you've got these people following you with tracking devices and shit, they don't seem like the kind of people to be playing with.

The words went through one ear and out the other. "Don't you have a car that I can borrow?"

Beeju reluctantly threw him a set of keys. "Yeah, take the white Camry at the end of the block."

XXXX

Eric jumped on the expressway and left Harlem. He still couldn't believe that this was all a scheme. Ron always said that life is like chess. Always anticipate your opponent's next move. He reached on the dashboard and grabbed his phone. "Ron, I'm going to kill you when I see you."

"Eric, it's me. Who the hell is Ron?"

He blinked his eyes fast, and held the phone to his heart, relieved to hear his sister's voice. "Don't worry about that, thank god you're alright. What about Ma?"

"She's fine, we were both next doors at Mrs. Rosenbaum's when the house blew up. She said she tried to tell you, but you kept cutting her off."

"Where are you now?"

"At your Lawyer's office."

Eric felt his heart slipping out of place, as he imagined the worst. "Listen, get out of there, it's not safe."

"Eric, what is wrong with you? He's been good to us. We didn't have anybody else to turn to. They seemed to be very concerned about you as well. Didn't he help you get out of jail?"

"Yeah he did, but-"

"So what's the problem?"

"Listen. It's a long story. I'll be there in a minute."

"Oh, Eric, there's another guy in the next room, talking to Mr. Cooper, he told me to tell you hello."

"Who is it? what is his name?"

"He didn't say, all he said was, was that you two spent some time together."

Eric dropped the phone and stepped on the gas peddle.

XXXX

Police tape still surrounded this familiar home, but unlike before, he wasn't nervous, or cautious. At this point, he had nothing to lose, and everything to gain. When he walked up to the house, he used his elbow to bust out a small piece of glass, near the door handle in the back of the house. Once inside, he walked to the living room. He stood still for a moment and reflected on the image of Kathlin Harper when she was lying lifeless on the floor. He reached in his pocket, and pulled out the key that he found, with the yellow envelope.

He walked around the large chess table, that he bumped into the last time he was there. He ran his fingers under the sharp edges. He kicked both chairs out of the way and crouched down. He was hoping that his hunches were correct, but there was no such luck. He stood up, leaned over the chess table, and ran his hand across the board. He noticed that the velvet material that covered it, could be moved. He lifted it up by the edges and peeled it back revealing a smooth metal surface, with a keyhole in the middle of it. He put the key inside and turned it slowly when he felt the latched give, and the key wouldn't turn any further, he took it out. He pulled on one side of the table, which loosened up, then ran to the other side of the table, which easily slid out. Then he stood up and looked inside. All he could do was smile.

CHAPTER 50

Blane sat motionless in his car, Knowing he should've followed procedure. Detective Neal told him a day or to ago, that he should've arrested Eric sanders for murder. But instead of acting on that advice and concrete evidence, he wanted to wait. Now that waiting may have very well gotten his friend killed. There was no one else to Blane, but himself, and he knew that. He had to find Hawkeyes.

As he sat in his car, he heard the dispatch speak about a body being found, in a black BMW. It snapped him out of his gaze and triggered his memory. He remembered that Eric was being followed by one, so he ignored the Lieutenants request to see him, he started his car and rushed to the scene.

With his siren blaring, he reached the scene in record time, leaving tire marks six inches behind him. He flung his door open, hopped out and disregarded the yellow tape, that surrounded the car. He ducked underneath it, while crime technicians were collecting evidence. "How long has the body been here he asked.

"It's fresh, we just got the call an hour ago" One lab technician answered. "Who is he?"

"His license says, Benjamin Jones."

Blane walked around the car and checked to see if he could find any dents.

"What are you looking for Detective?"

"Well, he said, bending down on one knee. "In another case that I'm investigating, witnesses say that they saw a black BMW chasing a white Lexus. And that they were trying to run each other off of the road."

"What makes you think that this is the same car?"

"I really don't know, but once I heard about a body being found in a black BMW, I took a chance, so I'm here. The driver's side of the white Lexus had traces of black paint on it...Yup, now this car has dents, with scrapes of white paint on it. My witness also said that the driver of the BMW was black. So, what's the race of the victim?"

The technician looked up, then said. "Black"

Blane called in the name on the license and asked for a full print out on the victim. "How many times was he shot?"

"Nine or ten, we don't know exactly, until we find out from the morgue. Something is strange though."

"What's that?"

"There'snot much physical evidence."

"What do you mean?"

"There are no prints, either on the door handles, steering wheel, nothing. It's been wiped clean, and there's no shell casing on the outside of the vehicle. But the casing's from his forty-five was left in thc car."

"A forty-five huh?" Blane walked a few paces, then looked

around. Someone moved this car here."

"But why? Why would someone go through the trouble of all that, and risk being seen?"

"I think I have an idea," Blane said as he rushed to his car.

XXXX

Blane stopped his car, in the middle of 145th street, just a few blocks away from where the crime scene investigators were processing the BMW. He jumped out and spoke to a couple of guys who were standing on the sidewalk.

"Listen, guys, I'm not here to arrest anybody, I need to talk to Beeju. Tell him that Detective Blane wants to speak to him."

All of the men looked at one another, with a look on their faces that said, Who the hell is going to go into that building and tell Beeju that a Detective would like to talk to him.

Blane recognized the hesitation and said. "Listen to me, I'm not here to lock him up. I just want to talk to him, it's important. Tell him, it's about Eric Sanders."

One of the guys walked away, and within a few minutes, Beeju stuck his head out of the building. He waved his hand, indicating to Blane, to come inside.

As soon as he walked into the building, he spoke. "Listen to me, I don't care about what you're doing out here, that's for another division to handle, I'm with Homicide. Right now, all I'm concerned with is trying to catch some of these Wall Street guys, who I think has Eric mixed up in some deep shit."

"I know that you're affiliated with Eric, some kind of way.

He is wanted for the murder of three people. I've tried my best to give him the benefit of the doubt, but it's not looking good for him. Even with that, I still think that he is being set up. One of the people that he's being accused of killing, was killed with a forty-five. The same kind of shell casing that was found in a black BMW a few blocks away from here. Were you following Eric, or has someone following him?"

"No"

"Well, that was what he thought."

"He asked me the same thing, and I couldn't understand why."

Blane lowered his head in disbelief. "You mean you weren't following him?"

Beeju shook his head. "No, he owed me a little money for helping him out, but that's as far as it goes."

"Helping him out with what?...oh, you mean with the drugs he got caught with."

Beeju sucked his teeth. "Eric's no drug dealer. We knew each other from High School, that's all. He told me he had a problem, and needed some extra cash, so I said okay. All he had to do, was dropped off a duffle bag or two every now and then.-"

"One second," Blane said, putting up a finger, and turning his back. "I need to answer this. Yeah, Blane here, go ahead."

"Blane, the murdered guy is an ex-con, who just came from M.D.C." The Detective said.

"What, hold on. You've got to be kidding me. Listen, put me on hold, and find out if he was in the same cell block as Ron Harper and Eric Sanders."

"You got it, Hold on."

Blane turned back around, faced Beeju and asked. "What happened here tonight?"

Beeju looked away without saying a word.

"I know that BMW was moved from this block. I also know that a couple of guys was admitted to Columbian Presperterian earlier and is being treated for gunshot wounds. If I was a betting man, I would bet my life that those bullets came from the casings we found in that BMW. "

"Blane! Blane!"

"He heard his name being called from his cell phone. He put up another finger to Beeju. "Yeah, what've you got?"

"Your guy, Benjamin Jones Ron Harper, and Eric Sanders were all in the same cell block-"

"I knew it!" He yelled through gritted teeth. He closed his phone, then looked at Beeju, and gave him that don't bullshit me look. "Now I said that I wasn't going to arrest you, and I meant it. But I can have this whole block surrounded in a matter of minutes if you want to keep fucking me around."

"Okay listen, my guys were defending themselves. First of all, and second, Eric came over here hysterical, asking me about his mother's house. The next thing I know, some guy drove by and started shooting at us."

"What was he hysterical about?"

"His house, he said his house blew up, and he thought-"

Blane didn't stick around to hear the rest. He ran out of the building to his car and peeled off.

CHAPTER 51

Blane drove around cars and ran red lights, on his way to Eric's house. He heard about an explosion being investigated on his radio. But he had no idea how closely related it could be to his case. He now knew without a doubt, that Eric was being set up for murder, but by who?

He parked behind a car, whose windows were shattered, and he could smell the smoldering wood. The actual damage couldn't be seen until he got out of his car.

As he walked, he stopped in his tracts, he couldn't believe his eyes. Not much was left of the beautiful Brownstone he once sat in. A scraping sound coming from the side of the neighbor's house caught his attention. When he got closer, he noticed an old woman, sweeping glass into a pile.

"Excuse me, Ma'am." He said flashing his badge.

"Yes, can I help you, officer?"

"Yes, can you tell me where Mrs. Sanders is, please?"

"Is she in any kind of trouble?"

"No Ma'am, I just want to make sure that she's alright."

"Well, she and her daughter were with me when their house blew up."

"Thank god, where are they now?"

"They called a lawyer, so I guess they're with him."

"Do you happen to know what the lawyer's name?'

"I'm not sure, do I look like I have the best memory in the world son?"

"Please try," he said smiling.

"Uhm..Josh...Joe-"

"Joseph Cooper."

"Yes, that's it, Joseph Cooper. How did you know?"

"I'm just familiar with him, that's all. Thank you for your help."

"Your welcome young man, I hope that son of hers is okay as well."

"Why would you say that?"

"He was here earlier tonight, and it looked like he was hiding from someone. I was trying to talk to him, and let him know that his family was safe, but he kept looking around nervously and left in a hurry. He left his computer with me and said that he would be back to get it later. But I gave it to his mother when she left."

"Thank you, thank you for your help."

After thanking the elderly woman, he got into his car and drove off. He needed to find out what role Joseph Cooper was playing in this tangled web. Ron Harper, he thought, that son of a bitch. He enlisted Eric to steal that money, had him set up for murder, then hired someone to kill him, all to cover his tracts.

Now Blane was going to do everything in his power, to make

sure he never sees the light of day.

The Law offices of Cooper and Cooper were grand, and laces with the finest of furniture. One floor of the building was kept a little more modest, it was in remembrance of when they first started out. Barely recognized, they grew their small but effective firm, into one of the most prestigious in the City. And had over five hundred lawyers across the country. Joseph Cooper was more hands-on with the case files than his older brother, who chose to run the administrative aspects of the Company.

He had Mrs. Sanders and her daughter sit in one of the modest offices to wait for Eric. After giving them some refreshments, Mrs. Sanders needed to lie down. She rested on the couch, while Lisa watched Joseph Cooper talk to Ron Harper. Suddenly, she didn't feel as safe as she did earlier, but she didn't want to worry her mother. In the middle of their conversation, they stopped and looked in her direction. She quickly turned away, now knowing that Eric was right, It wasn't safe.

As they strolled past the office that his mother and sister were in, he gave her a nod, as if to say, that everything is going to be alright. She responded with a skepticallook. When Eric got to the Law Firm, he could see an entire floor with its lights still on. He got out, went to the building, and walked right past the security guard at the front desk. He stepped on the elevator, and paced back and forth, waiting to reach his floor, he was unable to get his mother off his mind. All he could think about was administering the harshest punishment possible, to whoever wanted to hurt his family. When the elevator stopped, and the door opened, he was greeted by Joseph Cooper.

"Eric how are you?" he said with open arms.

"Where is my family?" Eric yelled, with his hands around

Joseph's throat.

"They're in that office over there, they are safe."

"You better not hurt my family."

"Calm down, I'm not going to do anything to anybody, I'm a lawyer for God's sakes. Let's go talk in another room, someone wants to see you."

As they walked down the hall he noticed his sister and smiled, then they both looked at their mother who was still lying on the couch. When he walked into another office, Ron Harper said, Hello Eric, where the fuck is my money.

CHAPTER 52

Detective Blane made it to the station in a matter of minutes. When he walked in, officers and plane close Detective's patted him on the back. Some even shook his hand, extending their condolences.

"Blane!" One Detective yelled. "The Lieutenant said he wants to see you in his office right away. Before you do anything. Oh, and Blane, he said don't make him have to send for you a third time."

"Is Felic Hernann still sitting?"

"She hasn't moved a muscle."

How did they catch her?"

"Some cab driver said that he noticed how nervous she and another passenger was when the news about Brian Scott came across the radio. So he called it in, and we sent a unit to the location."

"Good, don't let anyone talk to her before I do."

"Got it."

As he made his way to the Lieutenant office, he passed his and Detective Neal's desk, with all the evidence they were going over, still in place. Before he knocked on the door, Blane tensed up. He knew what to expect, so he put on his suit of armor and prepared for the worst.

"Come in!" The lieutenant yelled.

When Blane opened the door, he was just getting off the phone, and in his usual baritone voice said. "That was the Mayor!, he wanted to know what was going on. And you know what I had to tell him."

Blane stood silent.

"Nothing, that's what I had to tell him, nothing! I couldn't tell him a damn thing, because I don't know what's going on. If you would be so kind, as to fill me in on your activities."

"Lieutenant, there's a big conspiracy going on, with these Wall Street guys-"

"Wall Street?"

"Fraud, Murder, multiple murder's really. And I'm right on top of the suspects."

"Not anymore your not. I was told to take you off of this case."

"Don't do this, not now. It's going to take someone else weeks to get briefed on this case."

The Lieutenant shook his head as Blane spoke, folded his hands and placed them on his desk. "I've put in too much time to lose my pension, Blane."

"You won't, just tell the Mayor that you spoke to me and that whatever I did, I did on my own. Without your approval. That will put all the blame on me. Listen, I'm close."

The Lieutenant leaned back in his chair, weighing and judging his options. "Listen, Blane, the Mayor was adamant about taking you off of this case. I've never heard him sound like that before."

"Come on. I have a potential witness waiting in the interrogation room as we speak."

"Are you sure you want to do this, you have a long careerahead of you."

Blane walked closer to the Lieutenant desk, leaned over, looked him in the eye and said. "Sarg, Neal was just helping me. He could've sat at his desk, processed some papers and in two years, be soaking up the sun in Florida. He believed in his oath, and as his friend, I at least owe him this."

"All right, I want this over with, as soon as possible."

Blane turned to leave, then stopped and asked. "Sarg, was his wife notified?"

"Yes, she was, earlier. Listen, don't beat yourself over the head with this. It wasn't your fault.We all live with the consequences of death, every time we put on that badge. You just do what you have to do, to bring those bastards to justice."

He nodded in agreement, then went straight to talk to Felic Hernann.

When he got to the interrogation room, he looked in the window and saw her sitting there, as if nothing was wrong. As if nothing happened. She was admiring herself in the mirror, lightly powdering her nose, and applying lipstick to her dried yet succulent lips. He wanted to run in and slap the shit out of her but knew he needed to maintain his composure.

"Blane, you have a call."

"From who?"

"A Sergeant Jim Kesler, out of Connecticut

"Tell him I'm not in, take a message." he didn't have time to hear the I told you so's and you should've. When he opened the door to talk to Felic. She turned to face him.

"Hello." She said in a cool calm and collective voice.

"Miss Hernan." Blane nodded. "How are you?"

"Detective, why in the world is there a warrant out for my arrest?"

"There's a lot going on right now, and I need to know if you are a part of it…well, are you a part of it, yes or no?"

"I'm not part of anything Detective."

Blane slammed both hands on the table and yelled. "Do I look stupid to you, don't play with me Miss Hernann. You mean to tell me, that you didn't have anything to do with that two hundred million being stolen from the firm."

She responded, but her head tilted a little. She was ready to break. He slid his chair closer to her, making her turn away, then he hit the table one last time. She jumped and wiped away a thin liquid substance from her nose. He already knew the answer to his next question but decided to ask anyway, just to see where she was at.

"Who was blackmailing Eric?"

"Brian!" she said, as the tears began to drop from her eyes.

"Brian, why?"

"He found out that Eric stole money from the Company's

accounts for Ron Harper."

"For Ron Harper. I thought you said that you didn't have anything to do with it. How did you know it was Brian?"

"I recognized the writing on the package that you held in your hand, at the Company. Eric told me that someone was trying to frame him, for a murder he didn't commit. That's all I know."

Miss Hernann, two officers lost their lives tonight, by a couple of gun-toting thugs. Who I think, is trying to retrieve that money for the Smitz Family Corp. Now listen, these guys are trying to kill Eric. So if you care, even a little bit abouthim, you'll let me know where I could find him."

"Detective, I have no idea where he could be." She said, still crying out of control.

"Okay Miss Hernann, calm down. Would you like to go to the lady's room to gather yourself?"

She nodded. "Yes, I would like that. Thank you."

Blane stuck his head out of the interrogation room and called a female officer to escort her to the lady's room. After she got up to leave, He walked around the table and picked up her suit jacket from the back of the chair. He stuck his hand in the right side pocket, then placed it back on the arm of the chair. Felic returned and sat without saying a word.

"Miss Hernann, I really have no reason to hold you. There isn't any evidence pointing in your direction. So I'm going to have to let you go. But let me give you a bit of advice. I suggest that you be careful. Everyone around you, or at least those who you are closely associated with, appears to be losing their lives. You could be next."

Felic stood up, put her jacket on, and slowly walked out of the room, without giving Blane a second look, she walked past the other officers, who casually glanced in her direction. Then she strolled out of the front door.

Outside of the station, she could be seen talking on her cell phone, and Blane wondered who she could be talking to. He told another Detective to have the assault team ready when he called.

"You're letting her go?" The Detective asked with a strange look on his face.

"Yeah, I have a hunch she will be going to wherever Eric Sanders is, and wherever he is, those murderous bastards will be close behind."

"Just place the call. We'll be ready."

"Oh mike, have a couple of Detectives stake out Ron Harpers Mansion in Connecticut, just in case he pops up there, and tell them to stay out of sight."

CHAPTER 53

Eric sat in front of his computer, with his eyes focused on the screen, never thinking it would come to this.

"What seems to be the problem?" Ron asked. "You've been working on that computer for a while now."

He didn't want Ron to know that he already had access to the money, so he said. "I'm having a little trouble, Brian had me send the money to a new account. Now I have to try and extract it."

"You should be familiar with that," Ron said sarcastically. "Eric, that account was to keep the Feds from discovering it, not to try and hide anything from you."

"I'm not sure of that, for some reason, I don't think I was supposed to live long enough to enjoy my share."

Ron cleared his throat. "Why would you say a thing like that Eric?"

"Oh I don't know, maybe it's because the Old Head has been trying to kill me ever since I transferred that money."

Ron and Joseph stared at one another.

"By the way, he's dead. You're going to have to kill me yourself."

Eric felt the tip of a gun graze the back of his head. "With no hesitation. " Rons said. "No hesitation at all. Now, get me my fucking money."

"He must have a lot of dirt on you, Mr. Cooper, in order for you to be helping him like this."

XXXX

Felic hopped out of her cab, looked around, then headed for the building. Blane stopped about ten cars behind her. And watched as she checked the time, then looked around as if she was waiting for someone. She took a deep breath, exhaled, then went inside.

He sat in his car and tried to listen to the sound that was barely audible. In order for him to close his case, he needed to hear everything that was being said.

XXXX

When Felic got off the elevator, Joseph Cooper came to block her path.

"Felic, what are you doing here-"

"Get out of my way Joseph. Where is Eric?" She looked over his shoulder and yelled. "Eric!, Eric!"

"Seems as if we have Company," Ron said.

Lisa stood up when she heard Eric's name being called.

Felic pushed past Joseph and started walking down the hall. As she walked past the first office, she glanced in Lisa's direction, then took a few more steps. She stopped and opened the office door, and said. "Eric stop whatever your doing, don't do it."

Lisa was squinting, trying to remember where she saw the woman before, but she couldn't place it.

Ron put the gun in his waist when she entered the room, then started clapping his hands. "Bravo, bravo, what a performance. You've done an excellent job."

Outside, Blane shifted in his seat.

Eric gave Felic a confused look, as Ron applauded.

She didn't tell you, we've been having an affair for a few years now, did she? How do you think you were able to get into the Company, without having your pending charges detected. All of those clothes, that nice rented apartment. She helped me, every step of the way. She even went so far, as to share herself with you. That wasn't part of my plan, but she did a good job at that too, don't you think?"

The computer blinked the words, Access Granted, but Eric sat motionlessly.

"Don't believe him, Eric, he's lying. "Felic nervously said.

He started to replay the course of events in his mind but didn't know what to believe. Some of the things Ron said was plausible, but after trying to have him killed, he just didn't know."

"I promise you, Eric, I had no idea what he was doing, all he wanted me to do, was help you get into the Company. When we met in that coffee shop, I didn't even know who you were, until you told me your name, beyond that point, I was in the dark."

Eric was still in a daze, there, but not there. Listening, but not listening. His focus was on the Computer.

She moved closer to him. "Eric, can't you see that he used me like he's using you?" She faced him, then screamed. "You knew I didn't kill those people in that car. Yet you made me think that, all of these years!"

"Shut your mouth!, you have the nerve to talk to me like that when I gave you everything. If Jeff would've gone along with my plans, to take back control of the Company, none fo this would've ever happened. Instead, he decided that he was going to tell the Board of my plans, I just couldn't let that happen. So I decided to call his wife and let her know that he was having an affair with his secretary. And that they were at the party together. When she got near the house I used your car, to make her swerve into the trees. Then I crashed your car and put you inside to make it look like an accident. 'This was my message to him, to keep his mouth shut, but it did more than that, it drove him crazy. So don't try and go against me, everyone that does dies".

Now Eric, if you want to live, and save the lives of your family, transfer that money now. And by the way, hand me the key you found in that drawer."

Eric reached in his pocket, and tossed it over to Ron, while Felic stood silent.

CHAPTER 54

Outside, Detective Blane couldn't believe what he was hearing, Ron Harper was confessing to multiple crimes and the fact that his hunches were correct about Eric, was a plus. Just when he reached to pick up his radio, one of his recent fears was again about to meet him face to face. The three men who killed his partner was getting out of a car.

He called into dispatch. "This is Detective Blane, send the tactical unit, and all available cars to the offices of Joseph Cooper, ASAP! The suspects of the murder of two officers are there."

He wanted to follow the procedure and wait, but his mind was already made up. Hawkeyes was a dead man. He watched as all three men walk across the street, adjusting their fully automatic weapons under their jackets. When they got closer to the building, one of the men started to reach into his jacket but was prevented by Hawkeyes. He could no longer wait for back up. He put two extra clips in his pockets and crawled out of the passenger's side door. He crouched down behind the cars that were lined on the sidewalk until he was directly across from the building. When he looked inside, he saw why one of the men was drawing their weapons. A lone security guard sat at the desk, reclined in his chair, with his headphones over his ears.

While the three men rode up on one elevator, the only sounds that could be heard were guns being cocked, back and forth.

"Shoot everything in sight," Hawkeyes said while he prepared for the festivities.

Lisa was still pacing the floor when she heard the elevator door open. When she turned to look, her eyes widened with fear. Before they could release one shot, she dived on her mother.

XXXX

Detective Blane sat on the ground behind a car, trying to wait a little longer before going in. But it was to no avail. The sound of rapid gunfire made him jump up. When he looked at the building, all he saw was flashing lights. It reminded him of the Poperatzi taking pictures of a star on the red carpet. He got up and ran across the street, with his gun in one hand, and badge in the other. He busted through the front door and yelled.

"Call 911, and tell them that Detective Blane needs assistance and that shots had been fired, by suspected cop killers."

The security guard was stuck and afraid to move until Blane yelled again.

"Now!"

It shook the security guard from his foundation and made him reach for the phone.

When Blane reached the stairs, stragglers who worked for the firm, were reluctant to pass him, until he flashed his badge. With each flight, he cautiously allowed a few workers at a time to walk past him.

Hawkeyes and the other two Albanians were still firing at

everything in sight. Ron was grazed on the arm spinning him into a wall. Eric and Felic dropped to the floor, next to the computer, while plywood, glass and office supplies littered the room. When the firing stopped, the name Eric could be heard throughout the building. He instantly thought about his family and was about to get up, but Felic grabbed him by the arm.

"Eric, don't make me have to look for you!" Hawkeyes yelled as he walked down the hall, over broken glass. All I want is that money. I need you to send it to the account that I gave you, or you will die."

"Don't send my money to anyone else Eric, I don't care if the whole damn army was shooting at us. Don't you do it, or I'll kill you myself." Ron shouted from the other side of the room, pointing his gun at Eric.

"Send it to them, before we die, Eric," Felic whispered with conviction.

Eric didn't know who he should listen to, but he knew that he had to do something. He opened his computer and started to type at a fast pace.

XXXX

He eased through the stairwell door and kneeled behind on the office desk. He could see the three men walking down the hall. He sat on the floor and leaned his back against the desk, then checked his pockets, to make sure he had extra clips. He sat up on one knee and watched as they stopped in front of an office.

As Hawkeyes stood at the office door, He noticed Ron Harper leaning against the wall, holding his shoulder. "Get up," Hawkeyes ordered. While he focused his attention on Eric. "Did you send that money Eric"

"I'm doing it now," Eric responded

Everyone paused at the sound of police sirens outside.

One of the men walked over to the window and looked out. "Damn it looks like the whole police force is out there."

At that moment, Blane stood up and yelled. "Freeze, put-" He wasnt even allowed to finish his sentence. He was met by a hail of bullets, making him return to his nest.

Eric looked at Hawkeyes and yelled. "It's done."

Felic looked at Ron and noticed his hand slowly rising from the side of his body. When he pointed his gun at Eric, she screamed. "Eric watch out!" then jumped in front of him, just in time to catch the bullet that was intended for his heart.

When Blane heard the shot, he knew that it would be now or never. He jumped up, and fired several shots, hitting one man twice in the chest, throwing him on to his back. At the same time, a powerful shot shattered the window and caused anther man to slump to the floor. When Blane realized it was snipper fire coming from across the street, he yelled out. "Stay down! stay down!" As he got closer to the office, he saw a side door closing.

XXXX

"They went through that door," Eric said pointing.

"Are you two alright? Blane asked as a slew of officers came rushing in.

"She's hit, jumped right in front of a bullet for me."

"Blane, are you good?the officer asked.

"Yeah, I'm alright. Get paramedics up here, and alert the task force, and tell them that other suspects are in the building."

Blane crouched near the side door, and cautiously went inside. He held his weapon with both hands. The door led to another office, which took you to a fire exit. He kicked it open, jumped back, then took his time going inside. He took a few steps at a time and kept his Glock in firing position. Once he got to the last flight of stairs, he stuck his head out, and it was almost blown off. He ducked back and wiped the dust from the concrete off his face.

"Give yourself up," Blane yelled. "There's nowhere to go, the building is surrounded."

"Alright, I hear you, but before I do, just stick your head back out from behind the wall first. After that, I'll turn myself in." Hawkeyes yelled, then laughed.

The reflection of blue and white lights permeated the inside of the stairwell. And caused Hawkeyes to quickly go over the outcome in his mind. He thought for a minute. Then yelled in his Albanian accent. "Detective, I knew it would come to this, Just you and me." He ducked after he received some gunfire of his own. "But I thought that there was a chance I would be able to get the money and run. So long for that idea huh...what do you say we count to ten, then come out firing like the cowboys of old."

"I'm no cowboy, and this is not the wild wild west. How about you give yourself up, and we can talk about the cowboys of old, at the station."

Hawkeyes laughed uncontrollably, then said. " I'm not going to be able to do that Detective. It's been fun."

Blane peeked around the wall and watched as Hawkeyes shot through the glass door, and ran outside.

His run was short-lived, as red dots consumed his body, and rapid gunshots laid him to rest. Blane ran out of the building, with his hands in the air, until he was properly identified.

His Sergeant ran over to him and asked. " Blane are you sure these are the men who killed my officers?"

"Positive, I looked them right in their faces, before they started shooting."

"Good, get a report to me by tomorrow."

Felic and one of the three men were rushed to the hospital in a serious but stable condition. When Blane looked to his left, he saw Eric in handcuffs being escorted by police. And his mother and sister were being treated for minor injuries.

"Wait wait wait!" Blane said as he ran towards the squad car. "Hold on a minute. Eric., I'm going to let the Prosecuting Attorney know what your role was in all of this. Just be patient."

"I was thinking about my mother's medical bill, that's all. I never expected it to reach this level."

Blane tapped the hood of the car and said. "Take off." He walked between squad cars, and crime scene technicians, and sat on the curb next to Eric's family. "How you guys feeling?"

"You mean besides being scared half to death, we're fine." Mrs. Sanders said.

"We were hiding in an office under the table," Lisa added.

“Well thank god that table was big enough for the both of you.”

They smiled at Blane’s statement.

“For both of us and Mr. Cooper. “Lisa said.

“You know what, I forgot all about him. Where is he anyway?

“I heard an officer say that they were taking him in for questioning.”

Mrs. Sanders reached for Blane’s hand once again and said. “Please help my son, he just got mixed up with the wrong group of people.”

“I’m going to do everything in my power.”

“Thank you, Detective...oh, get yourself some sleep. You look like you’ve been up for a week straight.”

Blane smiled, then stood up. “I will, If I need to talk to you, where will I be able to reach you?

“For now, we’ll be with Mrs. Rosenboun, our next-door neighbor.”

“Is that woman going to be alright? Lisa asked.

“What woman?”

“The one who got shot. I’ve seen her somewhere before, but I just can’t remember where.”

CHAPTER 55

The sound of police radios could be heard echoing in the darkness of the night, while flickers of light concentrated on one area. The aroma of freshly dug dirt invaded their nostrils, as the anxiety spread throughout the group. Cadaver dogs were barking without remorse, breathing hard and flinging tongues vigorously. They were waiting to receive their prize.

Halfway down what could be a makeshift grave, an officer touched a rough patch with his shovel. He used his flashlight, and a small brush to dust away from the earth, exposing the stiffness of a human hand.

"Sergeant, it's a females hand." An officer yelled.

Working on a hunch that the body of Kathlin Harper was buried on the grounds of the Harper's residence. Sergeant Jim Kesler brought out a crew of fifty men and women, plus a dozen cadaver dogs, to swarm the property.

A pair of dogs descended on a site in the back of the house, in a heavily wooded area, indicating possible human remains.

Now that a body was found, it was time to figure out the cause of death.

XXXX

Ron entered his house through the wine cellar, with his arm still bleeding. He was just grazed, but it was still enough to leave a gash. He rushed upstairs, took off his jacket and shirt, then poured a whole bottle of alcohol on his arm. He screamed through the towel that he placed in his mouth, then wrapped his arm in gauze. After putting on a new shirt he reached on the top shelf in the closet and pulled out two large duffel bags. He made his way to the living room, stopped, and stood over one of his most prized possessions, his king-sized chess table. He pulled off the velvet cloth, then put in the key he got from Eric at Joseph Coopers Law firm, then unlocked it. He stepped to each side of the table and pulled it back, but when he looked inside, he instantly fell to his knees. Shock and disappointment engulfed him. All that was left was a small piece of paper. He reached inside and grabbed it. When he focused his eyes on the words, he couldn't do anything, but give a faint smile.

"Freeze Mr. harper. I want you to slowly put your hands on the top of your head, and turn around."

Ron paused for a minute and thought about his options, but there weren't many.

"Hands over your head Mr. Harper! The officer said a second time.

There was no way out, he clutched the small piece of paper and placed his hands behind his head.

Once he was cuffed and taken into custody, the Detectives read the note that was in his hand but couldn't make any sense of it.

XXXX

While Blane was on his way home, he received another call, that informed him of Ron Harper's apprehension, and the urgent message left for him, from Sergeant Jim Kesler.

CHAPTER 56

When he reached the Autopsy Division, at the Connecticut Medical Center, he hopped out of his car and hurried inside. He ran to a dest where a young lady was sitting and asked. "Can you tell me where I can find Sergeant Jim Kesler-"

"Blane! " Kesler yelled. "I'm over here."

"Jim, how did you know-"

"I had a feeling on the night of her disappearance, the smeared blood stopped at the door, so I automatically thought that she was placed in something and taken away from the property, plus the dogs lost her scent at the door."

"Did they start on her to determine the cause of death?

"Not yet, follow me. Do you have the stomach for it?"

"I can handle anything," Blane said, preparing to enter the autopsy lab. When they went in, he stood off to the side and waited for the procedure to begin. "Can you at least assume how she was killed."

"It appears as if she was shot by a small-caliber handgun."

When the medical examiner pulled back the sheet, Blane's eyes almost popped out of his head. He was speechless and temporarily frozen in his spot.

"Blane, what's the problem?"

His mouth was open, but he wasn't able to speak.

"Blane! Kesler yelled while he pushed his arm."

"That's not Kathlin Harper," Blane said as he walked closer to the gurney.

"That's not her?" what do you mean that's not her. If it's not her, who else could it be?"

"Angela Redford, a witness who gave a statement against Ron Harper, concerning the car crash."

"Hold on, Ron is in jail right?"

"Not anymore, he made bail this morning."

"Well, he couldn't have been responsible for this."

"I doubt it very seriously, from the composition of the body, I would say she's been dead, at least longer than seventy-two hours." The Medical Examiner said.

"Well, your right, we can't put that one on him," Blane said, staring at Angela Redford's lifeless body.

"I'll send a team back out to the house, to give it another sweep. I'll call you if I find anything." Kesler said.

XXXX

The night was aging, and Blane could barely keep his eyes open. Just when he thought the worst was over, there was another crime to be solved. Angela Redford, who could've killed her, Blane said to himself. The answer to that question would have to wait. There was still one thing bothering him, he just couldn't pinpoint what it was.

CHAPTER 57

First thing in the morning, Blane left his condo. Feeling rejuvenated, he jumped in his Range Rover and headed for the station. While he sat in the morning traffic, he couldn't help but think about all the good, in people. The job had a tendency to expose you to the worst, that the City had to offer. But he knew the kind-hearted far outweighed the rest. He watched and smiled, as someone helped an elderly person across the street. A young boy was helping his friend up, after falling off of a bike, the carnet to him slowed down, so another could pass. Yup, he was convinced, life was filled with more good than bad.

Once he reached the station, that shiny outlook on life started to fade, there were people being locked up for every type of crime imaginable.

Before he could even close the door of his truck, the congratulations started coming in.

"Good job Blane." An officer yelled.

"Way to go." Another said.

The inside of the station was no different, it erupted in applause, even the Sergeant was in attendance. He accepted the congratulations with grace, as he walked over to his desk. Once there, he stood for a minute, glaring at the photos that Detective and himself were studying. The applause became bittersweet.

"Blane, our suspect is in stable condition, and Felic Hernann is going to be fine as well, The bullet went straight through. Listen, a couple of guys went over to interview Angela Redford's husband. And he told them, that she was being fired from R.H. Holdings. He said that she was terribly upset about it, so she called Brian Scott. He told her to meet him somewhere so that he could explain to her why, and discuss her severance package.

"Did the Husband say where she was supposed to meet him at?"

"She didn't say. When she left, that was the last time he heard from her. Anyway, Detective's found a small-caliber handgun in Scott's apartment. So I told them to send it to ballistics, to see if he bullet in Mrs. Redford came from that gun."

"Thanks, Serg." He said, lowering his head.

"Don't be too hard on yourself, it's not your fault she's dead... Oh, and Blane, the funeral's tomorrow."

Blane sat at his desk and went over all the evidence that he and Detective Neal was sharing with each other the night before. The Sergeant wanted a report on his desk before the end of the day, and he wanted to make sure all of his t's were crossed and I's dotted. He listened intensely to the taped conversation from Joseph Cooper's law firm, to see if he missed anything.

Hours had passed since he sat down. He could no longer control the urge to sleep. He fell headfirst on the report that he was filing.

"Blane!, Blane!" the Sergeant yelled, trying to wake him up. But he didn't respond until he felt himself being pushed and shoved. He jumped up and reached for his gun.

"Easy, easy," The Sergeant said. "Are you all right?"

"Yeah, I'm fine."

"You think you need to see the in house psychologist?"

"I'm fine," he said, in an adamant tone.

"I'll set it up anyway."

CHAPTER 58

By now, both Ron Harper and Eric Sanders were both processed back into the comfort of their cells. Only this time they were in different dorms. While Ron awaited his fate on various charges, Eric was hoping that his charges could somehow be dropped.

Blane pulled in front of the Hospital and parked, he wanted to talk to Felic, to see how she was doing. Once he got to the floor where she was at, he asked a nurse to allow him to examine her clothing. The nurse complied, and he was taken to a storage unit on the same floor. The nurse brought out a basket and handed it to him. He pulled out her suit jacket and started to search for it. He stuck his hand into the pocket and pulled out a small listening device, that he placed there when she went to the bathroom back at the station. He turned to the nurse and said. "Thank you, do you think I could talk to Miss Hernann for a few minutes?"

"Sure, no problem, follow me."

She took him down the hall to see her, but two small children and a woman were by her side. He stood at the door and waited for her visitors to leave. Even in the Hospital, he thought, bandaged and laid up in bed. She still looked gorgeous.

She was kissing her visitor's goodbye when he was opening the door.

"We love you mommy." the small children said as they left.

"I love you too," Felic responded then blew kisses in their direction.

The woman who walked out of the room looked Blane up and down as she walked past.

He focused his attention on Felic. When he got closer, he could see the bandages peeking through her pajama top as she tried to adjust herself in bed.

"Hello, Detective."

"How you doing Blane asked.

"I'm fine, I told them that I'm ready to get out of here." She said as she leaned up.

"Slow down, not so fast. They said that they need to monitor you for a while. Listen Felic, you will have to stay in custody for a while, until they figure this thing out, and everything is settled. But I'm confident that once the facts come out about your involvement in all of this, you'll be released."

"Thank you for everything Detective, thank you."

"Don't mention it, you just lay back and get some rest."

On his way out of the room, he saw the same nurse and asked. "Excuse me, I hate to bother you, but I would like to speak to the other patient that was brought in with the young lady last night."

"Detective, I can't do that, the Doctors left strict instructions for me to follow."

"I promise you, it won't take long. I just need to ask a few questions."

She thought about it a minute, then buckled under pressure. She escorted him to a room around the corner, that was being watched by an officer.

"Hey Blane, nice job last night."

"Thanks, Is he strong enough to talk?"

"I was told not to let anyone in Blane, sorry."

"Come on man, just one quick question."

He looked inside at the patient, then back at Blane. "One minute. No more. I don't want to be doing paperwork for the rest of my life."

"You got it, one minute."

He stepped inside the room and walked up to the bed. The suspect was still a little hazy, but conscious. When he saw Blane, he went to cover his face.

"What do you want to do, finish the job?"

"I don't want to hurt you, Ijust want to know one thing. How much was the Smitz family paying you, to try and get their money back for them?"

"Smitz who"?

"The Smitz family"

"I have no idea, who you....Oh,m we were told to use that name, as a way to appear believable."

"Times up Blane." The officer at the door said.

"Hold on, one more question," Blane responded as he turned to face the officer.

"I don't want to lose my job, Blane."

"You won't lose your job-"

"If you help me, then I'll help you." the suspect said.

"If you help me, I'll personally talk to the prosecutor for you."

It now became a staring contest between the officer, Blane, and the suspect.

The silence was broken by the suspect. "It was my partner who was talking to the person on the phone."

"What person, who?"

"I don't know for sure, I guess it was a woman. Every time he got off of the phone, he would say, she wants us to go here or there.

She wanted us to scare Brian Scott, that's when you saw us at his office. She also wanted us to shake up this kid, I can't remember his name. Then last time he spoke to her, she told him to go to that lawyer's office downtown. That's all alI know."

"Let's go, Blane."

"Okay, I'm coming."

"Make sure you talk to that prosecutor for me." The suspect yelled as Blane hurried out the door.

"Blane, you alright?" The officer asked. "You look like you saw a ghost."

"Yeah, yeah, I'm alright. I'm just trying to figure something out that's all. Thanks for letting me talk to him. It was a big help."

Blane shook his head as he walked out of the Hospital. Ron

Harper must've found out what Brian Scott was up to, and came up with another plan.

XXXX

Detective Neal and Detective Laso received a full honors departure from the Department. Over five hundred officers, from throughout the tri-state area, were at attendance, to pay tribute to their fallen comrades. The governor and the Mayor spoke of the resilience of the NYPD. Detective Blane and his SErgeant stood off to the side and spoke during the ceremony.

"Why haven't you given me your report yet Blane?"

"Something is bothering me. I thought this case was all wrapped up until I spoke to the surviving suspect. He said something, that's been on my mind all night, I'm still trying to figure it out."

"I know you, Blane. This case is over, so I want whatever you've got, on my desk. The Captain is breathing down my neck."

"Okay, okay, I got it, don't worry."

CHAPTER 59

Manhattan Federal court, was the center of the world, for one brief moment in time. It's been two weeks since the deaths of the two Detectives, and the case was still fresh in the public mindsNormally they would move on to the next crime, but this one involved too many twists and turns, that they couldn't let go. Even Hollywood came calling.

The U.S. Attorney Richard Goldstone was making his way in the courtroom, after being hounded by media outlets outside.

"Richard!, Richard" Blane called out.

"Detective, I'm busy, what's up?"

"What's the status of Eric Sander's?"

He let out a loud sigh, then said, "Well, as of now, he still has that cocaine charge against him. And we're not clear whether he was forced, or under his own will, when he stole that money. One thing I can tell you is that we're not charging him with murder."

Blane shook his hand in appreciation. "Why not?"

"Oh, you'll see in a minute."

"Huh, I don't understand."

"Patience, You'll see."

"Okay, what about Felic Hernann?"

She was released yesterday. It's a small question of the depth she went to assist Ron Harper, but for the most part, she's been through a lot, Now that asshole who participated in the killings of two officers, it's over for him. I see no less that thirty to life."

"That's good," Blane said, pumping his fist in the air.

"As you well know, ballistics has already proven, that the old guy from the BMW, killed that day trader Shawn Pope."

"Uh-huh."

"And that small-caliber handgun that was found in Brian Scott's apartment, was attributed to the death of Angela Beset-"

"You mean Redford, Angela Redford, Beset was her maiden name."

"Alright, well since they are all deceased, those cases are closed." He looked around and realized that the proceedings were about to begin, and said Blane, I got to go...Oh, Ron Harper is being charged with the murder of Brian Scott ."

"What?"

"I'll talk to you later."

Blane took his seat and waited for the proceedings to begin.

"All rise, for the Honorable Judge Anderson." The Court Officer yelled

"She banged the gavel, giving an indication for everyone to sit down. "Mr. Goldston, are we ready yet?"

"Yes your Honor, we're ready,"

“I see there’s no Joseph Cooper this time around.”

“That’s correct your Honor, my name is Steven Burell. Mr. Cooper will not, nor anyone from his firm, be involved in the defense, due to the conflict of interest it posses.”

“All right then, Let’s proceed.”

When Ron Harper turned to face the crowd, he noticed Detective Blane in attendance. He gave a sarcastic smirk, then faced front.

“Your Honor, Mr. Harper has been given a superseding indictment, containing some of the old charges. Only this time, we’ve added one extra count of fraud, and one count of murder, in furtherance of those crimes.”

“Your Honor please, there isn’t any witness to the murder, No evidence-”

There is a witness your Honor, One who will testify to what she saw. She is here today. For weeks I’ve had her in protective custody, for fear of her life.”

While Ron Harper whispered with his attorney, everyone turned around to see who it was. When the door swung open, the courtroom burst into pandemonium. Ron Harper’s eyes bulged he swallowed hard and clenched his fist.

Detective Blane stood up and walked out of the courtroom. He thought to himself, how in the world is Kathlin Harper still alive.

XXXX

On the drive to see Mrs. Sanders, Blane was ready to move on to the next case, he had enough of this one. Kathlin Harper alive, he shook his head. What about all of that blood at the scene, that matched hers. The evidence of the body being dragged. Then there was the picture of Eric standing over her dead body. All of these images bothered him.

He exited the highway and made his way to 116th street. He parked and went to Mrs. Rosenboun's house. He could still smell the hints of burnt wood next door.

"Hello Detective, how are you?"

"Fine Mrs. Rosenboun, a little stressed, but I'll make it. How about you?"

"I'm alright Detective, still waiting for my insurance to replace these storm windows."

"Is Mrs. Sander's around?"

"Yes, she's here. Go inside."

When they walked into the living room, he saw her sitting on the couch. "Hey Mrs. Sander's, how are you feeling?"

"I'm doing better Detective. I see you came by empty-handed. Where is my son?"

"Hold on Mrs. Sanders, it takes time. They just want to clear everything up. From what I hear, he should be alright." He looked to the side. "Hello Lisa"

"Detective," she answered in a flirtatious tone, then turned to leave the room.

Mrs. Sanders pulled on Blane's arm and said. "She's single you know."

He smiled and lowered his head.

"We saw you on T.V walking out of the courtroom." Mrs. Sanders said. "I can't believe that woman is still alive."

"You and me both."

"How is Eric holding up in that jail?"

"He's strong, he'll make it."

"He should've never went there in the first place."

"Why do you say that?"

"Well, I told them what I saw."

"Told who what?"

"That day when Eric was arrested."

"You mean for the cocaine."

"Yes, I went to the police station, to tell them what I saw."

"And what was that?"

"Well, I was standing in my kitchen window, when I saw an officer taking money out of a bag in Eric's trunk. Then he put something from his police car, back in the bag."

Blane slid to the edge of his seat and asked with enthusiasm. "Mrs. Rosenboun, are you sure?"

"I may be eighty-two, but I'm not blind. I said that I might not have the best memory in the world, I didn't say anything about my sight."

"Blane jumped up and gave them both a kiss, then headed for the door.

"Detective." Lisa yelled, "How's that woman doing?"

"What woman?"

"You know, the one who was taken to the hospital that night."

"Oh, your talking about Felic Hernann. She was released from custody yesterday."

"Now, I remember where I saw her before. She was in the passenger seat of Joseph Cooper's car when he came to drop off a package for Eric. I remember clearly now because when I looked at her, she turned away as if she was trying to avoid eye contact with me."

Blane dashed out of the door, with only one destination in mind. He picked up his phone and called a Detective at the station.

"Hello, Homicide Division-"

"Yeah, this is Blane. I need you to secure subpoenas for Felic Hernanns phone records, and our perps, who killed Neal in that Harper's case. Check out Friday nights, around nine, from Mrs. Hernann's phone to theirs. Tell the Court that I need this done asap. This case is far from over."

CHAPTER 60

Blane reached the station in record time, he jumped out of his car and ran inside. He was greeted before he could speak.

"Blane, how the hell are you?"

"I'm good Pete, Listen, an elderly woman by the name of Rosenboun said she came up here to file a complaint, about a crime she was a witness to."

"How long ago?"

"Maybe six, seven or eight months ago."

"That wasn't my shift, but it should've been logged in, let me check."

Blane waited as patiently as he possibly could, while Pete scanned the computer.

"Rosenboun you said right?"

"Yeah, that's right?"

"Got it, it says here that she made a complaint."

"Print out the complaint for me, shouldn't it be part of the police report?"

"Hey I'm just playing secretary here, what do you want from

me?"

"Your right, point taken."

"He grabbed the report and stepped off to the side to read it. He noticed that the two arresting officers, gave completely different accounts, as to the events of that morning. Mrs. Rosenboun, is kind of old, he thought but he decided to talk to both officers Rodriguez and Pertelli anyway.

They were both notified of Blane's request to speak with them, so they came to the Homicide division to see him. When officer Rodriguez arrived at the Division, he was met with uncertain stares. He didn't know what to think, a million things were running through his mind. One thing he knew for sure, was that he wasn't there to be promoted to Detective. Blane stuck his head out of the interrogation room and called him inside.

"What's going on Blane? I've got more important things to be doing with my time."

"I understand, you could check with the Sergeant if you like. He authorized me to call you in."

"All right." He said nervously. "So what's the problem."

Blane leaned across the table and asked. "Why did you put two Kilos of cocaine inside of Eric Sander's bag?"

"Why what? You've got the wrong man. I-"

"Look, you know me, I'm after other things, bigger fish. What you tell me remains in this room."

While Rodriquez held his head down and contemplated. Blane called in officer Pertelli.

When Pertelli walked in, he instantly became defensive.

“What’s up Blane?” he said and slammed the door. “What’s this all about?”

“I already spoke to your partner and told him what I know. Now you know me, I’m after something, and it’s damn sure not either of you. So what I’m going to do, is step out for a minute, and allow the two of you to talk.”

Blane stepped out for a few moments and could see the tension between the two. When they looked at him, he opened the door and walked back inside.

“So, what are we going to do here?”

“Officer Pertelli spoke for both of them. “Look Blane it’s not cocaine, it’s two bricks of flour.”

“Flour!” Blane yelled and gave them both a confused look. “Why in the world would you put flour in his bag?”

Officer Pertelli shifted to the edge of his seat. “I met this woman at the bar, and she–”

“What bar?”

“The bar most of the guys here go to after work.”

“Okay, I’m listening.”

“She offered me two hundred thousand, to set up some guy. She said she wanted me to put two Kilos of coke in his car.”

“Did this person say why?”

“I didn’t ask why?”

“Okay, so what did you do?”

“After watching Sander’s routine for a while, I noticed that every other day, he came out of his house with a duffel bag in his hand. Like clockwork. I just waited for the right time to arrest him."

"But instead of cocaine, you put flour in his bag. Is that correct?"

"Exactly."

"Right after you took the money out, am I right?"

Pertelli now lowered his head and nodded in disgust.

"So you arrested him on the basis of drug possession, relying on a small amount to go to the testing lab."

"I knew that once he went to trial, it would've been found out that it wasn't cocaine, and he would've been let go."

"You're sure she didn't say why?"

"All she said, was that once he's locked up in MDC, she'll handle the rest.

Blane jumped up and pushed his chair to the wall, then ran out fo the room. He went down the hall, to the Homicide Division. He pulled out a picture from his desk drawer, then ran back to the officers he was questioning. With the pictures in his hand, he asked. "Is this the woman who gave you the money?"

Officer Pertelli reached out for the photo, then shook his head. "No, that's not her."

"Are you sure, it's been a while, look at it again."

"I said it's not her!" Pertelli responded.

Frustrated, Blane slammed the photo on the table. "All right then, we're finished here. If I have any more questions, I'll contact you."

After the two officers left the room, Blane sat back and wondered. This Pertelli guy must be trying to protect her. But if so, why? He put the pictures in his pocket and headed for the MDC Holding facility.

XXXX

At MDC, Blane spoke with the Lieutenant, who was on duty, at the jail. He wanted to know what the procedures were, regarding inmates who are assigned to dorms. Basically, he wanted to know who placed Ron Harper in the same cellblock with Eric Sanders. The Lieutenant called for the Correctional Officer, who was working last night. Once the officer entered the room, Blane introduced himself, and the Lieutenant walked out.

"How you doing?," Blane asked. "Have a seat. My name is Detective Blane, I have a couple of important questions to ask you, is that all right with you?"

"Sure, No problem, shoot."

"Were you or anyone in this prison paid any amount of money, to house Ron Harper with Eric Sanders, or vice versa?"

He gave Blane a skeptical look, then said. "Am I going to lose my job?"

"That's not up to me to decide, but I can tell you, as of right now. This stays between me and you."

The officer sat silent for a minute, then looked around the room. "Yes, a woman gave me twenty-five thousand, to put them into the same cellblock. All she said, is that she needed them to meet. So I gave a little extra food and cigarettes, to a guy in the same dorm as them, to make sure they ended up in the same cell."

"Let me guess. His name was Benjamin Jones, but everyone called him Old Head."

"How did you know that".

Blane ignored the question, then pulled out a picture, and handed it to him. "Is this the woman?"

The officer grabbed the photo, looked at it and said. "No, that's not her."

"Are you sure?" Blane asked in a frustrated voice.

"I'm positive, that's not the woman who spoke to me."

XXXX

The drive to the station was a grueling one. Blane processed all of the information in his head. This one baffled him. Maybe Felic paid someone to approach these men for her. He didn't know, but what he did know, was that all of the players in the game were accounted for.

Back at the Homicide Division, he opened up a small note pad. One he usually keeps cross-referencing his information. While he flicked through page after page, a little card dropped out, and fell on the desk With all that was going on, he forgot that it was found in Eric's computer. On it was an account number that Hawkeyes wanted him to send the money to. To Blane, the number seemed familiar. As he stared at it, he realized that it was the same account number, that Brian wanted him to send the money to. How could two different people give Eric the same account number? It just didn't make any sense. He thought.

"Hey, Blane." A Detective said. "Got those numbers for you."

He handed Blane a stack of papers, then sat next to him. "Nowhere is Felic Hernann's phone records for that night. At around 9:00 PM, She did make a call, but it wasn't to either of our suspects."

"Damn." Blane blurted out in disappointment.

"Hold on, not so fast. One of our suspects received a call around 9:00 PM as well."

"Okay, a coincidence. What does that tell us?"

"Out of all the numbers, on all of these records, there's only one that is the same. I have them highlighted."

"Yeah, I see, this number right here," Blane said pointing to the number.

"You got it. A funny thing happened when I studied the calls."

"What's that?"

"I noticed a pattern for that night."

Blane looked at the papers strangely

"Here, let me show you." The Detective said, reaching for the papers. With a pen in his hand, he pointed. "Check this out, At 9:05, Felic Hernann made a call to this number here, right."

"Okay, I'm following you."

"Now at 9:07, the number she called, made a call to our dead suspect's phone, which lasted less than a minute."

"Did you find out who's number this."

The Detective smiled, shifted through the stack, and pulled out one page. "This is the best part." He said as he handed it to Blane."

"Oh shit, you've got to be kidding me?"

"I felt the same way, I couldn't believe it."

He shook the Detective's hand, then ran to the Lieutenant's office. "Hey your not going to believe what I'm about to show you."

CHAPTER 61

The flight was relaxing, and everyone appeared to be eagerly awaiting their arrival. The stewardesses dressed as twins walked up and down the isles with bright smiles on their faces attending to everyone's needs.

Blane stared into the clouds, he now had all the pieces to the puzzle and needed to tie up one loose end. A voice came over the speaker breaking his train of thought.

"Everyone Please return to your seats and fasten your seatbelts. We are about to land."

Once on the ground, Blane checked his watch, gathered his bags and headed for the exit. Outside, he and his team were greeted by local authorities, who told them that everything was in place and that they should leave immediately. When they reached the Costa Rican Bank, Blane expressed his gratitude to the police chief.

"I appreciate you allowing me and my team to execute these warrants."

"We normally don't operate in this manner, but once we were informed of the killing of two officers, we had no choice. We may be from different parts of the world, but we are bound together by a common cause."

They stood near the bank and waited patiently. Blane was in classic mode, casually dressed, with his hands behind his back, proudly displaying his badge and firearm. They watched as the two of them exited the bank, hand in hand. As they walked, a look of apprehension invaded their faces, causing them to pause.

"Detective Blane, what seems to be the problem?" Felic asked as if she didn't know.

He managed to force a sarcastic smirk, before saying. "Your good Miss Hernann. For a minute there, you almost had me. Young woman, taken advantage of, by big Wall Street Businessmen. It almost worked, but you slipped. Everyone I interviewed, even the surviving suspect, kept saying she. She said this, she said that, and I swore it was you. But I couldn't get confirmation, every time I showed your picture, they would say, that's not her. I couldn't figure it out. Then I remembered, you made a call that night after you left the station. And when I followed you, those Albanians showed up."

She shrugged, "What does that have to do with me, I didn't call them."

"You didn't call them, but you called someone else, who in turn called them. So I got the name of the person you called, found a photo, then went back to all the people I interviewed. Guess what, they Identified you, Kathlin."

Their hands clasped tighter together.

"The two of you devised this plan from the start, didn't you? I've got to hand it to you, you almost got away with it. Take them away".

As the officers placed them under arrest and read them their rights, Blane turned to look at them. They silently returned the stare, as shame and disappointment left nine hundred and ninety-eight words to describe the look on their faces.

CHAPTER 62

Clouds scattered to expose the bright morning blue, and announce the quickness of a sleepless City. In the midst of engine fuel and steam covered manholes, batches of coffee and donuts could be detected in the morning air. Pedestrians peddled the sidewalks while strays scrounged for their meals. The Big Apple, he said to himself, there's no other city in the world he would rather protect and serve.

The reconstruction of the Sanders Brownstone was underway, and Blane could see Eric's mother supervising the process.

"There's Detective Blane." She said as he pulled up.

When he got out, they gave each other a lasting hug.

Thank you for helping my son Detective."

"No problem, it was my pleasure," Blane replied as if it was an easy thing to do. He looked over his shoulder and saw Mrs. Rosenboun.

"Hello, Detective."

"Hey, how are you?"

"My old bones are a little sore, but I'll live."

Eric and Lisa came outside to find out what all the hugging was for and saw Detective Blane. Eric walked over to talk to him, while Lisa stood on the porch and waived.

"Well, well, well, if it isn't our multi-millionaire," Blane said as Eric got closer.

"Yeah right," Eric said then smiled. I wish, almost though, huh"

"I see the treatment is working, she looks a whole lot better."

"Yeah, the Doctor said she should make a full recovery. What's going to happen to Felic and Mrs. Harper?"

"As of now, the U.S. Attorney is thinking about bringing a broad conspiracy against all of them. Regardless of the outcome, they are going to receive long sentences."

After a brief moment of silence, he continued. "I hear you made out."

"Yeah, R.H.Holdings hired me to help with their security systems, can you believe that life is crazy. Something is still bothering though, why did they choose me?"

"Really, it never was about you. Once they decided to bring Ron Harper down, Felic told Kathlin about your computer club, so she went down there to find anyone she could. It just so happens that you were leaving the building, at the exact time that she was pulling up. So she decided at that moment to use you.

"Okay then, why would she give Mr. Scott one account number, and then the Albanians another?"

"You see, you missed something, I almost missed it too, until I slowed down and was able to see it. They gave Brian Scott the number after they found out that he was supposed to kill Mrs. Harper and make it appear as if you did it. So instead of actually killing her, they faked her death and waited for you to come over. They wanted the security cameras to catch you standing over her. Then blackmail you into sending them money to that so-called different account."

"Look Felic and Kathlin didn't want to have to share that money with anyone, Not you, not Brian, and certainly not Ron. They had to make Brian think that Ron was holding out on him, then they had to make Ron think that Brian was trying to steal it from him. The Albanians were just added security, they were a distraction for you because it really didn't matter where you sent that money."

"What do you mean?"

"All the account numbers were the same."

"Are you serious?" Eric asked in shock.

"And the only one who could retrieve it was Felic, it was in her name. Ron had no idea that she would betray him, not after all he'd done for her,"

"Wow, I can't believe I missed that."

Lisa yelled from the porch. "Are you going to come in and get something to eat Detective, or stay out there all day?"

"Thank you, but I have something that I need to do. But would you like to go out to dinner sometime?"

She stared, smiled, but didn't respond.

Well, are you going to give me an answer, or just stand there all day?"

A loud yes came from inside the house. She turned around, not wanting to reveal her blush, then said. "That would be nice."

Eric and Blane faced each other, to shake hands, then Eric turned to leave. But before he could get far, Blane yelled.

"Hey Eric, what was the key for?"

Eric paused, swallowed hard, and with his back still facing Blane, answered. "I gave it to Ron Harper remember."

"Yeah, I remember, but what was it for? When I spoke to Mr. Harper, he said two million dollars was stolen from his house."

"Did he say by who?"

"He wouldn't say, but when my officers arrested him, he was clutching a piece of paper, with a quote written on it, which said. "Oh, what a tangled web we weave-"

"When at first we practice to deceive." Sir Walter Scott." Eric finished Blane's sentence, then walked into the house.,

XXXX

At the local bar, the same place where Kathlin met officer Pertelli. Detective Blane sat at a table with Sergeant Jim Kesler. He placed three glasses in front of them, and a large bowl. He ripped open a bottle of Jack Daniels, then filled all three glasses. Each time they took a shot, Blane emptied the third glass in the bowl. They didn't speak or utter a single word, and no one in the bar bothered them. They knew that he was keeping his promise to Detective Neal.

THE END

ABOUT THE AUTHOR

Stan C Gaillard was born Feb 2nd in the Bronx NY to loving hard working parents. He loved to draw which ultimately took him to the school of Art and Design. A Kid looking to capture the scenes floating inside his head until life came knocking at his door. By the age of sixteen, he saw how life would come to steal his youth and the talent he grew to love.

For the next twenty-five years, the struggle to survive would take him down roads that would teach him to escape and eventually begin a new path with a love for reading and the art to write.

Follow this writer as he shares the love of writing and introduce his first novel of the high life, heavy hitters and dark streets of the big city, and those who try to find a way out.

He is now married and lives in Howard County, MD.

CPSIA information can be obtained
at www.ICGtesting.com
Printed in the USA
LVHW082008090620
657726LV00008B/1821